Toxic Exposure

Toxic Exposure

by
Mark R. Sneller

Published by Fresh Air Press

Visit Mark's website at
marksneller.com

This edition was prepared for publication by
Ghost River Images
5350 East Fourth Street
Tucson, Arizona 85711
www.ghostriverimages.com

ISBN 978-1-7330238-4-9

Library of Congress Control Number: 2020919834

Printed in the United States of America
November, 2020

Other books Mark R. Sneller:

A Breath of Fresh Air

Greener Cleaner Indoor Air–a Guide
   to Healthier Living–2nd Edition

Dying to Read

The Mars Virus

The City Beneath the Earth

In Progress books:

*The Fight at the Poker Game and Other
Stories*

The Magical Powers of Lazlo Pearce

Dedication

To my grandparents who raised me from the age of three.

To my grandmother from Odessa, Russia, who permitted me to allocate my growing collection of paperbacks to a little cupboard in a little hallway in our small home, and who fed and cared for me. She endured me well, especially while I wrote and read to her my first one-page stories.

To my grandfather who grew up on a farm in Lithuania and who worked his small dime store in a poor section of Los Angeles. He overcame holdups and worked six days a week and ordered me to stop playing baseball in the streets and help him in the store.

My greatest regret? I never asked them about their own stories.

ONE

Two linebackers, formerly associated with the University of Oklahoma football team, loomed in the doorway of the Loose Cannon Bar and Grill in Norman, Oklahoma, backlit by the porch light. Moths fluttering around the outside lighting cast strange and enlarged shadows on the interior of the tavern wall. Inside, a random collection of college students were starting to get acquainted over pitchers of beer this Saturday post-game night.

Loud Oklahoma bluegrass music playing on a jukebox nearly overrode the conversations. Twenty feet of bar counter and all the tables were fully occupied. Mostly jocks and jock wannabees hung out there along with the usual assortment of co-eds. Peanut shells littered the floor and baskets of peanuts and popcorn sat atop the drink-strewn tables.

The tavern occupants totally supported the football team that had won another home victory. A few football players had already come and gone, having consumed their share of beer. At this late hour, only the students remained to celebrate, as if they needed any excuse to do so.

Manny and Lem Baxter appeared to sway slightly, first against the door frame, then against each other. Manny took a step forward, staggered into and rococheted off the end of the bar counter to the nearest table. He met with misfortune when he ran into Jeffrey Shenero.

At five-eleven and 185 pounds, Shenero wouldn't have stood a chance against the disgraced former football player in a face-to-face matchup across the scrimmage line. However, this was real life and Jeff Shenero's beer had splattered over his shirt, with the bulk of the liquid a lake in his lap. Jeff rose from the table, quickly turned toward his assailant, and hooked a nasty right fist into the man's nose to break it. Two of his front teeth were included in the transaction.

The man who had stumbled into Jeff had the reputation of being a a small town steam roller from Texas who had a rape charge pending against him in Oklahoma and who had been dismissed from the team.

Lem remained standing in the doorway trying to hang on to a promising future and, at the same time, try to control an out of control brother destined for prison.

Manny Baxter was in excess of three hundred pounds and stood six inches taller than Jeff. That didn't stop him from falling backward from Jeff's punch. He landed solidly on his rear in front of the bar amidst the peanut shells on the floor. When he did so, the room vibrated. Fortunately, construction in the area took into account the occasional earthquake in their reinforcement protocols.

Blood spurted from Manny's nose and he began to complain about getting hit with a cheap shot; this, while he felt his nose with hands which instantly became filled with blood.

Frank Bennett, seated next to Jeff, another sophomore, had pushed back his chair. He set his beer mug on the table and his cigarette in the ash tray.

Lem, not too steady himself, came over to the table and tried to help Manny to his feet. Manny overcame shock from the surprise punch, which quickly turned to embarrassment and then to rage. He shrugged off his brother and began bellowing at Jeff, "I'm going to get you. I'm going to kill you." The giant struggled to get to his feet, but kept slipping in the peanut shells.

"Bring your grandmother to help you," replied Jeff, standing to face the man, waiting for him to get up, totally prepared to repeat the punch. Lem managed to grab his enraged brother and drag him out the door. Patrons jumped to their feet saying "right on" hoping to enter into a good barroom brawl, but were soon disappointed. The excitement had ended almost as quickly as it had started.

Jeff dusted the beer from his lap, regained his seat, and poured himself another glass of beer. To him, a beer glass was a euphemism for an Oklahoma shot glass.

"Bastard cut into my drinkin' time," Jeff muttered.

Only minutes later, when the city police showed up, no evidence existed of the previous turmoil—the blood had been swept over with another layer of peanut shells, a table or two had been reset, and the bluegrass played on.

"Manny raising a fuss," shrugged the barkeep. "He decided to leave early."

As the evening progressed, Jeff and Frank returned to their conversation. Frank, always ready to enter a fray, had reseated himself.

Some two decades later Jeff was to become involved in a bigger fight, once again with Frank as his backup.

Frank stood three inches taller than Jeff and ten pounds heavier. He played catcher on the university baseball team, now in his second year. He was on a baseball scholarship, a rising star recruited from the national championship Norman High team and enrolled in physical sciences to become a general science major. He chose this to be his personal road to law school with a specialization of environmental law. He and Jeff had become friends in high school after Frank had moved to Norman from Alaska.

"As you know, I prefer to own a bat in times of trouble, but my common sense tells me to use greater weapons, such as belittling and intimidation through the use of words, when necessary," summarized Frank.

"Right. That's why you stood up when the fight started," quipped Jeff. "To call them names. I'll drink to that," he concluded.

Jeff was a declared scientist also on an athletic scholarship for water polo. He'd begun to shave his head completely, long before it became fashionable. With his almond shaped eyes and high cheekbones it gave him an Asian appearance. Then he added, "For the sake of purity, one must absolve oneself of temptation. Therefore, if any liquor is within eyesight, the alcohol must be consumed to deny its temptation."

To pass the time, Jeff drunkenly explained to Frank that his four grandparents had come to this country in the early part of the Twentieth Century from Eastern Europe during pre-Russian Revolution days. They had settled and met in Oklahoma City, in a small European enclave of farmers and ranchers where their children, Jeff's parents, met and married.

Shortly after marriage, his parents moved from the big city down to Norman where they believed better opportunities could be found. Jeff's mother found employment as a teacher at a local elementary school, a school that prided itself in its quality staff and dedicated students. His father got a part-time job in a pastry shop where Jeff spent his summers learning to bake bread and design pastries that quickly became popular with their clientele. His mother was an excellent teacher and over time rose to the rank of principal.

TWO

Frank had spent his early years in Seward. He lived close to a girl a year younger whom he knew as Mary Moore—nicknamed Megan, each in their separate 700 square foot homes. Their fathers jointly owned a charter fishing boat, one among hundreds in the Seward marina. They went to school together and helped operate the boat.

Frank and Megan shared many quiet and fun-filled moments playing board games and Ping Pong or going for long walks along the waterfront to watch the luxury liners park in the Prince William Sound.

Every school-child learned that Seward was located 225 miles south of Anchorage, a beautiful little drive along the Seward Highway. William Seward, Abraham Lincoln's Secretary of the Interior, purchased Alaska from the Russians in 1867 for seven million dollars. News of the purchase soon became a national scandal known as Seward's Folly. After all, who in their right mind, would want to pay that much money for a "frozen hunk of rock" two–and-a-half times the size of the State of Texas? It didn't take long for the purchase to prove its merit. The ongoing trade in otter and sealskins flourished, as did world-class fishing in the rich waters. Two gold strikes didn't hurt; nor did the eventual discovery of oil in Prudhoe Bay to the far north of the state, along with a growing trade in tourism.

Actually living in Seward, however, translated into hand-to-mouth, day-to-day survival for its less than three thousand population. Charter fishing boats required that people sign up for services, which in Frank and Megan's case, mostly applied during the late spring through fall months when they would get the tourist spillover after the larger boats had been filled.

During the summers and weekends, the two kids would scrub the deck, check the poles and reels, keep the engine full of gas, clean the toilet, and complete a hundred other chores necessary to maintain a boat, including finding a way to pay the rent on their boat slip. Then they'd go out for four-to-eight hour jaunts, cut the gills of the fish that were caught in order to bleed them once they were on-board (this was necessary to prevent any blood-borne parasites from entering the meat), and hose the deck of slop and blood. Once back at the slip, they helped load fish onto carts, which they would haul to the filleting tables.

While Frank loved the challenge of work and the successful completion of a hard task, Megan deplored physical labor and only partially completed her chores leaving the rest of her duties for Frank to finish.

Winters were rough when no tourists arrived. Frank stayed home alone, or stayed with Megan and her folks, or at the homes of other friends, and walked to school. His dad went to Anchorage and frequently stayed there for weeks working various jobs, mostly cleaning boats in the harbor.

Frank's mother died when he was two and he didn't remember her. His father raised him, in a manner of speaking. For the most part, Frank raised himself, and to him, that was all right. When you're a kid things are what they are, even if the world sucks.

Megan got into Frank's pants when they were still in junior high school. Although a lot of guys could make the claim that she broke them in, Frank liked to think the two of them had a special connection.

During tourist season, both of their fathers would hit the bottle after work, or when there was no work, but never during a charter. They also liked to gamble. Megan's father, nicknamed Hap for some reason, was an okay guy while Frank's father could remember a million jokes and always had a new one to tell. They both gambled one night a week with a friend who had a gambling parlor onboard his ship.

Hap maintained a reputation of being a smart gambler who knew when to say "No." As a result, more often than not, there would be food on the family table. Hap's basic rule: never drink on a gambling night. There were six other nights in the week to get loaded.

Megan's mother, Debra, stayed at home and sipped rum on the rocks for a career. When Frank went over to stay the evening, he'd usually find her corpulent body sprawled on the sofa like a drunk on a park bench, with the radio on and a bottle on the floor next to her. The occasional magazine over her face made the picture complete.

Sometime in their very early lives, Hap brought home a gaming set, complete with cards, dice, and a toy roulette wheel to show the kids how the House had control over the client. He even brought home a battery-operated slot machine, some eight inches in height. He spent a considerable amount of time teaching the kids how to shoot craps and play Twenty-One. In his opinion, the rest of the games were junk. He advised them to choose a game in which you can make right or wrong decisions, not one that decides for you, otherwise, it's not a game.

Frank and Megan had one big difference between them. Gambling caught her like a net catches a fish; Frank could wait until he turned twenty-one. Even then, he only gambled once every couple of months in order to kill a Friday or Saturday night, when a good or a bad lay couldn't be found.

According to Hap, you gambled and played "Twenty-One" for real when you turned twenty-one. Apparently, that was too long for Megan to wait. She'd practice on her own; they both did. By the time the two were in junior high, they had become skilled in a number of serious games and made a few welcome dollars on the side showing other kids how to play.

When Megan gambled it, it drew spectators. To Frank's young mind, when you're young, you see an idiosyncrasy, some quirk in another kid and that's all there is to it. When they get older that quirk stands out and when they get still older it tends to define who they are. Megan played for all the marbles all the time; except for when she might be setting someone up for a fall.

Megan didn't have any great beauty, but friends are friends. She began to smoke in junior high, and more times than Frank cared to count, he'd see her take shots of her mother's rum when the old gal lay unconscious and Hap was out somewhere. Frank considered that Hap might have had a girlfriend on the side.

The turning point in Frank's life came during his final year of junior high school. His father died of a brain aneurysm and his aunt and uncle, who lived in Norman, were notified and flew up to Seward to bring back Frank to live with them.

Aunt Flo and Uncle Bob were solid decent folks. She served as assistant manager at a department store and he owned an accounting business employing several people. Thus, for Frank, poverty came to an abrupt end as he said "goodbye" to Seward and Megan and said "hello" to upper middle-class America.

Studies and baseball took up Frank's time in high school. He and Megan wrote back and forth. To Frank's eye, she'd turned out cute, if one were allowed some flexibility in the word.

Not long after high school graduation Frank received a letter from her in which she said she got married to a nice guy up in Seward and she wasn't even pregnant when she did so. According to her, the guy was two years her senior—Bernie something or other, whom she'd met at a party. Bernie went to trade school and got a good job as a repairman in a new industry, computer technology.

From Frank's other friends back in Seward, he had learned that Bernie soon made enough money to help support Megan's penchant for drinking. Once she learned to dress properly and to look more mature, she developed a penchant for going down into Canada to gamble. After a few short years of watching his wife gamble away his money, Bernie announced to the world he was through with her, filing for bankruptcy and divorce on the same day. He owed the Internal Revenue Service sixteen thousand dollars in back taxes.

At the same time that Frank began college at the University of Oklahoma, Megan stopped all her correspondence with him.

THREE

At the Loose Cannon, the two men, who shared a couple of classes, ate ribs, drank, and exchanged war stories together until closing. Frank confessed that, although his aunt and uncle were pleased to have him live with them while he went to school, he wanted some independence. He couldn't take the college dorm scene and needed a new place to live. While having fun had its place, Frank needed to study.

Even at eighteen, Jeff owned a nice little three-bedroom home on Allenhurst Street east of the university, a short five minute drive from the school. Jeff explained to Frank that he only had one roommate at the moment who had announced his departure at the end of the month, and offered Frank a room at his home for ninety dollars a month. Frank accepted the offer.

"It's your house?" Frank asked, his words slurring. "I thought you lived in a rental. How'd you get it?"

"Oh, a couple of years ago, during summer break during high school here in Norman, I saved enough from the bakery and from collecting and selling soda cans and flew to India. When I was in Delhi, I made friends with a man who owned a sitar factory. I paid him fifty dollars to make me a hand-made ivory inlaid instrument. I had it shipped back to my parent's home here. The next summer, I traveled to Oregon and found a piece of land that I loved, so I sold the sitar for a great price and made a down payment on the land. After I graduated the next May and got accepted to OU, I sold the land to make the down payment for my home."

Several days later and shortly after Frank had moved in with Jeff, a student named Billy Kirk telephoned and said that he was responding to an ad Jeff had placed in the school paper for a roommate. Billy explained about his journalism interest and his status as a sophomore.

The three men bonded instantly, despite Billy's flaws of being too handsome and too impeccably dressed to suit either Jeff or Frank. Nobody suffered from a lack of ladies, however, Kirk set the standards. He possessed an abundance of jet black hair that he slicked back, laid back ears, and blue eyes set beneath perfectly sculpted eyebrows. This put impossible pressures on the other two to match the class of women Billy dated.

The next summer, before the start of their junior year, the three men decided to have a barbecue at the house. Jeff invited several of his water polo jocks and scientist friends, Frank invited a few of his baseball buddies and general science friends, and Billy invited a number of his journalism classmates.

The large group was grilling hotdogs and burgers, but mostly drinking beer. Jeff had established two pits complete with backstops for the game of horseshoes in the rear expanse of lawn. Country-Western music played on the radio. Many of the attendees had a date. Jeff brought his latest girlfriend, a meter-maid named Linda, who didn't have a lot of brains or looks, but made up for it in other ways. If Jeff would ask her if she wanted to drink a gallon of wine and watch TV, she'd probably say, "Okaayy, sounds like fun." Or, "Would you like to smoke a couple of joints and play in bed all night?" Her response might be, "Alll riigght, sounds like fun."

Frank had overstepped his bounds, worked up a lot of nerve, and asked out a woman who'd recently graduated with a degree in philosophy and had been accepted into law school, his own destination. The woman seemed like she might be a good date, if only for the night. She possessed a high degree of intelligence and in his mind, seemed to be a stuck-up snob. Still, he didn't mind showing her off.

Billy left the party early to pick up his date and soon returned with Miss Oklahoma. She stood close to five-ten, three inches shorter than Billy. A blond with shoulder-length ringlets, she also had blue eyes and wore a black halter-top and a short black Hawaiian floral print sarong slit up one side decorated with red Hibiscus flowers. Red sandals completed the ensemble. Everyone already knew of Lucinda Evans. She preferred to be called Lu rather than Lucy. To his credit, Billy never tried to show off. He was just good at whatever he did.

Billy's family had moved into the Oklahoma City area in the 1880s. His great-grandfather founded and operated the *Oklahoma City Storm*, a newspaper that ran legitimate news stories alongside legitimate scandal. The mix became a popular read for local residents. The name Kirk became legend in the state, in part because of the Kirks' social skills and in part because of their handsome lineage. Millions in the bank didn't hurt their notoriety.

As a fourth generation newspaperman, Billy grew up writing journalism from the earliest years under the tutelage of his father, presently senior editor of one of the papers, the *Oklahoman*, which served Oklahoma City, Tulsa, Norman, and the townships of Bowlegs and Maud. You had to go through Bowlegs to get to Maud, as the saying went. Some years later Billy's father purchased *The Oklahoman*.

Billy wanted to move into the arena of television, the first of his father's children to have such aspirations. His roommates had not the slightest doubt he would achieve his goal.

Frank had an active imagination. Many times he and Billy would discuss simple news events of the day and spin them into realms that ranged from the absurd and comedic to the tragic. These exercises would serve them well later in their respective careers.

Jeff lived a comedy of errors and like Billy, things always seemed to work out for him. Whether fate played a hand, or whether positive attitude acted as the determinant, no one could say. As a bioscience major with a physical education minor he was never fast enough to make the swim team, but the coach told him that he was aggressive enough to be a starter in the rough sport of water polo. Before too long, the man had enough skill and leadership capabilities to become team captain.

Jeff always bemoaned the fact that he had never made it to six feet in height. Early in their relationship, Billy had accused him of having a Mongolian ancestry because of his facial features. Jeff took it as a compliment.

"Jeff, five-eleven is only a number," Frank told him once. "If you change inches to centimeters, it will seem like a lot more."

To which Jeff might reply something like, "Frank, that's like standing on one leg on a scale to see if you weigh less, or converting the pounds to kilograms so the number will be smaller. It is what it is."

"Okay, be insecure all your life. You'll never amount to anything," Frank had responded, sounding like a mother trying to motivate a son whom she felt certain would become rich and famous.

A few evenings after the barbecue, the three roommates lazed in Jeff's living room, listening to The Who and watching lightning flash outside, seemingly in rhythm to the music. Jeff had decorated the room with several posters: one of a frizzy-haired scientist pouring a vaporous liquid into a beaker, one of the periodic table of elements, and another with numerous color photographs depicting mushrooms of the world.

Jeff slouched in a bean bag chair beneath a fourth poster; a two-by-five-foot picture of the galaxy as seen from Earth. He had dotted the prominent stars and constellations with fluorescent paint of varying colors. A black light illuminated the framed master-piece.

Jeff enjoyed the wind and the big Oklahoma sky. Whenever possible, he kept the windows and doors open for a good cross-breeze, but not this stormy night. .

"You know, guys," Jeff began, "how dreams are so bizarre you want to deny them? You want to say, 'This dream is so strange, even for me, that it must belong to somebody else. It must have gotten loose from their head and floated around until it found mine to land in by mistake'."

"Happens to me all the time, except to say that life is the dream," philosophized Billy, as he took another drag from his joint.

Frank removed a cigarette from a box and lit it.

Jeff continued, "Well, you know that physical conditioning class I took? I spent most of my time in synchronized swimming."

"I thought you were taking karate?" asked Frank, taking a drag from the joint passed to him from Billy.

"I am," responded Jeff.

"You mean swimming with the caps and the girls?" Billy inquired, suddenly more interested.

"Believe me, I don't seek pain as pleasure. However, I have learned that it can provide unexpected rewards."

"Yeah, like whatever, man," contributed Billy.

"We're listening," Frank said, ignoring Billy, wondering if Jeff was leading into some sadomasochistic realm—perhaps about to confess that he might be coming out of the closet as an S and M worshipper.

Jeff continued his tale. "I entered the class late for various scheduling reasons. The class required that for a six-week period, three times a week, everybody would train in a sport that was not their major activity to gain experience."

Billy made a sign of going to sleep by dropping his head suddenly and making snoring sounds.

"As the last man to enter the class, I got assigned to synchronized swimming. Let's face it. This is an assignment that no serious manly jock is going to volunteer for. Come on, who wants to train in a dainty and delicate effeminate sport? Time to turn in your man card, right?

"Here I am, inside the familiar chain-linked pool area—-not as a competitive water polo player, but as a member of the women's synchronized swim team. I introduced myself to the coach and to the six babes who comprised the team. They had already been warned to expect a male to join them.

"For the next six weeks, three days a week, for forty-five minutes at a time, I trained with the women."

"That works," Billy quipped.

"Hey, they hurt me. Try holding your breath under water for over a minute, with your feet pointing upward. Then you paddle halfway across the pool, using only your hands and shoulders, with your ankles showing above water. Then you do the other half of the pool with the knees showing. Then you come up for air and put your arms straight up and go the long way across the pool, back and forth. The coach is yelling, 'Legs only, and keep your arms all the way up over your head—reach for the sky. That means you, *Mister* Shenero'."

"She actually called you mister? That's cool," Frank said.

Jeff rolled on with his story. "She grabs a megaphone that could be heard underwater and yells, 'Now pike. Young man, please keep up. You're out of timing with the rest of the girls. Let's go, team, hands to the right, hands to the left, pike again...she went on and on. Let's get the music going. Today we're going to listen to Tchaikovsky's Overture of 1812 and followed by Ravel's Bolero'."

Frank tried to picture Jeff, a recently declared future scientist, in his nylon Speedos, svelte, cut, pecs galore, six-pack stomach, thighs made of steel—it was hard to have sympathy for him.

"After they left me for dead the first day, these women, who had to be aliens from another planet, trained for another hour-and-a-half on their own without having me to worry about.

"To make matters worse, after the first class, the coach called me to her office and confided, "I know you're a swimmer of sorts and a player of water polo. That's evident. So, I'm thinking you must have some athletic ability. But we really need you to not hold up the class. I have girls to train and meets to prepare for. Please try harder'."

"Where's your lawyer when you need one?" Billy quipped, looking at Frank. "So what'd you do then?"

"I tried harder next time. My stomach burned and my ankles swelled. My heart tried its best to burst, and my lungs had left me to find another body more suitable for its God-meant functions.

"Over the weeks I became stronger, passed the course, and made a friend or two.

"End of story," said Billy, popping open another beer.

"Not quite," responded Jeff. "In fact, at the end of my last day, I was standing inside the chain-link fence that surrounded the pool and looked out as sweating jocks came rumbling back from their macho activities having left blood, sweat and tears on the track and in the weight room.

"Apparently the girls had been scheming together to reward me. Six of the babes attired in clinging bathing suits surrounded me, with arms about my shoulders and waist; this, as the slathering heavyweights walked past the pool area on the way back to class. They saw me and grabbed onto the chain-link fence and shook it, demanding entrance into my domain."

"Did you get any phone numbers?" Frank asked.

"Seven," said Jeff.

"Seven?" declared Billy. "But there were only six girls in the class. Oh, shit, you mean the coach..."

Jeff smiled in reply.

FOUR

For the next two-and-a-half years the three room-mates lived together until they all received their Bachelor's Degrees. Jeff graduated with a specialty in biological sciences and got accepted into Micro-biology/Biochemistry graduate school with a full scholarship from the National Institutes of Health and Infectious Diseases. His interest was in the field of Medical Mycology, the field of medically import-ant fungi.

And Jeff, on a fast track for a Ph.D., received it several yeass later, based on his almost unparalleled excellence in his field of study. He applied for the position of interim Assistant Professor of Microbi-ology at OU and was accepted for the position—the youngest person to do so in the department. After several years, he got promoted to Associate Profes-sor.

Jeff also opened a business of monitoring indoor air and investigating mold-related issues for the private and public sector. He married one of his clients and soon had two sons with her. He still maintained the Allenhurst home as a rental and later purchased a larger residence, enough to accommodate a growing family.

Frank got accepted into law school at OU and directed his attention toward environmental law. By 1986, Frank passed his bar exam on the first attempt and moved into a small home he rented in the town of Moore, located halfway between Norman and the big city and destined to be leveled by a tornado a few years later,

After receiving his Bachelor's in Journalism, Billy was offered the promotion to Assistant City Editor of the *Oklahoma Storm,* but turned down the position to accept another one. KOKO-TV hired him for his looks and his ability to speak correct English to serve as a of fill-in news reporter, a position he coveted as a starting point. He married Lucinda Evans, the forme Miss Oklahoma, whom he had continued to date since their first get together at the barbecue years before. They began to grow a brood of handsome blue-eyed children.

A small but rapidly growing airline company out of Oklahoma City hired Frank within weeks of passing the bar exam. His presentation during the interview, his mathematical skills, and, as he would soon find out, his lack of business experience in the big world all contributed to his hiring.

Frank's primary duties entailed doctoring their

books, which was hinted at, but not disclosed during the interview. The job had flexible hours and paid well with opportunity for advancement and came with paid vacations and health coverage. He held the auspicious title of Environmental Consultant, a title which he wore on his proudly wore on his sleeve. He quickly became disenchanted with the job's activities.

The airline supported a subsidiary business of degreasing engine and wheel parts from airplanes. The company dumped their old and used trichloroethylene, otherwise known as TCE, into porous soil, thus potentially contaminating the fresh water supply.

The company would buy TCE in fifty-five gallon drums from supplier number one, all by the book. On the side, they would pay cash under the table at a greatly reduced rate for another batch of TCE from supplier number two. The original batch would show in the audit when it was sent for recycling, the other batch would not. The illegal batch, already used, went into a tanker truck and driven into the backwoods to be dumped. Frank's job entailed two major parts: to ensure the books were right for the Environmental Protection Agency and state auditors, and to represent the company in any environmental issues that might arise in general.

Along with the criminality of the job, Frank had a serious ethical problem. However, years before, while before growing up in Seward, he'd decided in favor of possessing a lot of money in lieu of being the possessor of abject poverty. While he could survive at either end, he preferred not to be in the middle. He might call it a personality flaw based on bad upbringing.

The second year of the job he also became married to one of the daughters of the company vice president, so he moved out of his rental home and moved into his wife's house in the city.

When he could get away, Frank frequently visited Jeff at his office at the university in Norman, or at his home there, and assisted him with his indoor air quality investigations, a field that also fascinated him. He had often contemplated that the two of them might have made a great team, if the practice of law had not captured his heart.

One day, during the beginning of his third year on the job, Frank received a letter from Megan at his post office box, presently employed by a casino in Oklahoma City. She wondered if he could call her to rehash old times.

When they first met in her apartment, the visit was casual. She revealed that she had gotten jobs in various casinos dealing Black Jack, occasionally acting as croupier at craps tables. After answering an ad, she had secured a good job at a casino on Cherokee land outside the city limits. She told Frank her secrets and he revealed his—a pact they'd made as children and had always kept. That is, except for what he actually did for the airline. That secret was for him and him alone.

Like Frank, the airline also employed his wife

and she had commitments to her job. Her duties required her occasional departure from the city for negotiation purposes. For his part, Frank also had the freedom to move about, as long as he maintained proper care of the books.

The evening of their third date, two months after they had first met, Frank and Megan shared numerous drinks and engaged in a long-overdue sordid and torrid one-night stand. In pillow talk borne of alcohol-driven recklessness, Frank related to Megan how much his job bothered him and that he might go to jail before his life had even begun.

There is never a good way to get blackmailed. To Frank, the way Megan did it tasted particularly sour, if only because she had crossed the line regarding their trust and their forever pact about truth telling. During their night in the sack, she turned to him in the very early morning hours and said, "Frankie, I need money."

"Don't we all," he said, casually.

"No, I'm serious." She took a large swallow from a glass of warm rum left over from the previous evening and lit a cigarette, as she leaned back against the headboard. "I owe big money to very serious people and I have negotiated a payoff settlement."

Frank sat up and leaned against the headboard. "How much?"

"Maybe a couple hundred thousand with thirty percent interest, so call the debt around three hundred thousand, give or take."

"Damn, Megan, let me guess." Frank took a stab

in the dark with a blunt instrument, not likely to miss the mark. "Gambling."

"Very good." The scratchiness of the words in her tobacco challenged vocal cords was matched by her sarcasm. "Let's say new management came in and they let me get stinking drunk on my day off and gamble. I dug myself into a six-foot grave."

"Hell, lady, if your daddy were alive, he'd never approve of your mixing the two habits. On your friends' part, that's not a good way to run a business, screwing over your own employees. From what I'm hearing, though, nothing personal, but it sounds to me like you really pissed somebody off, like somebody in the casino management and that you're leaving a lot out of the story. I'd say you're not being totally honest with me."

Megan remained silent for a few moments, then said, "Frankie, the details of the story don't matter. What does matter is that I need money."

"Which tells me the answer to my question is 'yes'. Well, I don't have that kind of money, Meg. Even if I did, how would I get paid back, if I did lend you the bucks?"

"What does your wife do? Doesn't she have money?"

"What!" Frank exclaimed, narrowing his eyes and boring into her. "My wife doesn't have anything to do with you or this conversation. Leave her out of this."

"It came from desperation, Frankie. You're my last resort. I have nowhere else to go. These are nasty people and I'm lucky to get off with a payout. Permit me to be blunt so you can understand this question. First, how much can you pay me monthly? And second, who said anything about a loan?"

"I can't and won't pay you anything, Megan. Plain talk. Let's figure this out."

She cut him off, looking almost diabolical with her short hair sticking up in places. "Okay, Frankie. Figure this out. How are you going to stay out of prison once the Feds find out about how you poison people for a living and how do you explain to your employers why you took them down and how is your wife going to pay the bills while you're away and especially when she finds out about you and me?"

Totally speechless and stunned, a hot flush ran up Frank's face. He'd always felt like crap since the day he'd started his job, but he'd become adept at burying his feelings. It had turned him into a bitter man underneath his smooth façade with a bitterness that continue to grow almost daily. Megan had definitely hit him where it hurt the most.

Before he could stammer a reply, Megan, in her unique style, gulped the last of the liquor in the glass, took a deep drag from her cigarette and stubbed it out in the liquor glass. Casually, she threw the sheets off her naked body, wanting more, but Frank was in no mood. He quickly dressed and walked out.

After that night, Megan and Frank parted company, if one didn't count the monthly checks he sent her over the next four years. He began honing his outside contacts, stayed with his job until she had been paid off completely, and continued to sweat with the full knowledge that the devil-woman might come back into his life at any time.

He eased out of the airline accounting business. Still living in Oklahoma City, he obtained employment as an environmental attorney for the Oklahoma Petroleum and Gas industry, otherwise known as OPG. This time he worked strictly as a lawyer on behalf of the company's legitimate interests—a reborn man with old memories.

FIVE

There was always something wrong with Mary Sue Tamsen—lead poisoning, exposure to pesticides and radon, latex sensitivity, chemical sensitivity, allergies, and even mad cow disease—whatever the current trend might be. To define Mary Sue as a hypochondriac would be to say that rotten fish have a bad odor. However, separating fact from fiction, in her case, proved to be an impossibility.

At five-two and one hundred thin pounds, her most recent jobs included working as a cosmetic salesperson in a department store, cash register clerk in a small grocery store, and bowling alley shoe check-out expert. Although loathe to do so and in times of near famine, she had also worked as a carpenter's assistant doing small repairs in homes, along with very personal jobs for the carpenter, for which he paid her side money.

Over time, she let herself go to a point nearing disintegration. She had long since developed deep grooves in her face, most of which could be attributed to smoking, drinking and hard living. Always thinking, always scheming, she openly bragged to her neighbors about never having cooked a meal in her life, except when she got paid for it.

Mary Sue had married Bud, the most recent of her husbands. She brought into the marriage a two-year-old daughter, Wendy, father unknown.

After a year of marriage, she gave her husband a son, whose fathering was also suspect. After the child's birth, Mary Sue claimed to have a chronic yeast infection and couldn't have sex anymore. Except for rare occasions when the infection "minimalized," she could no longer provide wifely services for her husband.

Bud Tamsen dropped the scoop of his front end loader. He turned off the ignition and stepped down from the machine, tilting his Oklahoma Sooners baseball cap downward, as the wind whistled across the City of Norman landfill. Swirls of dirt and trash became airborne, much of it flapping against his clothing and stinging his cheek.

The northern horizon roiled with black storm clouds and darkness threatened to rule the day. Wind entered the low-pressure area and towering pitch black cumulonimbus clouds served as a flag demarking the approach of yet another rapidly moving and serious thunderstorm.

Wishing he had invested in a face mask for times like these, Bud inhaled both large and microscopic particles of debris as he walked the fifty yards to his battered 1985 Ford 150 pickup. Thankful for the completion of another average day, he did not look forward to another dull night with his complaining wife and two children.

Bud drove seven miles to The Touchdown Tavern and parked himself on a barstool, greeting the other regulars getting off work.

If Bud Tamsen had died, the world hadn't yet learned of it. Doubtless, the man served as an extra in *Night of the Living Dead* with no breath to cloud a mirror. The man stood average height, with thinning light brown hair with a colorless personality. He possessed no jokes to tell at the bar and could never remember any that had been told to him. A drooping white mustache served as the highlight to a poorly designed facial ensemble, as wanting as his personality. Bar patrons had nicknamed him Rushmore, because of the stone face he perpetually wore.

Sitting there, Bud knew exactly what his wife would say when he got home. "'Buddy, here's what I'm thinking'," she would proclaim, "'and I wish you wouldn't drink beer, it makes you stink so much; you should try rum or vodka, and you smell from work, and change deodorants while you're at it'." He would find her at the mirror, as she gave him her opening salvo, her statement of welcome, rarely turning away from the mirror when she did so.

No doubt, she would call him 'Buddy', a clear indication that he would soon hear another of her famous schemes that had kept them in painful debt for virtually their entire marriage. When they had married, he'd possessed good money. Now he languished as another minimum wage worker with a secret stash for drinking; a stash no man in his right mind would tell his wife about.

When Bud left the bar, the storm had progressed nicely. He pulled his cap lower and sloshed through the pelting rain to his pickup. It took him ten minutes to drive home. When he did arrive at seven o'clock, he immediately checked the refrigerator for something to eat and found it typically wanting. He made a sandwich of left-over baloney, threw some mustard onto the bread, and opened a cold can of soda.

With sandwich in hand, Bud turned on the TV. Several minutes later, he sauntered into the master bath in time to see his wife apply a layer of hypo-allergenic facial cream.

The mirror served as Mary Sue's best friend and worst enemy, depending on the time of day she viewed herself. A tumbler containing the usual rum-on-the-rocks rested on the commode top next to an ashtray containing a smoldering cigarette. The bathroom fan hummed, "to pull in some fresh air—something everybody needs," according to her.

Their daughter, Wendy, seventeen going on eighteen, spent most of her after school hours and most weekends at her boyfriend's house. Not particularly fashion conscious, she preferred to wear loose clothing, bordering on baggy. She was strikingly handsome and wore her dark brown hair lengthy, sometimes straight, occasionally curled—no curlers, thank you. Their thirteen-year-old son, Karl, spent evenings in his room playing video games.

Mary Sue began her latest presentation. "Anyway, I think this deadly toxic black mold could be the cause of all my problems and the other medical problems we've all had."

Bud nodded slowly, aware that his wife always wore the same torn green cotton bathrobe and slippers. She didn't like to wear anything underneath the robe. Curlers, the small variety, another of her trademarks, adorned her short blond hair. He mused that the combination of curlers and her small face made her appear to have a pointy head. He needed to give deep thought to what his wife had said regarding the medical problems experienced by his family members. Try as he might, nothing came to mind.

Tornado warning sirens began to wail. At that moment, Bud noticed a water stain developing in one corner of the ceiling.

"We got a leak," he said.

"Damn, Buddy, I checked the roof this morning, too, as soon as I heard about the storm coming in."

"You went up on the roof? You?"

"Yes," Mary Sue gave her simple response, smiling broadly.

"What a piece of bad luck," said Bud in reply to her comment about the roof leak.

"I wouldn't exactly call it bad luck, dear."

"What do you mean?" he asked suspiciously.

"Buddy, haven't I always taken care of you and the children?" she asked, unabashedly.

"Uh, well, I guess," he uttered, not willing to get into another ugly fight about her suspected extra-marital affairs along with her excuses not to care for him during his times of dire need.

His wife continued, "I've got an idea, a plan, but I need you with me on this. It's a plan to make us rich. Are you following what I'm saying?"

Bud did his best not to roll his eyes skyward. "Damn it woman," he said dully, "maybe you should stop pissing away my money with your online gambling."

"Sometimes I win."

"Why don't you go to a casino and lose it right?" To Bud, that seemed a legitimate question.

"No thanks. I don't do casinos anymore," she replied.

Bud wanted to say something about her usually getting too plastered to drive to a casino, but let it go. However, with wrestling matches looming on the TV and with him also having had a few too many, he felt courageous. "Gee, dear, here's an idea. Why don't you take, oh, say, a few twenties, lay them in the toilet, and pull the handle. That way you'll save gas money without having to drive to the casino."

Another plan, another scheme—a gambler who wanted to give it one more try. How much had he lost on her plans? Virtually everything. Mary Sue gave him a cold stare.

"Okay, Okay, I'm listening," he said, "But do we have to talk about this in the bathroom?"

His wife grabbed her supplies to follow her husband into their sterile bedroom, devoid of reading materials save the latest tabloid. She set the items on the nightstand, then pushed him lightly down onto the bed. "Listen," she said in a half-whisper, smoke still coming from her mouth like a fire-breathing dragon in the first stage of ignition-sequence-countdown. "I jimmied a couple of shingles on the roof above the bathroom to make it leak."

"So?" asked Bud, not understanding the next move on the chessboard.

"So, the roof leaks."

"That was clever," he said sarcastically. "And?"

"And we will get water damage to the ceiling," she responded.

Bud shook his head back and forth in two quick motions. "So?"

Mary Sue paused in feigned exasperation, took a long drag and blew out a lung-full of smoke. "So deadly toxic black mold will develop in our home," she stated, as a matter of indisputable fact.

"It will?"

"Yes, it will. Trust me. I saw it on TV and I looked it up on the Internet."

"You did? I mean, why is it deadly? What did they say on TV?" said Bud, perhaps more than a little concerned, since both he and his wife held great trust in television reporting, especially when she backed up the information by the Internet and the tabloids. That made a powerful matched trio second to none.

Mary Sue placed one foot on the bed, exposing

her upper thigh, a purposeful tease, saw she was getting the bate nibbled at and added, "On top of that, I called up the handyman guy who lives next door and he thought the same thing might be possible."

Bud turned down his mouth as an expression of respect for his wife's thorough investigative skills.

Mary Sue set the hook. "You look here, Buddy," she proclaimed. "This is our big chance."

"I'm confused," said Bud, trying to not stare at her thigh, which was the most he'd seen of her exposed body for quite some time.

"My research proves we have a chance to make some serious money. Are you with me? Real money; and not a lot of inconvenience involved. And it won't interfere with your work schedule. Oh, and not a cent will be spent out of our pockets," she quickly added, as if reading his mind.

Bud felt like asking if she was going to say something about never having steered him wrong. His better judgment prevailed, and he bit the words before they could issue forth. To Bud's way of thinking, her statement did suggest she might back off gambling for a short while, as usually occurred when she involved herself in a new get-rich scheme that required extra cash.

"I'm with you," he said dully, in reality not interested, but playing along with her drama to get it over with at the same time. This evening's professional wrestling match promised to be brutal.

Here's what I'm talking about," said Mary Sue, almost one-time beauty queen runner-up of her high school prom—albeit the school was quite small.

The moment she began to explain, Karl walked into the bedroom, taking a break from his usual round of videogames. "What's for dinner?" he asked.

Their son had a goofy look about him. With black spiked hair, tee shirt and blue jeans, he was of average height and weight, but possessed a serious overbite and his ears stuck out. In fact, thought Bud, not for the first time, *he looks more like the temporary handyman who lives next door than he does me.*

Suddenly conscious of her exposed thigh, Mary Sue pulled her leg from the bed and stood up. "Go ahead and order a pizza, if you want, sweetie," she told Karl. The top to her robe had pulled open to expose a good portion of her medium-sized well-shaped breasts, compliments of an expensive surgeon.

Karl watched her as she cinched up the robe.

"Honey, give Karl some money, will you?" If nothing else, Mary Sue loved her children.

Bud fished in his pockets and put together enough for a large pizza, hoping there would be enough left over for him.

"Thanks, Dad," Karl said, and departed.

"Bring me back the change, Karl," Bud demanded.

"Don't I always?" asked the boy.

"No." Turning his attention back to his wife, Bud checked his watch at the same time. "So get to it. What are you telling me? And hurry up about it."

"What I'm telling you is that the leak in the bathroom will grow mold in two or three days. If we say we are sick from the mold then we can sue the insurance company."

"That's dumb. If we report the problem and they fix it, then that's that." said Bud.

"Suppose we don't report it because we don't notice it?" said Mary Sue, as she pulled a fresh pack of cigarettes from the pocket of her robe, deftly opened the pack with her hands and teeth, tapped out a cigarette and lit it from the first, without paying attention to the ashes falling to the floor. She turned to the nightstand and stubbed out the first one, then turned back to her husband.

"Why should they pay anything other than normal repairs?" he asked.

"Because we are going to get in a fight with them from start to finish, Buddy."

"Excuse me, but what's the big deal with mold, anyway?"

Mary Sue took a deep breath. "Dearie, in case you haven't been paying attention, mold is the hot news in the country. It's the rage. Everybody knows about it. It's on Oprah and all the news channels. It's what causes people to get sick from everything."

"Everything?"

"Pretty much. Mold is a dirty word. People get scared when you say the word."

"Doesn't everybody get mold, I mean in their house and stuff?" Bud asked, thinking back to a piece of green moldy cheese he ate out of the refrigerator the day before.

"Of course," Mary Sue added in her best tutorial tone. "That's the point. That's why everybody's sick. It grows on and between the walls, on the ceilings, on clothes, and even on people."

"How does it grow on people?" Bud was starting to itch.

"Did you ever hear of ringworm or Canada?"

"I heard of ringworm. Isn't Canada a country?"

"I meant candida, or something like that. You know, yeast infections in women like I got."

"Oh yeah, you been complaining about having that deadly disease for years," her husband complained, coldly.

Mary Sue ignored him. "And all kinds of molds can make you die. So, we're going to wait a few days, then call it in. Our insurance company is All American Insurance. They will send out a claims adjuster who will go up on the roof. He will say that normal wear did not cause the leak and they aren't going to pay anything. We say he's full of it and nobody in this house goes up on the roof and he doesn't know what he's talking about. While they're dicking around, the leak will get worse and mold will grow. The way these things work, when they do come to their senses and decide to help us, it will take them forever to fix the problem, that is, if we play our cards right. Meanwhile, the problem in the house gets worse."

Mary Sue was on a roll. "How we're going to make money is to find lawyers who will file a suit for bad faith and illness as a result of All American's negligence," she concluded.

"What negligence? What illness?" Bud asked, completely out of his element.

"They were negligent in fixing the problem," she answered. "They took their sweet time to fix our home and we all suffered from their..." here she struggled to find a suitable word, then "...slowness."

She didn't understand the nuances, but she was referring to the duty of an insurance company to provide the services it promises in a timely manner. This can be tied to breach of contract. Separate from this is a bad faith issue, that is, a paid-for promise to provide the services for which the insured is paying them to provide.

Then Bud nodded very slowly, scratched his head, took his wife's cigarette out of her hand and put it in his own mouth. "Got it. It's not extortion, because it's true. So, how much do you think we can get and now that I think about it, I've been feeling really crappy since this whole water leak thing started what...three days ago?"

"It started three days ago. As for the other part, I don't know how much money, maybe a few thousand dollars."

"Is that before or after we pay off the lawyers?"

"I'm not that far yet," she said. "What do you think?"

"I say we deserve it."

"Damn right we do and so do the kids. Let's not forget their health," contributed Mary Sue.

Bud dropped his voice, as if the walls had ears or

worse, as if the government were listening. "How do we work the sick part into it?"

"I'm not sure, yet," she said. "I need to think more. For the present time, let's let things percolate."

Unable to bite his tongue anymore, Bud threw out a fastball, "I hope this isn't another one of your great loser schemes".

"Hey," she said, very defensively, "once in a while I can be right, even if it is by accident."

"Yeah? Sure beats being wrong on purpose," Bud stated forcefully and more directly than Mary Sue had seen in some time.

Bud checked his watch, stood, and hurried off to catch the wrestling matches on the tube.

SIX

Ten days and two storms later, in early July, Bud and Mary Sue Tamsen spoke with, and filed a claim with Steve Hirshfield, adjuster with All American Insurance, for water damage to the bathroom ceiling. They thought it might be a roof leak and Mary Sue expressed her growing concern for the presence of mold. The large multi-colored stain on the ceiling increased in size daily and had grown to two feet in diameter, covering part of the ceiling corner and growing down two walls over the shower. The stains, initially marginated, were filling in with various colors, mostly green with patches of black.

Hirshfield told them that All American Insurance was inundated with storm claims a lot worse than theirs, and it would take an inspector another ten days to get out to the house.

At this time, Bud and Mary Sue began to worry in earnest and wondered whether the rapidly growing multi-colored staining could pose a real health threat. At that point, Bud felt certain his wife had roped him into yet another scheme that heading south even faster than the stain.

Mary Sue claimed illness whenever she entered the master bath so they placed it off-limits. They closed the door to the bathroom, and stuffed a towel beneath the door. Unbeknownst to them, this caused the humidity level in the room to increase, resulting in accelerated mold growth. They began using the hall bath which they shared with their children. Mary Sue brought along her robe, smoke, and rum.

After the roof inspection, it took another week for the Tamsens to receive a report from All American Insurance denying their claim. In a letter from their carrier, the adjuster reported a loosened shingle had been found over the master bath and that subsequent damage to the underlying structure was not due to natural causes.

On cue, in the latter part of July, Mary Sue called and harassed the adjuster and demanded to speak with the district supervisor. This man supported the finding of the inspector and the conclusion reached by the adjuster. It had been a month since the stain had first appeared.

"What do you think?" Mary Sue raged while speaking with the district supervisor, "Because my husband came home from work with a bad leg xor something so I got up Bn the middle of the night and climbed onto the roof while he and my children were sleeping and pried up a shingle? You have got to be kidding."

Finally, in early August, over one month after the initial roof leak had been reported, and under nagging pressure and threats, All American Insurance relented and hired Bob Jones, Restoration, Inc., to repair the bathroom and the roof. The company had used Bob Jones over the years for such instances.

Bob Jones Restoration set up an appointment with Mary Sue three days after their directive from All American and, still in early August, came out to the house to do their work. This they did, following standard guidelines.

Bob Jones, Inc. critically contained the master suite and hauled the furnishings out the back sliding door to the rear covered patio and then took them around to the garage. They totally cleaned and used state-of-the-art vacuuming suction to vacuum the furnishings after their removal from the home.

Bob Jones covered the bedroom carpet with heavy gauge plastic and separately contained the bathroom, which they found exceedingly nasty with the corner of the ceiling having dropped from the weight of the moisture. They bagged the contaminated materials, dropped the remainder of the ceiling, pulled the vanity, removed the shower surround, cut the walls and followed all the procedures necessary to ensure that no mold escaped into the home proper and that none remained of any consequence. Finally, they placed a HEPA air filter in the bathroom and another one in the bedroom.

From the bedroom side, only a zipper opening

placed in heavy gauge plastic with a double entry could be observed leading into the stipped out bathroom. These activities were classed as standard operating procedures followed nationwide by reputable remediation companies. Only clearance testing and rebuild remained to complete the project.

From the moment she and her husband reported the water damage to their bathroom ceiling, Mary Sue had expressed her concern regarding the presence of mold and possible illness from it. To her, mold had become a four-letter word. She was in her element, much as a slug slithers in slime of its own making.

She did more research on the Internet and learned enough to become extremely dangerous to most of those who entered her sphere of influence, especially Dr. Shenero.

Some insurance companies pay the remediation company directly for their work, pay separately to another vender for clearance testing, and pay the homeowner enough money to reconstruct their residence. As long as the dollars paid out did not exceed a certain amount, All American usually followed the policy of paying everything to the client, who could then disburse the money to the agencies that did the work. To All American, it simplified their bookkeeping. To the recipients of the money, it frequently spelled trouble.

SEVEN

Dr. Jeffrey Shenero prided himself on being able to perform his own microscopy whenever possible. Nationally certified as a mold identification and enumeration expert, he trusted independent labs up to a point. They over simplified their reports and could solve a lot of problems by using slightly different procedures. Instead, in his opinion, they complicated issues by lumping categories of molds to the extent that indoor mold couldn't be distinguished from outdoor mold.

Jeff maintained two offices. His two room private office was located on Campus Corner across from the university where he would take an occasional nap and operate his consulting business. He once told Carmen, his secretary, "Try falling asleep at a binocular microscope. Both eyes get punched at the same time as you nod downward. Whatever you see after that is a sight for sore eyes."

The smaller cramped second office was situated on campus in the microbiology building. Three mornings a week, Jeff taught an early morning class of medical mycology along with three separate lab sections of eighteen students each. He also taught basic microbiology with one lab section and a course in public health.

With the exception of actual work and exercise time, Jeff and Frank spent time together. Once a week, when Jeff could get away, he drove to the city to visit Frank and his wife in the evenings. At least once a week, Frank was at Jeff's office, mostly to look at Carmen. Occasionally he would visit Jeff at his home to get fed by his wife until a few years ago when she left the scientist to move back east. She had taken the two children with her.

Things had not gone smoothly for the Sheneros. Because of Jeff's eccentricities and outspoken nature, he had become, according to her, an embarrassment to the family.

Jeff's cell phone vibrated as Bob Jones' workers were finishing their job at the Tamsen home. He returned the call to Bob, an old associate, and who owned the company. This particular afternoon Frank had arrived at Jeff's office at the point when Jeff had concluded the call. Carmen gave Frank a wave of the hand and went back to her computer.

"Bob Jones," Jeff stated to Frank.

Frank nodded. He leaned up against the door frame that separated the outer from the inner office and facing inward where Jeff sat at one computer, Carmen at another with printer-fax machine set upon a separate table. A single folding chair leaned against one wall that Jeff had decorated with pictures of historic scientists.

Frank said, "I know that name. Didn't you tell me that Bob had some personal problems at home and some medical issues?"

Jeff replied, "Yeah, but that's all I know. He does good work. The grapevine is quiet, so I guess all is well. Anyway, Bob told me he finished a job yesterday and needs me to do clearance testing. Want to come along?"

"If I can get away," said Frank. He pulled out his pocket calendar and apologized, "Sorry, buddy, can't make it on this one. Major OPG meeting." He came to regret having missed the appointment with his friend.

Jeff propped his feet up on one corner of the desk, the only area not strewn with junk: computer screen, mouse, monitor, radio, weather receiver, old culture plates, contact samples, microscope, tally counters and tally sheets, bills, scientific papers, notes from jobs finished and samples from jobs that still needed to be analyzed.

Jeff always suggested to his secretary, "Carmen, if you don't know where to put something, just put it on my desk so I'll always know where to look for it."

Jeff could never find a thing he was looking for when he worked alone on Carmen's days off and frequently needed to call her at home to locate an item. Always the eternal quipster, Jeff held Groucho

Marx as one of his ultimate heroes, tirelessly celebrating the twists and turns of the English language. Therefore, according to him, Jeff considered himself a dis-organizational genius, and frequently proclaimed that he needs to re-disorganize his office in order to locate lost items.

Carmen, on the other hand, was well organized and put items where they belonged. She also had a beauty that could not be ignored, with her tight figure, flawless complexion, and long black hair.

Frank asked, "What's the deal on the job?"

Jeff leaded back in his spring-loaded chair, shrugged, and answered, "Master suite, a couple of closets. Basic stuff. I'm supposed to expect a call from a women named Tamsen. Bob calls her a very concerned woman and to be wary."

Frank grimaced, "Oh, one of those, huh?"

Neither man laughed. A very concerned person was a euphemism for a person who wouldn't let go of a concept, regardless of the facts presented to them, except in rare cases.

All American Insurance had hired Bob Jones, Inc., their usual go-to company, for a remediation job rated at about a seven out of ten, as these things go; better than a whole home flood and worse than a water supply line leak behind a toilet. Here the ceiling and walls of several areas were involved.

Jeff continued recounting the conversation. "According to Bob, the home incurred extensive damage. The Tamsens had that bathroom baked in. Lots of humidity. Mold everywhere. About what you'd expect. The trouble is, he could contain and easily dispose of the mold; not so the woman. She wouldn't stop talking about mold and what it had already done to her family'."

They'd all circled the block on the issue of mold complaints versus health issues numerous times. All the remediation companies dealt with the problem on a weekly, if not daily basis. Within only a two-year period, liability insurance had increased as much as ten-fold where mold matters were concerned, in part, thanks to a couple of high profile cases that had made the news.

In addition, the entire insurance industry had taken a hit on nine-eleven. As an outgrowth of that disaster, it became necessary to settle the larger claims first, and the average claims got backed up in terms of attention afforded to them. They were still playing catch up, years later.

In Jeff's opinion, once television started the nationwide reporting about toxic mold, everybody decided this was as good a time as any to blame their problems on someone or something else. Viewers increased in numbers and so did advertisers. The trend that followed was a natural one as people saw an easy way to make big money without having to work too hard at it. In Jeff's experience, many insurance companies didn't help, since they would rather pay somebody to shut up rather than to fight in court. The rare legitimate claim of injury due to mold existed when tied to respiratory symptoms, but these claims were at a level far lower than the frequency of non-legitimate claims for every other kind of illness attributed to mold. If mold claims made it to court, they were being thrown out almost as fast as they came in, unless a jury could be convened.

Jeff then related the rest of the conversation to Frank. "After I asked Bob about why Mrs. Tamsen complained so much, he said, ruefully, 'Beats me, Jeff. We went above and beyond the call of duty. We critically contained every area we worked in, as per SOP. Hell, man, you've come in after us and you've never found anything, other than a stray spore. Right'?"

Bob and Jeff knew that the guidelines Bob spoke of were in the past and the industry had moved beyond the initial recommendations that came from the State of New York. Besides, the remediation guidelines were never meant to deal with the "perception versus reality doctrine," as Jeff and Frank both called it, a theme Jeff constantly preached at mold detection and remediation seminars. These seminars were directed toward hundreds of real estate personnel during state accreditation seminars. Jeff became saddled with the task of ensuring that full disclosure of water damage in the sale of a home must be part of the buying and selling process. When asked why he supported mold remediation if he didn't believe mold to be a problem over and above allergy and asthma issues, he would reply, "Somebody has to be the voice of reason."

Every legitimate person in the field of remediation and clearance did their best to avoid any terms relating to health. "Is it dangerous? Was it danger-ous? Is it safe to move in?" Those terms were way too general. As Jeff had once stated, 'Like incest, the answer to those questions could be termed 'it's relative'.

Jeff went on. "So Bob tells me that Mrs. Tamsen complained of various illnesses and her sensitivity to mold. Hell man, we'd sealed the studs, scrubbed the air, HEPA vacuumed the contents of her *entire* home and cleaned the air ducts. We left her home *clean*'.

"Anyway, he needs me to find what he might have missed, to go into the containment areas and take measurements, you know, do my thing and let him know if I find anything. Then he'll come back and fix the problem; nothing complicated."

An hour after Frank left his friend to go to an appointment, Mary Sue Tamsen called Jeff who listened to the woman whine and moan about how Jones' crew screwed up her dream home and the en-tire inside of the house was covered with mold in-cluding contents, structure—absolutely everything.

"Well, Missus Tamsen, if things are so bad, why don't you leave and deal with the problem from a safe location?" He'd given the same advice to doz-ens of people over the years.

Apparently, Mary Sue knew enough not to an-swer that question directly. Instead, she insisted on a meeting immediately. Dr. Shenero could see for himself the mess Jones and his people had created.

EIGHT

The next morning, a Saturday, Jeff arrived at the Tamsen household.

He found himself in an average neighborhood for the lower middle class, somewhat rundown, with an overgrown lawn that needed serious attention to its margins. An old Chevy set up on blocks decorated the center of the lawn. A single car garage completed the ensemble.

Jeff parked at the curb and pulled a tripod and a case from the back seat. He a work bag full of equipment over one shoulder.

Got to stick to the straight and narrow with this one, Jeff cautioned himself.

He knocked and a few moments later a middle-aged woman answered the door, greeted him cordially, and bade him enter the Tamsen domicile. The heavy makeup on her face failed to disguise the deep crease lines around her nose and mouth. Her cheeks had begun to wrinkle. Without makeup she might pass for a senior citizen. She wore an overtight pink halter top and pink short shorts with white sneakers and pink socks. Her short tightly curled hair gave her head a pointy appearance. "Please come in. May I call you Doctor Shenero?"

Jeff wore his work uniform, a tan long sleeve shirt with tan slacks. Totally innocuous. "All right, thank you. If it's okay, I'm on a limited time schedule and I'll take a little look around while I run my tests. Let's see, where's your master bath?" He needed to get in and out in a hurry, but do his job efficiently.

The Tamsen home consisted of a very basic wood stucco frame residence measuring about fourteen hundred square feet with modest furnishings. A large television and entertainment center occupied most of the west wall of the living room.

Mary Sue moved behind him to shut the front door. "Be careful when you walk or touch anything because all the furniture and walls are covered with this slimy lavender colored mold. Your feet will stick to the carpet, so be careful. Look at it." she directed, sweeping her hand around the room.

Jeff moved toward the living room wall in order to take a closer look. He saw nothing amiss. If slimy lavender colored mold were present, he could send in one of his graduate students to write a first-of-a-kind report on it.

Over the years Jeff had inspected hundreds of seriously contaminated homes in which as much as thirty thousand gallons had cascaded freely across the rooms--water damage caused by anything from a broken water supply line to the fridge ice maker, or to the under-counter reverse osmosis water purifier, or to flooding and roofs blown off during storms. He knew of at least fifty ways a home could suffer water damage. Water on walls of plaster board walls usually meant mold would be present, either on the walls, inside them, or both.

Jeff's feet had slushed under the worst of home-flooding conditions, but they never slid from slime. "Excuse me, ma'am, there's no such thing as lavender mold," he explained, looking up, down and around. He didn't need to get too technical with her. "Sometimes green mold can take over a home, but this isn't one of the times."

"Oh, then actually I guess the mold on the walls and furniture does have a greenish cast, depends on how you look at it." She canted her head to look at the structure and contents of the home in a side-wise manner.

"My husband and I had to move into our son's room and put him in with his sister," she threw in, as an attempt to gain sympathy for the plight of her suffering family.

Jeff smelled a set-up all the way, but curiosity got the best of him, along with a sense of professionalism. He should have walked out the door, right at the slimy part and not looked back. You'd think these people would come up with a better story, knowing a professional mycologist would be the person who came to conduct the testing, he thought.

Something undefinable drove him onward. Later,

his dark side considered that it might be because he wanted to dive into quicksand and see how long it would take him to crawl out. No, this wasn't about mold, it was about somebody who pissed him off at the intuitive level, somebody who needed to be confronted on a bigger stage.

The scene continued to play on. The Tamsens could have yelled that Santa Claus had caused their problems and even then would have received some payment from the insurance company. Court awards for damages were costly, and something the company would try to avoid. Perhaps ten payouts might equal one jury award. Payoffs to schools were among the worst, according to what others in field had told him, but in Jeff's opinion, insurance had caused a lot of their own grief. Okay, maybe incompetent professionals in any field didn't help matters either, Jeff owned.

Jeff looked at the polyethylene sheeting covering the doorway to the master suite in order to locate the problem area. Then he went back outdoors and set up his tripod. He pulled out a long extension cord and a pump from his small equipment suitcase and set up the tripod some distance for the house, plugging the unit into a porch outlet he had noted upon his arrival. He labeled a cassette and inserted it into the hose at the end of the pump and set the hose into the top of the tripod. He ran the pump for several minutes and took notes.

Then he put his equipment together and re-entered the house. He unzipped the containment at the master bedroom and entered. His client followed behind him before he could close the zipper.

"You shouldn't be in here," he admonished her.

"Why not?" she asked.

He knew the house belonged to her and she could do what she wanted. He had no authority to order her out, only to appeal to her common sense.

"Because that's why these rooms are contained. We don't need extra spores from outside in here and we don't need that containment open any longer than necessary," Jeff said. "We need to get the truest readings as possible inside here."

"But you came in and you don't have protection," the housewife stated.

"Because I trust the people who hire me," Jeff replied.

Mary Sue said nothing. A response either way could get her into trouble down the road.

Jeff found the master bedroom devoid of furnishings, a portion of the ceiling gone with rafters exposed.

An air scrubber noisily pulled air through a HEPA filter. The top half of the bedroom walls were cut including a large portion or the master closet. The home had been constructed during an era in which home occupants required few clothes—some casual wear, some work clothes for the husband, a couple of semi-dress outfits, something for church, something for junk wear. Rooms and closets were small.

In the bedroom, Jeff repeated the testing procedure while Mary Sue hovered over him taking notes of her own while he periodically moved the tripod and pump to obtain representative air samples. Then he entered through the plastic covering the door to the bath. She followed.

The bath measured six feet-by-eight feet. Before being completely stripped, the simple bathroom housed a single towel cabinet to the right of the door, a single vanity to its left, a medicine cabinet above the sink, a commode to the left of the sink, a shower with step-in tub and a small linen closet. Not much else. Two people could fit into the room. It would be tight.

"Be careful, the wood has mold all over it," warned Mary Sue.

"Not really. And you shouldn't be in here, either." Jeff inspected the dozen or so studs on all four sides, representing all that remained of the tub-shower arrangement.

"What are those dark stains?" she asked, pointing to one of the vertical studs. "And what about the mold growing on the door hinges or the mold that on the toilet seat?" she continued.

Jeff tried to wrap his mind around the realization that this depressed middle-aged hag had once been configured into a younger looking hag.

"They're pine pitch and were there when the home they framed the home decades ago," Jeff said. "A little of this is wood rot; it's been there when the wood came from the yard. Besides, it was all contained inside the wall cavity and what's inside the wall stays inside the wall as long as the walls are dry. And mold doesn't grow on door hinges or toilet seats."

As Jeff stood examining the wall studs on the side of the shower, Mary Sue brushed closely and slowly past him facing his back and pointed to occasional stains on other two-by-fours. Then she said softly, "Doctor, there's still mold on the other wood. I can *feel* it. Originally, I also saw mold on the mirror and on the metal hinges of the doors. I took pictures."

"Tell you what," Jeff said, needing to get out. "Let me run tests, go back to the lab and see what the microscope says."

While he understood more than most people about the wide variety of fungi and could grow on or in people, there had to be the right circumstances for this to occur. None of them were present in this household. Normally, he would be concerned with the types and locations of the spores. Secondarily, he would pay attention to the total spore count. His equipment would collect it all.

On his way out the front door, Mary Sue pleaded with him to please return and conduct more tests in the remainder of the home.

"Tell you what," he offered somewhat defiantly, "If I do, it will be because I need to, not because you want me to." At that, he left the home of the Tamsens. As he did so, Jeff congratulated himself for refusing to do more, and at the same time, cursing himself for doing the job at all, especially for a woman who reeked of poisonous vibes.

Back at the lab, Jeff felt compelled to check out

the samples in order to determine whether a problem existed. In objective scientist mode, he wondered what it might be that lurked in the household to make this woman claim that his own feet and the feet of her family would stick to the floor.

His work finished, Jeff found some four thousand spores outdoors, while none were found indoors. Normally, he would expect to find some inside of a containment after remediation for a variety of reason. One reason might be that the filtration was poor, or a small portion of mold growth had been missed. Frequently, outdoor species associated with lawns and wild grasses found their way inside the containment because they were carried on the clothing of persons such as himself. In this instance, however, no spores were present at all. The job was very thorough. He found no other particles of consequence, only the normal occasional skin cell. Any carpet or clothing fibers had been filtered out.

Jeff explained his findings by telephone to Bob Jones, the man who hired him, and explained that what he saw was the dictionary definition of clean air. Jeff's job was completed. Bob could give the report to the client, if he so desired, although Bob's duty was to All American, who had, in turn, hired him. Jeff prepared a short written report and emailed it. Done and over with.

The following day, Bob called back and said that Mary Sue was more insistent than ever that the symptoms in her family were worsening, complaining about her, loss of appetite, sleeplessness, coughing, and respiratory distress.

"Oh, and Jeff, she wants you to conduct more tests," Bob told him, knowing Jeff's answer.

"Not going to happen, Jeff responded icily. "Even if she wants to hire me separately to conduct and independent investigation, I'm not going back. I never want to see that woman again. She's bad luck."

Jeff knew a con job when he saw one. She must have spoken with a neighbor over the back fence along with the ladies in the salon and coupled their inputs with what she had read.

When he discussed the visit with Frank the next day, Jeff expressed the thought that if this woman and her girlfriends stood around the street corner like guys did and asked what each wanted to be when they grew up, guys might say they aspired to be a race car driver, a doctor or mechanic or pro ball player. Had Mary Sue responded to such an inquiry, she might have replied by saying that she wanted to be a con artist who would suck her family into some get-rich-quick schemes. There could be no other explanation for her behavior. At what point does a person lose touch to such an extent?

After his years of experience, Jeff had never received a complaint about the length of his reports in which he summarized his findings in the fewest possible words. Once in a while, a special case required a longer report. No fluff, no puff. Jeff didn't believe in padding. Ask, if you want more details. His business grew thanks to his brevity and his candor. He learned early on that if one took sides, the other side would bite him. Therefore, he simply presented the facts and his interpretation of them.

Jeff turned to his computer and wrote his single page report and made a statement that if anyone wanted exact details they could ask. Since Bob Jones hired him, Jones received the single page—a simple letter of clearance, not a tome. After all, how many pages are required to say there is no mold? He titled the report, "Clearance Testing: Inspection and Monitoring of Tamsen home for Mold."

In September, one month after Jeff submitted his report to Bob Jones, the Tamsens received a check for eight thousand four hundred dollars from All American to cover expenses related to remediation, testing, and repairs of the home meant to include Bob Jones and Jeff Shenero for their initial work.

When Bud found his wife in her usual position in front of the mirror in the hall bath, she showed him the check. "Great job," Mary Sue," exclaimed Bud taking the check from her and reading the amount awarded them. "But how are we going to make any money if we have to pay this Jones company and this scientist guy and get the house fixed too?" he queried.

"First of all, we're not going to pay anybody. Second, we're not going to get the house fixed" Then she explained her plan to Bud.

From that point on, the spokesperson for the Tamsen family, Mary Sue, complained bitterly about their worsening medical problems. The containment remained in place and the bedroom and bath remained off-limits to the family.

Because Mary Sue had initiated the call to Jeff's office, she was deemed the responsible party. Over the course of the next several weeks, Carmen made a number of calls to the household and sent reminder letters to no avail. Mary Sue claimed the insurance company was going to pay the bill but couldn't remember the name of the adjuster. Carmen then called Bob Jones's office who told her they had the same problem with the housewife and provided her with the adjuster's name. Carmen spoke with Hirshfield who stated that Mary Sue had already been paid and it was out of his hands.

Carmen suggested to Jeff that they file suit against her in small claims court, to which Jeff replied, "Just because we get a judgment against her doesn't mean she'll pay. Drop it. She's bad luck. I never want to hear her name again."

NINE

Mary Sue's projects kept her busy during the month of October. Once she had the check in hand, she contacted Kressler and Associates, Attorneys at Law, in Oklahoma City. This firm specialized in lawsuits against insurance companies and agreed to meet with her and her husband..

Anthony Kressler stood six-foot-four. He had played football in college, followed by a short stint in the pros. However, some years later, the man could be officially classified as obese. According to him, he recently lost forty pounds. According to everybody else, nobody noticed. His head sported a small amount of hair that could have been pasted on. Even a bad comb-over would have looked better.

Kressler always wore a dark blue or black double-breasted suit with either a yellow, flowered, or paisley tie. Priding himself on out-of-court settlements, Kressler didn't mind the occasional jury trial. With a jury, you either lost your investment, as far as time spent on the case, or struck it big; seldom in-between.

The attorney's offices were located in the penthouse of an old twelve-story bank building, two blocks from the state courthouse.

Upon speaking with Mary Sue Tamsen three days earlier, Kressler saw a winnable case. His intuition told him good money could be made. Based on experience he knew that All American Insurance almost always paid off under pressure. His mission was to apply that pressure. Attorneys have to eat, too.

Across the desk from Kressler sat a clean, neatly dressed couple. To the attorney, they appeared to be simple folks who obviously came from a decent middle-class background; a couple grievously wronged by an insurance carrier who didn't want to pay their clients what they deserved and the bastards dragged their feet when the time came for them to man-up and fix the problem. All the poor family ever wanted was to have their ceiling fixed and their roof repaired.

Kressler offered, "So, let me understand this. You haven't entered the master suite since the time Dr. Shenero paid you a visit because you knew your health would worsen. Is that right?" their attorney contributed.

The couple nodded vigorously.

Kressler folded his hands on the desk. "Have you been paid yet for the repairs by your insurance company?"

"Yes sir. We received over eight thousand dollars," said Bud proudly.

"And did I mention that I've felt ill since that all started?" Mary Sue interjected.

"Yes, of course. You mentioned that on the phone and earlier in our conversation, as well as a moment ago," said the attorney, who could clearly hear the trumpets calling. "So, folks, please, tell me all about these problems you and your family are having."

After listening to Mary Sue go through a well-memorized laundry list of complaints, Kressler expressed sympathy with their plight and promised to prepare the necessary papers.

"We are going to need a medical report for the records," Kressler told them. "Everybody's going to want a copy of that."

The Tamsens looked at each other trying to figure out what to do next. Kressler held up his hand as an "Okay, don't worry" gesture. "There is a good doctor I know of who specializes in cases like yours. I'll give you his name and be sure to mention that I sent you to him. Campbell is his name and he's right here in the city."

On a bright and perfect day, Bud and Mary Sue left the law office in mid-town Oklahoma City and got in their car, which was located in the parking lot associated with the building. Their Chevy Malibu had incurred serious damage to a rear quarter panel and needed of a tail light from a rear-end accident three years earlier. Red plastic tape covered the damaged tail light. They had received money to repair the car, but never got around to getting it fixed.

However, they had gotten around to spending the repair money. The car's interior was decorated with pizza boxes, fast food bags, empty soda cans, along with other items critical for survival in the Twenty-First Century.

Bud began the conversation as he drove the short distance south to their home in Norman. "I sure hope this guy knows what he's doing. This little trip, what with haircut and shopping and all, cost me a day's pay."

Ignoring him, Mary Sue smiled, "I like him. I think he's going to get us the money we deserve."

"I'll hand it to you, dear, I think you've hit a winner this time around."

"We'll see," she said. "I think lady-luck may come our way, call it 'lucky seven'. By the way, I think you look very handsome today."

Later the same day, emboldened after having spoken with Kressler, Mary Sue made her next move. She fearlessly made a call to her claims adjuster. She told Hirshfield that she and her family were ill from the remediation performed by Bob Jones Restoration, Inc., insisting he that hire another company to inspect and test for mold.

Hirshfield had reluctantly approved the payment for Tamsens' repair bills. He also placed their name on the insurance industry's watch list through word-of-mouth and not through any traceable written form. This wasn't because of the paltry sum they received, but because everyone could smell trouble brewing from the start. Hirshfield didn't like where this was going, but he had an obligation to assist the client; a client they couldn't drop without setting themselves up for a lawsuit. As if by design, Hirshfield found himself between two very thorny places. Things became more complicated when Bob Jones wanted to know what happened to his money, while Jeff suspected he knew what happened to his.

Safe Home Environmental out of Oklahoma City came in and conducted air and swab tests in all rooms of the house. The latter included count determinations for both total mold spore and live spore. One week later, Safe Home reported that no mold related to indoor contamination could be found of any consequence and charged All American twelve hundred dollars for the tests. On a single low-dollar contract, the money went directly to Safe Home. This time All American paid them directly.

Mary Sue complained bitterly to her adjuster. "Then why are we all sick, Mr. Hirshfield?"

"I don't know, but apparently mold is not the cause," Hirshfield, replied, politely. He always tried to be courteous to a client.

"Well, apparently mold *is* the cause," she answered softly. She hung up and next called Dr. Charles Campbell, whom Kressler had recommended to set up an appointment for a medical workup for herself, her husband and the two children.

The business park housing Campbell's office presented an expensive air. Ample lawns and Southern Magnolia trees were plentiful in the neighborhood to provide a soft homey feeling, unlike the concrete and asphalt business parks common to other areas of the city.

Certain tight circles perceived Campbell to be a highly recommended specialist in mold toxicity who catered to wealthy clientele nationwide. The man appearance was fairly non-descript, his face sallow, and stood the same height as Bud with thinning brown hair. Like Bud, exercise and diet control did not appear to be on list of priority of any new year's resolution. His office manager, a portly, but experienced nurse practitioner, interviewed both husband, wife, Karl and Wendy, taking copious notes. Once the notes were placed in a file folder, she and the doctor conducted a standard series of tests, collected several vials of blood from each patient, and ran a panel of allergy skin tests on each member of the family.

He charged the family eight thousand dollars for the workup. "Normally, I charge a lot more for your requirements, but since Mr. Kressler called and told me to expect you ...well," his voice trailed off.

Campbell saw the frown on the faces of his new clients and added, "Unfortunately, it is our long-standing policy not to release any medical information until this bill is paid in full."

"That's about what we got from the insurance company. Hell, we can't fix our own house if we wanted to, now," Bud complained.

"Don't worry, dear," Mary Sue said smilingly, patting his arm. "Everything's under control." She pulled out her credit card and paid the bill.

TEN

Campbell put the Tamsens' case on the fast-track and submitted a copy of his findings to the beleaguered Tamsen family, as well as to Kressler.

Kressler spoke with Campbell in detail about his report, took notes, and digested what he had heard. He wrote his own brief of where the situation stood today. Then he called James Hirshfield for a heart-to heart talk.

In late November, Mary Sue received a phone call.

"Mrs. Tamsen, I have good news for you," said Kressler. "We have a settlement."

The attorney took a deep breath. "I don't want you to be angry with me, but I did what I thought would be best in your case. For that reason, I didn't call you for your opinion, but went ahead and trusted to my experience in these matters. After I explained to All American Insurance about what a jury would do to them should we go to trial showing bad faith and breach of contract on their part, your insurance carrier made me a couple of offers and I refused them both. To be perfectly honest, since I am an honest man, I told them I would consult with you for your opinion."

Mary Sue stubbed out her cigarette and took a seat at the dining room table. She wore a gray sweatshirt and sweatpants. She had never been a great fan of exercise and wore sneakers for comfort, not for sport. "Yes," she almost whispered, as if speaking out loud might chase away favorable spirits.

"Are you with me, so far?"

"Yes, yes, of course," she said, shakily. She had won and lost a fortune at the gaming tables; could she hope for ten or maybe twenty thousand here with Kressler?

"Well, of course, I didn't consult with you, as you know, but told them I did, so if anybody asks, you can say I called you, which I am doing, in all honesty."

"Yes, of course."

"Are you sitting down, Mary Sue? May I call you Mary Sue?

"Yes, of course." She couldn't stop stammering the repetitious three-word mantra.

She could hear the big man take a deep breath on the other end of the line. She saw more years of being married to another loser of a husband—she deserved so much more than being buried in a ditch for a lifetime. *Bitch in a ditch*, she thought to herself.

"What would you say to a one hundred forty

thousand dollars," he said at last.

Silence.

"Mary Sue?"

"How much did you say?" Her voice sounded like that of a robot dropped off a cliff.

Kressler repeated himself, then said, "Of course, you wouldn't get it all, since you and your husband signed a contingency fee arrangement for us to receive forty percent of the amount. This would amount to $56,000 for us and $84,000 thousand for you. You should be receiving a check for this amount from our office within thirty days. I hope our arrangement is agreeable?"

Mary Sue sat stunned for an instant, as though she had been pole axed. That was ten times what they had received on their first check. Excitement began to creep into her voice. The amount they would receive at one time would take some time to digest. "Yes, I mean, thank you, Mr. Kressler. But how..."

"I explained real life to them, that's all," Kressler interrupted. "I explained that they pay out this amount every day to wealthy people who own wealthy homes with expensive possessions and their homes get flooded, or whatever, and here you are, simple people who want to get on with life and that a jury might side with you if it came down to it, especially with the medical report in my possession.

"You folks have a nice day and if I can help you with any other matters, consider my door always open to you and your lovely family."

Several hours later Bud Tamsen came home, sweaty and smelly. This time Mary Sue didn't make an issue of it.

"Goddamn air conditioning in the cab didn't work today," he said, greeting his wife in the bathroom where her present project entailed pulling out a bad eyebrow hair. She had taken a long hot shower in the hall bath and had dressed in casual clothing for the evening, which consisted of new blue jeans, new sneakers, and a new blouse.

Bud looked at her a little askance, wondering why she was not dressed inappropriately.

"In case you're wondering, we're all going out to dinner tonight. I haven't quite decided where, yet. Wendy will be home soon and is going with us. So why don't you take a shower so we can get out of here."

Bud wasn't ready to go anywhere. He'd had a hot day and needed to relax.

After looking at him, Mary Sue rescinded her promise to herself that she would give him something special for the night. Instead she said, "I got a call from our attorney today."

"What attorney?" he asked, completely oblivious.

"Kressler. The one we went to see."

"Oh, yeah, okay," he said. "So what's up with him?"

His wife looked herself in the mirror and continued to detail her face. "So he gave us some good news."

"And?" Bud queried, weary of playing his wife's word games.

"He said that we're going to get $84,000 from the insurance company," she replied, so casually Bud thought she was teasing.

Bud stood in place and stared at her not knowing what to say. At last he replied in his usual monotone voice, "Is that before or after attorney's fees?"

"It's after and it's ours," his wife said. "We'll be getting the check in the mail within thirty days. Now, go get changed. We're going out to dinner."

Her flat statement and her unusual behavior strongly suggested to Bud that what she had told him smacked of truth. Reluctantly, he did as requested. Going out to eat would work.

Earlier, Mary Sue had phoned Wendy at her boyfriend's and directed her to get a ride home because they were all going out. She then told Karl to turn off the TV and to change shirts for the same reason. Once Wendy arrived home a short time later, the family departed for the destination Mary Sue had decided upon.

Lobster and More provided a typical seafood selection of farm-bred salmon "fed with only the finest of soy products" along with "fresh lobster flown in from the coast." Which of three coasts the seafood had arrive from wasn't specified. Steaks, hamburgers and salads also filled the menu.

The walls of the restaurant were decorated with the usual boat anchors, paddles, and pictures of whaling vessels plowing through the high seas.

A busy, but not-too-crowded, Wednesday night permitted the Tamsen family to quickly settle into a private corner table for four.

Birthday and anniversary cheers and annoying songfests came from the staff, as they occasionally attacked a given table.

Nearly four years had passed since the family had visited the establishment, back when Bud received a Christmas bonus check for three hundred dollars. Since then, his bonuses had seriously decreased in proportion to lack of job dedication.

While Mary Sue exhibited a festive mood, Bud was somewhat reserved and unsure as to what Kressler might have really told her. He made a mental note to call the lawyer in the morning to find out the exact details of the transaction. He was about to broach the subject of the day when Wendy spoke about it first.

Wendy had become a handsome woman; aware, perceptive, and intelligent. She appeared to know more about life than she was willing to tell. She had quit high school to work full-time at a hair salon located in the wealthier district of Norman. Her boyfriend served as a part-time locker room attendant at the OU athletic complex. He had not quite defined his life's aspirations. The boy had turned eighteen years of age, a fact that troubled Mary Sue from the standpoint of statutory rape. Perhaps an older woman would keep him from getting into trouble.

Like her mother, Wendy knew how to barter. She

possessed swept back straight dark hair, combed at the temples, a slightly turned up nose, large dark eyes, semi-full lips and a thin, but well-proportioned body.

The waiter took their orders, staring at Wendy as he did so. Karl asked for a cheeseburger and fries, Wendy and her mom took salmon steaks and Bud got the seafood sampler. Bud also ordered an appetizer of crab-stuffed mushrooms and a second helping of jumbo shrimp in sauce for the family and white wine for himself and his wife. The kids got sodas of their choice.

Testing the waters, Wendy said, "Somebody came into some money, otherwise we wouldn't be here. Right?"

Feeling new strength, Bud replied, "Looks like we actually did come into money, dear."

Wendy looked at her jug-eared brother, who shrugged. Pointing a finger at her temple, she said, "I figured that for a no-brainer."

"Not simply money, Wendy. We came into a lot of money, so we're celebrating," replied her mother. She led them into small talk for a few minutes.

Mary Sue felt in control; yet, considering Bud and the kids as variables, things could turn ugly. Her intuition told her not to trust him. Despite his occasional posturing, he was too compliant.

The waiter arrived and served the appetizers; a basket-full of sliced garlic bread and another dish with jumbo shrimp in garlic sauce. Karl's hand reached into the dishes first to extract the largest piece from each. Wendy cringed and foraged around in her purse for a small bottle of hand sanitizer. She applied a liberal amount onto her hands and forced the bottle into Karl's hands.

After a few minutes of appetizer sampling, Mary Sue presented the news. "Wendy, we came into eighty-four thousand dollars."

"Yeah, and monkeys are flying out of my ass," said Karl, nodding vigorously. He looked at his sister and licked sauce from his fingers.

Wendy leaned forward. "That much? I'll bite. So, let me guess, you're both trying to decide who gets what? Am I right?"

"We haven't gotten that far, yet," said Bud, looking at his wife.

Mary Sue smiled with a bearing only previously reserved for the highest of All Knowing Priests. "Something like that," were the words she selected from her vast vocabulary.

"No, not something like that; exactly like that," said Bud, who had nothing left to lose.

Wendy jumped in. "Well, how much does everybody get and what did we get it for?"

"Yeah, for what?" Karl, mumbled around a mouthful of garlic bread, not too distant from the manner in which he normally spoke.

Mary Sue took a breath. "Because we got a lawyer named Anthony Kressler and he sued the insurance company—the one we paid to protect us, because they didn't do it and took forever to fix our roof and so I...your father and I got him to help us, and the insurance company paid us the money because they owed us the money, and we are all taken care of so we don't need to worry about money anymore. On top of that, we're all sick from the mold in the house," she threw concluded emphatically.

Wendy sat thunderstruck at the news of riches, the fact that she her mother proclaimed her to be ill, and the fact that deadly mold might probably be in the house. Indeed, all four of the Tamsens were trying to wrap their heads around the news.

Mary Sue pressed on. "I called Mr. Kressler back this afternoon and confirmed what he told me earlier in the morning and also talked to him about our illnesses." At that, she then listed a multitude of ailments that each of them had endured "...since the whole problem began with the insurance company, Bob Jones, Dr. Shenero, Safe Home Environmental—you know, the ones who messed up our lives."

Bud permitted a little thrill of excitement to course through his body. His wife had bigger plans. He could smell it, feel it.

The waiter brought salads to the table. The family remained silent for a few moments, each nibbling, with the exception of Karl who shoved forkfuls into to his mouth.

"Well, now's as good a time as any to decide who's going to get what," Wendy stated, flatly.

"Yeah," asked Karl, "how much do I get?"

Bud stepped in, "We already told you both that haven't decided yet. Besides, the check won't be here for a while."

"Well, since we're talking about it, I want to go to beauty school and I need a car and new clothes."

"I want a car," said Karl. "And there's other stuff I want to get, too."

Mary Sue smiled. "Well, let's celebrate tonight. I'm sure we will all work things out."

"You can bet your ass we will," said Bud.

"What do mean by that, Bud?" asked Mary Sue. "You don't need to talk in that tone in front of the kids."

"Oh, it won't be the first time they've heard me talk that way," he said.

"And, since you want to know, what I mean is, I'm going to make sure this money gets split the right way, not your way," Bud concluded.

Mary Sue felt a flush creep up her face. Bud was rarely this blunt in front of the children. He needed to be defused. She smiled and said "Of course, dear." At that moment decided she'd better cool his jets tonight. If it came down to it, maybe two nights in a row.

The following week Mary Sue met with Kressler once again. She told him about their individual medical issues at home, which were worsening by the day. This had nothing to do with bad faith or breach of contract, did it? It had to do with neglect by the people All American had sent to repair their home, didn't it? This was a matter of family health, or a word that rhymed with it.

Kressler listened patiently and told Mary Sue to keep a diary to record their illnesses and the approximate dates they had begun. He hinted that it didn't matter what they claimed. This case begged to be heard by a jury.

ELEVEN

Three weeks later, in early December, the Tamsens received a certified letter containing the check Kressler had promised. No taxes needed to be paid on an award settlement. Bud told his wife he wouldn't co-sign the check unless they split the money evenly. He brought along a drinking buddy from work to witness her agreement. Once they both signed off on the certified letter, the couple went to their bank and opened two separate accounts, in addition to the single joint account they held, each depositing forty-two thousand dollars. In a short period of time, Mary Sue had seen $140,000 go down to $84,000 go down to $42,000. She needed to buy something for herself before the money dissipated completely.

Once outside the bank, a stiff breeze hit them head on and blew Bud's baseball cap off his head. He retrieved it while Mary Sue waited for him. They bent forward into the wind until they reached the car and climbed in. Then Mary Sue turned to her husband. "Well, tell me, Bud, did I do good or did I do good?"

Bud checked himself in the rear-view mirror and smoothed down his remaining hair, feeling much better about himself having money in the bank and having gotten laid, such as it was, sometime before. He turned to her and replied, "You set us up for life, Mary Sue. You finally came through. You're a true high roller, as you would say."

Another two weeks passed. Nearing Christmas, Mary Sue's great inclination was to divorce Bud, take half of his share of the money in the settlement, keep the house and the kids, and get child support. However, reality dictated she keep him on board for the next round. Plus, being a devout religious person, she could not do such as thing at this time of the year, but she had followed Kressler's advice. She purchased a small notebook, and backdated a sequence of events to the best of her recollections. These included daily complaints from each of her family members.

In early February of the following year, Mary Sue continued to read about the dangers of mold on the Internet. She read all the tabloids she could get, and listened to all the neighbors who would speak to her. The time had come to make her next move. She continued to subtly comment to her husband and her children about problems they didn't know they had until they saw her ploy without her having said so.

She also believed herself to be up-to-date regarding lawsuits filed around the country pertaining to mold and health-related issues. These suits were directed against remediation companies and insurance carriers, and the awards could be staggering. She also learned that virtually all decisions made in favor of the plaintiff were reversed on appeal. She would cross that bridge when she came to it.

Mary Sue called Anthony Kressler one more time. "Mr. Kressler, I kept the diary you asked me to keep and I have quite a few notes about what has happened to us. Our symptoms are getting worse and my joints even ache and it all goes back to Bob Jones, and this Shenero guy, and Safe Home Environmental."

"I'm sure the insurance company is at fault, as well, don't you think, Mrs. Tamsen?" her attorney contributed.

"Absolutely," she agreed.

"Let's make them prove it didn't happen," he stated.

"Yes, I like that," Mary Sue readily agreed, feeling quite comfortable being on the side of truth and justice.

"Well, then, I want to schedule a deposition for you and your family. Would..." here he paused to check his schedule, "...say, next Wednesday at ten a.m. work for you? We want to get this in before the holidays."

"Yes sir, I'll make sure we're there. Thank you for everything you've done."

Lady Luck dealt the next card. Shortly after her

last meeting with Kressler, a small legitimate leak started in the roof over Karl's room, which Mary Sue and Bud had occupied since their master suite remained under containment. They had moved him into Wendy's room, and despite her frequent absences, she expressed great disapproval of the decision to move him into her space. Their home repair money had been spent on Campbell and Mary Sue would be damned if she was going to spend any of her award money on repairs to the home or to pay any bills pertaining thereto. She managed to convince Bud of the wisdom of her action, or inaction, and he followed suit.

Mary Sue demanded that Hirshfield provide yet another company to inspect the home to find out why the family's health was worsening, especially in light of their doctor's report. This report stated that the Tamsen's blood work had been conducted in Campbell's own laboratory, along with other tests (which she didn't specify or even understand) and which pointed to exposure to toxic mold in their home—the deadly type.

This time Hirshfield left the choice of a company up to her.

Mary Sue recalled something she had read online, amidst her daily ration of soap operas and Internet searches. She took a chance, went back to the computer, and called up her Bookmarks. There she saw it: Burke Remediation (BR), located in Tulsa, also serving OKC. From what she could gather, BR made it a habit of entering the home of a concerned client wearing respirators, and, if necessary, declare all contents and possessions contaminated, even if a trace of mold was found in the home that their experts considered suspicious. Reviews did not rate the company favorably, a small fact in the eyes of the beholder.

Over the phone she detailed her problem and two days later BR's van arrived. The three man crew entered the home and within a short time had dropped a portion of the damp ceiling in Karl's room and conducted air tests. With two bedrooms of the home uninhabitable, the Tamsen family moved into a motel.

Two days later BR reported finding several spores of the black mold *Stachybotrys* in the air of the room and condemned the entire home, including the contents, as being toxic and that all personal belongings had to be destroyed.

In late February, the Tamsens received another check; this one for fourteen thousand dollars for loss of their possessions. After giving half the money to Bud, Mary Sue spent most of the remaining money as a down payment for something she had always wanted: a Harley Davidson motorcycle. She had stashed the forty-two thousand for a rainy day.

Because Hirshfield had paid money for the loss of possessions, a good lawyer might construe that act as a tacit admission that All American acknowledged the presence of deadly mold in the home.

TWELVE

In contrast to Frank's character, Jeff was opinionated, but not intractable. New discoveries could change his mind. He could tolerate cowards, but not those guilty of seditious or traitorous acts. He had a vindictive streak a mile long and if you want to get into a big fight with him, just pretend to be nice and then try to stab him in the back or cheat him. This trait had been there ever since Frank could remember.

However, Jeff's biggest personal problem, in Frank's estimation, was that he didn't have any ass to hold up his pants. He kept hitching them up, tighten his belt as he might. And he was definitely not the suspender type. He readily acknowledged the problem and had once remarked that he had checked into getting an ass transplant, but all they had available at the moment was one that belonged to a four hundred pound fat lady that they were keeping on ice. Jeff passed on the deal and opted to remain assless.

In March of 2003, nine months after his initial visit to the Tamsen household, Jeff signed for certified documents at the post office, not knowing what they were. The letterhead said it was from the law firm of Kressler and Associates, located in Oklahoma City.

Mystified, he drove to his office and opened the thick envelope. He found that Kressler and Associates and the Tamsens had named Dr. Jeffrey Shenero in the lawsuit as a party at fault and negligent in his duty to the client. It also named All American Insurance, Safe Home Environmental, and Burke Remediation.

The suit against Jeff alleged that he should have inspected the entire home, and that he exhibited gross negligence in his work because he failed to find several species of deadly toxic mold, including the notorious black mold, which had been later discovered. This failure led to the severe illness of four family members. No dollar amount was specified.

Jeff felt like a traffic cop who heard an original story from a speeding motorist–a story he could tell at the station. He showed it to Carmen who shook her head slowly, wordlessly.

Jeff called Frank, who had already planned to be in Norman the following day, and gave him the document to read when he arrived at Jeff's office.

Frank slowly and carefully read it over and explained it to him. Then he set it down and said, "I thought you told me the house was clean."

Jeff was totally confused. "The containment was

one of the cleanest I've seen in a long time. Hell, man, you were here when I got the call from Bob. I did what I always do. I got hired to check out their master suite and that's what I did."

"Says here they are filing suit against you because you didn't find anything," said Frank.

"The gal's a left-threaded wing nut from the get go." Jeff was emphatic.

Frank picked up the phone. "Let's see if we can get you out of this. I'm going to call a friend of mine, another attorney. His name is Matthew Collins. He's got impeccable character and as good an attorney as I know."

Frank spoke into the phone for a few moments, then hung up the phone. "He couldn't get away until after work hours, so how's about we meet him at six-thirty in his office." Frank read over the papers again.

"Tell me about this guy," said Jeff.

"Sure. Matt's a great detective and a master prosecuting attorney. In court, he's just eccentric enough to pace and slouch, he picks at papers on various tables, then might spin around and ask the person on the stand if he or she might be gay to throw them off balance. He's about your height, but tending toward portly. He's got a full head of graying hair well-groomed and long. He "works out" every morning in the breakfast bar after walking on the treadmill at the laborious rate of two miles per hour while reading a newspaper.

"Oh, he's a meticulous researcher and can find

details that escape even my own eagle eye. If he takes the case, it would probably be his first mold job, just like it's your first time as a defendant. He's old school and undoubtedly knows things about winning a case that I won't know for another twenty years."

At five-o'clock the two men met at a diner and had a leisurely meal.

Matt's office was relatively close to the diner. It consisted of a renovated three bedroom house with a well-tended lawn, flower beds, and a picture window that opened onto the greenery of a small forest across the street comprised of London Plane Tree, Bald Cypress and Southern Magnolia.

Frank made the introductions and the men shook hands.

"So you're the famous doctor. I'll have to get your autograph for my collection."

"It'll cost you," responded Jeff, chuckling. He suddenly realized the irony of his statement and closed his mouth.

"Let's see what you got there, Frank," said Matt, as he returned to his desk chair while the two others sat in comfortable arm chairs across from him.

While Matt was reading the documents, occasionally going back and forth, Frank looked over at Jeff, wondering how he was going to handle this possible stain on his reputation, or if he even had a clue as to what was coming.

Matt finally put down the papers. "What happened, Jeff?"

Jeff explained the case again, his memory improving the more he got into the story. He summarized by stating that "No goddamn bastard freeloading deadbeats are going to get a cent of my money." The way he figured it, putting all his money into himself painted a lot better picture than pissing away the money to pay off the Tamsens. "Fuck 'em," soon become a regular part of his vocabulary whenever he referenced this case. If he decided to take the case, Matt just needed to keep Jeff from saying it in the courtroom.

Then Frank spoke with Matt in technical legal terms about the situation from his perspective as one who was familiar with the area of Jeff's expertise.

"I'm going to need you to help me on this one, Frank, for your experience in the field. I'll do the courtroom, you do the observation and consultation," Matt told him.

"Also, I need you to find out what you can about the Tamsens. These people smell like they make a career out of this sort of thing. My guess is to start with a call to All American Insurance, because they're also named in the suit, I'm certain they will be happy to share their information with you. You might try speaking with Steve Hirshfield. He's my agent with the company."

"Jeff, my fee to you will be fifteen thousand dollars. I expect the trial to last close to a week and there will be pre-and-post-trial hearings and meetings. I'll file for hourly fees with the court after the trial is completed, if we win, that is."

Jeff agreed and the men shook hands.

Matt was in new and old territory at the same time. He had a fair to good feeling about his chances in the case. In this instance, winning meant not losing. He didn't know mold, but he did know human idiosyncrasies. Jeff would help educate him on the mold part and Frank would help him link normal versus abnormal findings, standards that might exist, Jeff's role in the matter, and would serve as his reservoir of knowledge.

Jeff would be his own expert witness so they didn't need to spend good money to acquire another one.

Matt filed a counterclaim against the Tamsens for $15,000 to cover Jeff's projected upcoming expenses, which included attorney's fees and lost wages from his company. He also filed a motion for the judge to state *absolutely* why they had lost the case, if testimony warranted a finding against the good doctor. That would be necessary before sending the case on to appeal, if it came to that. To Matt, there appeared to be more 'ifs' in this case than most.

THIRTEEN

With the trial only days away, Anthony Kressler sat behind the desk that hid his massive frame. He rose when the Tamsen family entered in the paneled cherry-wood office; a sunny view of Oklahoma City shone through the many office windows. Slight aromas of sweet cigar smoke and lemon oil furniture polish lingered in the air.

"Please, do come in." Kressler walked around the front of the desk and greeted the couple with warm handshakes. "Good to meet you again, Bud." Their last meeting resulted in a decent amount of money for each of them; enough to feed a large number of men, women and children in any Third World country for a long time.

Meeting the children for the first time Kressler turned toward the daughter. Kressler beamed "Let's see, you must be Wendy. I've heard a lot of good things about you."

Mary Sue had expressly told Wendy to leave her

chewing gum behind so she would look as present-able as possible. She wouldn't be able to chew in court anyway, so she might as well get used to it.

"Yes, glad to meet you, Mr. Kressler." Her small hand disappeared into the giant's palm.

"Yeah, and I'm Karl," said the son. The boy looked up at Kressler, his eyes glittering with the promise of future fame and riches.

"My pleasure, Karl," said Kressler, with all the Victorian polish he could muster. He gave Karl a short handshake, as though seeking to avoid con-tracting whatever had given the boy his features. "Please be seated. Can I get you anything to drink?" He pushed the intercom without waiting for a re-sponse and asked his secretary to come and take their orders.

Kressler returned to his chair. It creaked in pain as he leaned back. "I called you in because, as you know, we will be going to trial in a few days. It doesn't look like a settlement will be reached this time, so a court trial is in our future."

"Cool," said Karl.

Kressler gave him a quick glance.

"Fine with me." Bud tried to act as manly as pos-sible, "Let's get to the fight. I'm ready."

Kressler took the baton. As a former All Ameri-can at Oklahoma State University and an NFL play-er for two seasons before his knees were destroyed, he responded, man to man. "I hear the challenge, Bud, so let's play ball. Are you with me?"

"Oh, yeah," said Bud, fired up, his voice still on

an even keel.

"By the way, you all look wonderful. Mrs. Tamsen, I might suggest you wear a little less makeup when you appear for your testimony. Nothing personal, you understand, I do love makeup, especially on pretty women, but the court takes a different view."

"Don't you worry about a thing, Mr. Kressler, I'll take care of it." Mary Sue batted her eyelashes at him and leaned forward enough for her cleavage to be exposed.

Kressler slowly and calmly leaned forward slightly, perhaps to have a better look, then leaned back. "We need to go over things I will be asking you and things the other side will be asking you. It's two against one. I mean, there are two of them and just me. There's George McKinney representing All American, Bob Jones, and Safe Home. Matt Collins will represent this Shenero character."

The attorney placed his elbows on the desk and brought his fingers together in a steepling motion with his thumbs hooked beneath his chin as he looked from Mary Sue to Bud, then to the children. He dropped them suddenly.

"These are two very high-powered and wealthy attorneys who will stop at nothing to discredit you, to make you say anything, to make it seem like you are lying. These two have quite a reputation. And we're going to need to be a team and stand up to their accusations and believe me, they might think they are doing the right thing, but they are getting very well paid for their antics. Now is the time to tell me that it's okay with you that I stand alone against these men, these challengers?" At the last word, Kressler glanced at Bud.

Mary Sue and Bud looked at each other. "That's why we hired you, Mr. Kressler," Mary Sue said trustingly. Her newly styled hair did little to detract from the appearance of grooves in her face that looked like dried tire tracks in a muddy road. She struggled to understand how less makeup might make her a better witness.

Kressler explained further. "The trial will occur in Norman, where you live. There won't be a jury. Only the judge will review the case."

A cloud passed over Mary Sue's face. She'd been practicing her testimony in the mirror with a jury in mind. "But I...we want a jury trial. We have to have one. What do you mean a judge will review our case?"

Kressler held up a large hand. "While this case can raise emotions, the reputation of Dr. Shenero in Norman is such that it could cause us to lose because there is a good chance we wouldn't get a majority decision. It would be tough to find people who haven't heard of him."

Bud declared, "Heck, we never heard of him. Anyway, aren't good people and great people get taken down all the time for their ..." Bud searched for a word.

"...negligence?" inserted Kressler.

"Yes," said Bud.

Kressler ignored Bod's comments about good and great people and went on to explain about a jury of eight in a civil suit as opposed to a jury of twelve in a criminal matter and why a judge is the best fit for their lawsuit, in his estimation.

Karl scratched his head. "What kind of stuff are they going to ask us?"

Kressler briefly studied the boy. The kid looked as though he would not be out of place in virtually every local venue from juvenile court to a school for the mentally challenged; schools such as Oxford, Harvard, MIT and the Sorbonne were not likely to be part of the boy's future. "Well...Karl, isn't it? That's a very good question, so let's talk about that right now.

"Today, we will go over the truth and how to say it. This will take a little time, so relax. It's not so much what anybody asks you, but how you answer. You can't lie on the witness stand, so tell things as you know them to be. It'll be my job to make it work.

"After today, we'll meet once more before the trial. I believe I have all your documents in order." He reached out and pulled a six-inch high stack of paper-filled manila folders toward himself.

The secretary came in with soft drinks and coffee for the family.

Kressler brought out papers to sign and shifted into teaching mode.

Matt held a number of papers in his hand. "These are copies of documents that Kressler filed with the court. They contain the list of witnesses he plans to call. These include Bob Jones, the four Tamsens, Burke Remediation owned and operated by a James Burke, Dr. Charles Campbell, and, of course, yourself." Here he nodded at Jeff.

Matt continued. "Help me with this. He names everyone above in the lawsuit and calls them parties at fault. But he doesn't place Safe Home on the witness list. Why would he do that?

"Jeff, let's start with Safe Home. What can you tell us?"

Jeff shrugged. "Sure. The company is owned by Julie Robinette. I've known Julie for over a decade. She's a Certified Industrial Hygienist with a Bachelor's Degree in Biological Sciences. She started her company up in the city with nothing and built it on integrity and efficiency."

"She learned about construction as she went along. We do a couple or three jobs a year together and talk shop at various in-state and out-of-state conventions. She's solid and the real deal."

Matt said, "That explains why they don't want to call her as a witness. Kressler doesn't want to wave a red flag in front of the judge and corroborate your testimony."

"They must know we're going to call her as a witness anyway," added Matt. "I've already submitted her name to the court and sent a copy to Kressler in return for the list he sent me."

Frank said, "Sure, but so what? She'll give her testimony that she didn't find anything and agrees with Jeff. Kressler will probably leave her alone. It's better than him trying to beat her down. That could be a big mistake and could backfire by magnifying her integrity."

Matt nodded. "What about this James Burke, Jeff?"

Jeff snorted. "A piece of work. If I'm A, he's Z. We're polar opposites. He's the ultimate extremist and a wealthy man because of it. Unlike Julie, he began in construction and took a lot of courses and went into the mold mitigation business. That's okay unto itself, no problem there, but this guy is crazy extreme. He cuts corners and doesn't understand the data he gets back from a lab. His claim to fame is that he's never had a job that failed. Of course, he's the one who interprets the reports that come back from the lab. Burke does some restoration after a fire, and cleanup after a messy body in a home from a shooting or a suicide, but mostly his company specializes in mold and charging three times the going rate. I've met him on a half-dozen occasions and wish I hadn't."

"Wow, Jeff, sounds like you're in love," quipped Frank.

Matt gave a brief smile. "Let's discuss what we're going to talk about and how we're going to do it."

FOURTEEN

For the lawyer, uninitiated or old dog, a courtroom is like a game of chance and a game of skill at the same time. The drama can be for a short duration or for the long haul. Its games can be self-satisfying and life changing in their rewards; its losses can be devastating and profound. The drama demands stage presence, knowledge, and experience. Add media or a jury and, win or lose, there is nothing like the hormone rush during a major case. The courtroom is a storybook.

"All rise," called the clerk of the court.

Everyone stood in the courtroom, on a Wednesday nine months after Jeff had conducted his testing.

Judge Linda Craycroft entered, ensconced in her black robe.

"Be seated," called the clerk.

Judge Craycroft took her seat at the bench and those in the courtroom took theirs.

"This matter concerns the plaintiffs Mr. and Mrs. Tamsen versus defendants All American Insurance, Bob Jones, Restoration, Inc., Safe Home Environmental, and Burke Remediation along with Jeffrey Shenero, Ph.D.," announced Judge Craycroft. "Do we have counsel for the plaintiffs and defendants present?"

The three attorneys, anointed by the court, stood and chimed almost in unison, "All here, Your Honor."

"And do we have the Plaintiffs Mr. Bud Tamsen, Mrs. Mary Sue Tamsen and the two children Wendy Tamsen, almost age eighteen age and Karl Tamsen, age fifteen?"

"All present, Your Honor," pronounced Anthony Kressler.

The judge to whom the case had been assigned, did not cater to rapists, assaulters, DUIs, check-kiters, child molesters, drug runners, wife beaters, and many other accused despots. Those cases were assigned to the judges who specialized in criminal proceedings. In Room 272, litigation involved civil cases and crimes that basically involved lawsuits.

As an environmental attorney, Frank could represent the plaintiff or the defense. On defense, he would sit in Matt's chair, to the immediate right of the defendant, Jeff. Today, he sat in the first row of spectator's seats, immediately behind his two friends with his head down in a relaxed pose. At the mention of the Plaintiff's names, he looked around. He casually looked at the spectators who were seated in the gallery. It was at that moment when he saw the Tamsen family. His jaw literally dropped and a strong jolt ran through his body; a tingling sensation ran down his entire spinal column, as he stared, incredulous. His heart raced. His eyes met those of the wife's for an instant, until he pulled them away. He leaned forward in his seat toward Jeff and in a loud whisper, said, "Jeff, is that her?"

Jeff glanced around behind him to his left. "Yep, the one and only."

Frank never connected the name Tamsen with this woman, and if Jeff had mentioned the name "Mary Sue," he might have thought it a coincidence—a name not uncommon in these parts.

He knew, of course, about the huge settlement All American Insurance paid to the Tamsens only months earlier, but he sat there thunderstruck. A stanza from a childhood poem he'd written slammed into his mind:

> Play with heat and get a fire,
> I run with fear and feel the chase,
> With widened eyes the flames leap higher,
> I've ended at my starting place.

Yes, there sat Mary Sue, all right, in all her rundown glory. Mary Sue Megan Moore Tamsen, childhood friend, former soulmate turned blackmailer—a woman with a lot of money and wanting more. His payments to her had been completed years before. At last he his bank account held a decent amount of money and he was happily married with children. Thankfully, his wife never learned of his short-term illicit soiree with this dark creature.

How many years ago had that been? He'd been working at the job a couple of years and wanted to quit then. That was before she made her demand which forced him to stay there another four years so he could afford to pay her off. He tried not to think about the alien entity called an ugly memory that struggled to take over his mind.

Her presence gave him a medley of mixed feelings, but at least she had been relegated to a fading memory, until suddenly, there she was again in full force. None of this would have happened had he gone with his friend to do the job. One look at her, one word to Jeff, and both would have turned and run like the roadrunner leaving a trail dust behind at the sight of the coyote. For now, it looked like piling on was about to occur with Jeff on the bottom.

George McKinney stood as the designated representative of All American Insurance. "Your Honor, Mister Jones asks to be excused from this morning's proceedings due to a family matter."

"Very well," said Judge Craycroft. "You may proceed."

Frank knew McKinney. They'd met a number of times at various conventions. Frank considered him to be smooth talking, mentally sharp, and extremely knowledgeable in the field of a variety of sciences, even when he was high on coke.

Frank also knew the Cleveland County Courthouse, a four story building located on South Peters in Norman. The building sat at the back of large lawns and wide walkways. Eight steps led to the first floor—the same courthouse where Frank had represented companies that hired him over the past years.

The back of the courtroom was comprised of four rows of twelve upholstered dark blue padded seats with a walkway splitting them down the middle and another walkway on either side that led to the main courtroom or to an entry-exit door. A low wooden wall separated the seats in the front row from the main courtroom.

If a person came all the way down the right hand side through a swinging gate into the primary portion, they would see a table labeled "Defense" with three seats that faced the judge's bench. To the left of the defense table stood another table, this one labeled "Plaintiff," with three seats available there, as well.

At the very front of the courtroom was the judge's bench with the clerk's table to the immediate left of the bench with the witness stand on the opposite side. The clerk held the exhibits that were presented by the various attorneys.

Finally, nine seats were located for jurors – eight for a civil trial and one for an alternate.

Kressler stood. "Your Honor, at this time we would like to call Mary Sue Tamsen to the stand."

Mary Sue stood, walked over to the clerk where she was sworn in, and took a seat at the witness stand. She wore a simple one-color blue cotton dress. Her hair appeared newly coiffed and her nails were polished a dark red. Frank noted that she also sported a boob job that she hadn't possessed during their last meeting. He had no doubt he'd paid for them both. To him it appeared as though the woman must have put money into herself, although not nearly enough.

FIFTEEN

"Please state your name for the record," began Kressler.

"Mary Sue Tamsen." She looked around the courtroom and made brief eye contact with Frank once again. He gave a short nod and wry smile. She straightened slightly and turned her eyes back to her attorney. Frank desperately hoped his presence might fluster her enough to make mistakes.

"Mrs. Tamsen, please tell us what happened when Bob Jones entered your dream home to fix the water damage to your bathroom ceiling," Kressler requested.

"Oh, it was awful. All American Insurance called and told me Mr. Jones would be coming over to the house. You know, with the ceiling leaking for months and months. Then, when he did show up he just stood there with a chainsaw in his hand and said he would fix my problem. Then he went into our bathroom and starting hitting the walls with a sledgehammer and then went into our closet and began hitting the ceiling and breaking it and sawing it, letting loose deadly toxic mold all over the house." She began to cry.

Frank began to wonder in earnest if she might be a lifelong subscriber to *Mad Magazine*. He thought to check the national remediation guidelines to see if they recommended remediation companies use sledgehammers and chainsaws during their work. While his profession revolved around a wide range of what one might call normal courtroom activities, here he faced something truly original. He tried to picture a man walking around with a sledgehammer tied to one side of his belt and a chainsaw latched onto the other side. It didn't work. Through spending on-the-job time with Jeff, he met Bob and virtually every other restoration contractor in town and none of them possessed these items for work purposes.

No doubt Kessler saw contingency fee dollar signs as floaters drifting around inside his eyeballs. He asked, "What happened next, Mrs. Tamsen?"

"Well, his workers came in and they went to my refrigerator and started drinking my husband's beer and turning on my radio and hauling deadly black mold out of my house because they found it all over the drywall and on the lumber and shower tiles, and the deadly toxic mold spores went everywhere and my entire family got sick. Now, we find out we're dying a slow and terrible death."

Mary Sue's speech accelerated to fever pitch as she told her tale straight out of H.P. Lovecraft's tales of horror.

Frank took a quick glance at Jeff and surmised he was probably calculating a ballistic trajectory in order to launch an object at the witness. Frank sent him a telepathic message to save his inner strength. He would need it.

"Mrs. Tamsen, didn't you try to stop him?" asked her attorney, obviously very concerned for his client's welfare.

She wiped her eyes with a tissue and poured a cup of water, both readily available at the witness stand. "I did," she began, with fear suddenly appearing in her eyes, "but the monster stood there in my face with the hammer in his hands and he was so much bigger than me and intimidating. What could I do?" She began to cry again.

Frank looked at Judge Craycroft, who appeared unmoved.

"Tell us what happened to your dream home, then." Kressler's concern and remorse seemed to deepen, as he drew out more of her tragedy.

"We'd done so much work to the front yard with natural landscaping...and we'd done so much with the interior and then Bob Jones came in and ruined everything and left trash all around and holes in the wall. Oh, God, it was terrible."

Frank recalled that Jeff had described to him the natural landscaping in the front yard, especially the dead vehicle. The recollection made him think a car situated thusly might be good for the ecosystem, like a sunken ocean liner allows for the growth of barnacles and small sea creatures that larger creatures can feed upon. In this case, the car might be a great eco-friendly place for black widow spiders to raise their young.

Frank's attention sharpened when Kressler asked his witness about Dr. Shenero and what occurred when he came to the door.

"Well," she said, "Mr. Hirshfield, my insurance adjuster, suggested I call Dr. Shenero as a mold expert. I called him and made an appointment so he could come to the home. Then, when he came, I told him to be careful when he walked because our hands stick to the furniture because it has mold all over it and the walls are covered with mold and he said there wasn't any mold he could see. He didn't want to believe me."

She stopped to take a breath and so did Frank. The suspense registered eleven on a scale of ten for drama.

"We walked into the bathroom where I showed him black toxic deadly mold on the wood behind the shower where the tiles used to be and he said it was stained wood. Anybody with half a brain could see mold. He said that mold doesn't grow on toilet seats or door hinges or the mirrors and basically he ignored everything I told him."

Jeff leaned toward Matt to say something, but Matt raised his hand to stop him. He wanted to listen closely and take notes.

In court, you could say the most ridiculous things, and as long as a jury could be swayed, you could be a winner. It was the one place where free speech reigned supreme, as long as you believed what you were saying, or, at least, give the appearance of believing it.

With witness continued telling her tale of horror. "Well, Dr. Shenero put up sort of a gadget in my bedroom and another one in the bathroom and I told him he could find mold all over the house if he would look, because you could see it all over what was left of the two-by-fours in the bathroom..."

"You mean the studs?" asked Kessler.

"Yes, and he really wouldn't look at them or anything.""Where do you and your family live at the moment, Mrs. Tamsen?" asked Kressler, almost in tears himself.

"Well, my...our daughter actually moved out when she turned eighteen and is going to beauty school and Bud...well, our marriage isn't going too well, so he moved into a place on his own and Karl is living with me in an apartment."

Poor suffering woman, Frank thought. Let's see, thanks to you, the liability insurance for companies in the remediation field increased from two thousand dollars a year with a five thousand dollar deductible to as much as twenty thousand dollars a year with ten thousand dollars deductible. And it went up for homeowners, as well.

His mind still reeled with the sight of Megan after all these years. It occurred to him that she might need the insurance money to pay off another debt, and, like any incurable gambler, had gotten into worse trouble than before. Maybe she didn't have anything left from her previous award. Part of him gloated at the thought. People like her never climbed out, only descended deeper.

The more he thought about it, the more he believed his premise. Here she sat, boldly asking for money, amount not yet announced to the world, and naming his best friend as one of the people she filed suit against to support her selfish interests.

He felt no sympathy for her; he only felt sorry for himself and for Jeff. All of his insecurities returned. Their friendship had become an expensive reality show turned sour. What had happened to that little girl who liked to play with toy slots, but who had complained about scrubbing the deck and scraping the barnacles off the hull? Maybe she'd gutted too many fish and decided at some point to gut the world instead. Was he the biggest fish she'd gutted? He thought about it and decided that no would be the answer.

For that matter, what had happened to that little boy who liked to be her companion? He had dumped poisons into the aquifer over many years. By any measure, what he might have done to people could be considered infinitely worse than what she was doing through all her machinations. At that moment, he felt sicker about it than he had felt in a long time.

From the witness stand, Mary Sue looked over at Frank and a tide of emotion ripped him to the core. Whether it came from her to him or from within him, he could not say. It bespoke of a deep sadness and a sense of confusion. They had grown up as trusted friends and she emerged years later to cut out his heart without any remorse, as if he were on the fileting table. She just wouldn't go away. A wave of horror overcame him. In an alternate universe, would he divorce his wife and marry this she-devil? What also hurt was the knowledge that, if he had never taken the bad job, he could never have been blackmailed. Two for the price of one.

No, he had paid his dues, if not to society, at least to himself. He realized his driving force all along had been to do some good for the world and this realization had begun as soon as he had quit the job; after all, he was an environmental attorney working against those who attempted to gain obscene profits from environmentally unfriendly ventures. The net end game must be positive.

With that concept, a cleansing feeling washed over him. He tried to push down the bitter realization that his own filleting knife would re-emerge whenever he felt like having a go at gutting himself.

Frank took a deep breath to pull himself out of his revere at the sound of Mary Sue's raspy voice.

"Well, with me out of work and all and sick and maybe even possibly getting a divorce and all, you know, that happened because of the mold and everything else going on, I managed to find an apartment. It's Karl and me."

An apartment? Not another home purchase? Not even a home rental? Maybe she actually had hit bottom, again, Frank thought, looking over at the kids, when Wendy sneezed, loud enough for everyone in the courtroom to hear. Obviously, the mold in the air had affected her overly sensitive body.

Jeff wanted Matt to work over the two kids when their time came, knowing that Kressler had coached them. Matt, being the consummate gentleman, told him nothing tangible would be gained by blasting them. In the long run, it might make them look un-professional, even shoddy in the eyes of the judge. Once again, their testimony did not relate to Jeff's competence. His work stood alone.

Judge Craycroft looked at the clock which read 10:12. "Let's take our mid-morning break. We'll re-convene at ten-thirty." The judge stood and departed the courtroom through a back door to the offices. Virtually the entire court, which included perhaps a dozen on-lookers, departed into the hallway be-tween courtroom, or went outdoors.

Jeff, Frank, and Matt headed outside, not saying a word on the stairwell. McKinney met up with them moments later near one of the lawns on a beautifully clear day. A light, cooling breeze brought them the smell of freshly mown lawn. A motorcycle raced by, barely making the signal change at the corner.

"Why the somber face, Jeff?" Matt asked.

Jeff looked wistful. "Oh, I was thinking that you can help people who are sick, but you probably can't help people who only think they're sick, and you definitely want to stay away from people who aren't sick, but want you to think they are."

"Too late for that now, buddy," Frank told him.

Jeff took a big stretch trying to work the kinks out of his muscles. "All right, counselors, what do you think?"

McKinney said, "Her testimony is so inaccurate as to befuddle the imagination." McKinney was a rail thin, very deliberate investigator who had met Frank while working opposite ends of an environmental case a number of years back, hitting it off as professional friends, as well as on a personal basis. He stood ramrod straight, as though he had graduated from West Point. "We can refute virtually every statement she made."

"No big deal," Frank said, "We're still in the first inning of a nine-inning ballgame. I wasn't impressed with her testimony."

Matt admonished, "Be careful not to celebrate a victory in the middle of a match. It's bad luck. That said, so far, she has yet to enter into testimony what Jeff had done wrong to warrant a suit against him. He submitted his notes, as requested, and they're quite plain to read. The truth will come out eventually when you get to the stand to refute her testimony." Here he looked at Jeff.

"When can I expect to get to the stand?" Jeff asked.

Matt replied, "Well, she still must be cross-examined. We need to hear from and cross-examine Dr. Campbell, as well as the husband and the two children followed by Bob Jones himself and Burke Remediation. Julie Robinette will be in there somewhere, too. All this should occur before you get called for defense testimony. Of course, the plaintiff's lawyer can always call you in any time before they complete their testimony."

"Huh?" Jeff looked startled.

McKinney, who always appeared not to have a care in the world about anything, suddenly looked at his watch. "Time to go back. Oh, by the way, All American offered them another hundred grand to settle. They refused the offer. Kressler told them to turn it down."

"My guess is that Mary Sue had probably told Kressler to turn it down," Frank added. "The family has already received around a paltry hundred grand over the past year.

"What's minimum wage these days?"

It didn't take a genius to figure it. Had they taken the offer, Kressler would get another forty. Not bad for a few phone calls and some paperwork. Frank hoped that the era of free handouts would change, or at least limit the amount of the payouts.

SIXTEEN

Still in the first day of the trial and back in the courtroom after the morning break, Mary Sue Tamsen dramatically presented more of her sob story about how Jeff only used one monitor in each of the rooms and how he performed a superficial inspection. She knew, because she stood right there watching him the whole time.

Craycroft shut down the court a little early for lunch at 11:45 making the comment that she needed to review another case.

McKinney went out by himself to return a number of phone calls. Matt, Jeff, and Frank took a short drive over to the Bigger Burger on Jenkins for lunch, immediately to the north of the university. Matt drove by himself citing the need to do some quick shopping for a few items his wife had ordered for a party they were slated to have that evening and said he'd have to leave lunch early.

The three found parking slots directly in front of

the establishment sandwiched between Lobster and More and the Game Day Bar. Over the years, only the prices changed, not the menu or the popularity. They still served a five-inch slab of hamburger meat between two six-inch sesame seed buns and you slop on your own fixings.

They trio sat at a window seat and tried not to be too obvious taking in the college co-eds passing by. Jeff began an easy laugh.

Matt gave his head a quick twitch upward. "What gives?"

"I was thinking about other crazy jobs I've had over the years and the people I've run into." He set down his hamburger.

"Such as?" inquired Frank.

"I went out to a guy's house one time where he met me outside. This guy was middle-aged and not too bad looking. He had a thing about newspapers. He opened the garage door and newspapers were stacked floor to ceiling in the middle section of the garage, with furniture taking up the rest of the space. So we go through the rows of newspapers with barely enough space to squeeze sideways. We make a few turns and finally I said, 'We are going to check the house, aren't we?'

"And the guy says, 'Actually, we're in the living room. Like I told you, I need you to check the home for mold'.

"I wander through the rest of the home and there is virtually nowhere to go or sit or do anything because there is stuff everywhere, including the bathrooms where he had stacked more newspapers and magazines. Potted plants sat in the tub and on the toilet seat cover."

"I'm curious. What could you do if you did find airborne mold, or mold anywhere for that matter?" Matt asked. "Hell, what would you do if you found mice or bats?"

"Exactly," Jeff said. "So I excused myself from the case and gave the man the name of a competitor I didn't like."

Jeff took a solid bite out of his burger and looked as if he had more to say. He finished his chew and went on. "I remember a couple of hospitals I got hired to check out. It turns out that the air handlers drew a hundred thousand cubic feet a minute through their filters. When I checked them, the filters had once been pleated, but were collapsed with all kinds of air by-pass going on around the edges. The physical plant people told me they changed the banks of filters every three months, as per manufacturers' recommendations, and here we were at the eight-week mark. They'd been doing this for years.

"So I checked the air of the various departments and found a very high amount of highly allergenic cornstarch particles in pediatrics, hematology, emergency care and other areas where they use latex gloves powdered with the stuff for ease of use. Lots of people are allergic to corn, including patients and hospital staff. Now it's in about everything we eat.

"On top of that, the builders had installed the air conditioning units on the roof on the side nearest the parking lot where they pulled in their fresh air."

Frank and Matt sat in rapt attention. Frank had heard enough of Jeff's stories over the years and had been there with him on a number of his adventures. There were always curious tales coming from the lips of this professor; one of the reasons why he liked to stay at his friend's side. Frank had always tried to integrate Jeff's skills into his own.

Jeff leaned back and continued. "One time a lady told me that one of her cats died and it was the worst day of her life. I told her I'd be happy to trade her for one of mine.

"My question to you is, compare any one of those stories with the trial we are going through. Which one is the strangest of all?" queried Jeff.

Matt looked at Frank, then to Jeff and said, "It's like people. There are different ways to be strange."

"Amen, to that," Jeff responded. "Just like there are a lot of ways to be smart."

"And a lot of ways to be stupid," Frank concluded, philosophically.

Matt then departed, which gave Frank the opportunity he wanted in order to speak with Jeff alone.

At that point Frank quickly told Jeff everything he could about Mary Sue Megan Moore Tamsen; their growing up, his first job, money, his guilt, meeting Mary Sue later, her blackmail, her courtroom appearance and how it all tied in.

Jeff let Frank spill it all out. He asked a couple of questions which Frank answered truthfully.

"Jeff, you've always been my best friend, you

know that. Just don't judge me too harshly—or, maybe I need that judgment to happen."

Jeff smiled, "Come on, Frank, friend's don't judge each other. They make constructive comments and take it all in stride. Shit, man, look at me. I wear my emotions on my sleeve. I can't control my tongue. I was an embarrassment to my family and my wife left me because of it and took the kids with her. To make matters worse, I'm still as outspoken as ever. Do you know why I'm actually jealous of you? At least you still have a beautiful woman and two beautiful children.

"You tell me, Frank, which of us is worse than the other one? Besides, you're out of both messes. It's over."

"Yeah, but you're in it now, buddy."

"Hell, this ain't nothin'," said Jeff emphatically. "How about the time I got jammed in a cave tunnel underground looking for mushrooms off Palau and the cave flooded with sea water." He touched a jagged scar that ran across his newly shaven head from his left eyebrow up two inches across his forehead. It had resulted from a gouge by a stalactite that he ran into while lying on his back trying to inch his way out of the tunnel in the stygian blackness.

"I was seriously scared for my life, Frank. Scarred for life, too." Jeff grinned at his own quip pointing to the scar on his forehead. "I'd have taken all your bad memories to avoid death."

"But you did, didn't you?" said Frank, smiling for the first time.

"And so will we all." Jeff stood and clapped his friend on the shoulder. "Now let's get to court for the next round."

Jeff knew full well that, win or lose, he'd have another scar-causing memory at the conclusion of this trial.

SEVENTEEN

At precisely 6:00 p.m, on the Friday before the trial began, Sandra Hudson turned on the television in her small apartment to catch the evening news. Her week of teaching had concluded and it was relax time.

Amidst the usual reports of traffic accidents and various renovation activities came a news flash about a trial that would begin on the following Wednesday, a picture of Mary Sue flashed on the screen. The reporter noted that the Tamsen family had filed suit against a number of persons and companies because they got sick from mold in their home. Sandra became so captivated by the story that she failed to hear the details of the report. But unquestionably, she knew that woman and waited for the 6:30 news on a different station.

At 7:01 she went on the Internet learning everything she could find out about mold. As a good investigator, she dug deeply into the literature, didn't like what she saw, and concentrated on surface fluff—facts everybody knew concerning the hazards of mold—nevermind that everybody was wrong. By Monday she was ready.

Sandra and Mary Sue met and had become friends in a battered woman's shelter (no children) in Oklahoma City years before, when Jeff, Frank, and Billy had become roommates in Norman.

Sandra had already been a resident of the shelter for eight months before Mary Sue moved in.

Five years before moving into the shelter Sandra had fallen under the auspices of various child protective agencies in Oklahoma who soon found her a foster home in the city. This, while continuing to provide counseling services to her.

Three days after she turned eighteen, Sandra left the home of her foster parents and never looked back.

She had planned ahead and had a job lined up in a clothing store. Soon she began dating a customer. On their fourth date, the man raped her and beat her senseless.

With the help of the police and female manager of the store, she found her way to the shelter, whose measures directed them toward integrating troubled women into society.

By the time Mary Sue moved in to the shelter, Sandra had turned nineteen, with Mary Sue some two years her senior.

The two friends contrasted in appearance.

Mary Sue stood a thin five-six, with short-to medium-length blond air she preferred to keep curled and wore her makeup in abundance.

Sandra could best be described as short and frumpy with medium length dark brown hair flipped up at the bottom, fleshy face, and large breasted. The latter she kept well hidden under several layers of clothing. Both her clothing and her face were drab.

Mary Sue, who had found employment as a cashier in a car wash, slept wherever she could and with whomever she could in order to survive. Her own personal trauma got her to the shelter immediately after a bed had become available. Thus, she and Sandra became roommates. Her recent past paralleled that of most of the women there; meeting a bad man and paying the penalty.

The shelter had a common area with television, large kitchen, a counseling office and numerous bedrooms with virtually all bedrooms holding two bunk beds with up to four women each. Each woman had her own nightstand. A separate bedroom held two live-in counselors. Three bathrooms were present in the facility and an outdoor fenced-in lawn and patio area offered evening relaxation and a place for smoking, an activity in which most shelter occupants engaged.

The shelter required each women to visit with a counselor three times weekly and to rotate duties in the facility. In order to pay for their stay, the shelter directed that each find a job. Turnovers were the norm, one of the common denominators of shelters in general.

Many homeowners in the neighborhood where the shelter was located were not happy to have an assortment of single homeless women living so close to them and shunned the dwelling as though it were a crack house. Others were more forgiving, perhaps having wayward daughters (or wives) of their own, and asked the staff if they could be of help in any way.

Members of the church who operated the shelter worked hard at finding part time work for the women, when they didn't run away.

Sandra and Mary Sue remained inseparable, as they tried to figure out where they were going with their lives, learning from each other.

When the work rotation schedule listed Mary Sue to spend the week in the kitchen, either assisting with meal preparation or washing dishes, she flatly refused and got assigned to assist in the housekeeping; that is, sweeping, vacuuming, and cleaning—chores to which she readily assisted as little as possible.

Counselors found her to be intractable, as well as lazy.

"Why are you even here?" they would ask.

Mary Sue had no ready answer. "Because I am divorced and have nowhere else to go," she would reply. However, she did have a few dollars saved.

Sandra, recently employed at a convenience store only a short bus ride from the shelter, had recommended Mary Sue for the swing-shift position at the store. Occasional stocking of the shelves and the refrigerators would be the most significant extent of her friend's ardor.

The time had arrived when the women decided to leave the shelter and go out into the world themselves, each with her own burden. They promised to stay in touch, but never did.

From Mary Sue, Sandra had learned that perseverance and effort can pay rewards in the absence of physical labor, and to always play for the highest stakes you could afford. And if you couldn't afford to play the high stakes, then find some way to get the backing, whatever it takes. And if you lost, you lost. Don't worry about it. Simply save up and start again. The big victory is a hundred times better than the big loss. Why? Because you shouldn't give a shit about losing. The part just comes along for the ride, like a troublesome hitchhiker.

From Sandra, Mary Sue had learned that there is such a thing as vengeance. If you're pissed at someone or something, say, life, for example, maybe a considerable amount of slow and deliberate planning is in order to fulfill your dreams. There is nothing wrong, indeed there is perhaps something special, about your target incurring a slow bleed.

Thus, well into her twenty-first year of age, Mary Sue obtained a job at a casino that had been established by the Cherokee Nation. She easily passed their interview in the facility near OKC with her ability to bullshit and her inside knowledge of the games. Management sent her to training school and she soon returned to a full-time employment position.

Sandra opted to go to junior college with an emphasis on theater arts. After receiving her Associate in Arts Degree she transferred some of her credits to upper division and attended the University of Oklahoma in Norman, this time majoring in education with the emphasis on elementary teaching. She chose psychology as her minor.

EIGHTEEN

At 12:50 p.m., the three men returned to the courthouse, entered through the checkpoint metal detector at the entrance, and walked the stairs to the second floor, Room 272.

At 1:02 p.m., Mary Sue again took the stand.

Kressler approached the witness to continue with his direct examination. "Could you please tell the court your medical problems since your encounter with Bob Jones and his crew and with Dr. Shenero?"

Mary Sue almost started speaking before Kressler had finished asking his question. "Yes. My family had and still has a terrible time dealing with this; it hurts to discuss our problems, you know, especially in public."

"Do your best, Mrs. Tamsen. You've lost a lot, but we need to hear about what happened after those men entered your dream home. I'm going to ask you a few painful questions. How do you feel now?"

Mary Sue poured herself some water and answered the first question. "I feel terrible, joints ache, and like my husband, there's no sex drive, depressed all the time, unable to take care of my home and children or to be a good mother, and even though my husband and I are getting divorced we care for each other... a terrible burden on all of us..."

Mary Sue poured herself another paper cup of water and drank it slowly, trying to compose herself.

A few minutes ago she was considering a divorce. Now she's getting one? thought Frank. He wanted to ask the bailiff to check the contents of the pitcher for the presence of downers.

His imagination flew off to a nether world, imagining booze being served at a trial. A smile crossed his lips: by law, the judge and the attorneys may down only two shots of hard liquor during a break while spectators may drink a single beer during breaks, as a fund raising method to needy children.

"This is so embarrassing," Mary Sue complained. "But in all honesty, my poor husband couldn't get an erection after we got exposed to all those deadly toxic molds. His back started hurting and he couldn't sit on the sofa without getting all slimy and feet sticky, and I know he felt inadequate as a man and his knees started hurting...oh..." Mary Sue quickly pulled a tissue from the box. Then she started to cry, dabbing at her eyes.

Kressler looked up at the judge. "I have no further questions of this witness, Your Honor."

"Mr. McKinney, you may begin cross examination," directed Craycroft.

McKinney stood and faced the witness.

This could be good, Frank brought his mind back on track.

McKinney couldn't wait to sink his teeth into Mary Sue's throat. The company he represented had already paid out a lot of good money to the Tamsen family—read Mary Sue.

George McKinney had moved to Oklahoma City from Plymouth, Massachusetts. A graduate of Yale University, he spent a number of very successful years in a law firm based in Plymouth. He had a strong science background and had experience in mold cases back east. He'd moved to Oklahoma City to escape the grind of high-pressure law.

"Mrs. Tamsen, Bob Jones gave you papers to sign before he began the job, did he not?" McKinney began.

"Yes."

McKinney displayed a handful of documents. "In fact, you signed in three different places regarding the fact you would not sue Bob Jones Restoration, didn't you?"

"Yes," responded the witness.

"And you received a disclaimer from Dr. Shenero stating that what he found or didn't find was only valid at the time of the testing. But you still sued him, didn't you?"

"Yes."

"And you also sued Bob Jones, didn't you?"

"Yes, but at the time I signed, sir," her voice raised in pitch somewhat, "I didn't know my family would be put in a life-threatening situation."

"Why did you also sue Burke Remediation? I mean, they said they found the problem in your son's bedroom, didn't they? I mean, you hired them yourself, didn't you?"

Kressler stood. "Objection, your honor. Multiple questions of the witness."

"I'll rephrase, Your Honor," said McKinney.

"Mrs. Tamsen, who do you think is at fault for your health problems?"

McKinney knew that the answer to his question went back to Kressler, who probably felt that more money could be forthcoming if he filed suit against more people.

"All of them," she almost shouted. "Because Burke found it, but didn't clean it up properly and made us destroy all our belongings. Because Bob Jones and Dr. Shenero caused our health problems. Because All American Insurance hired Bob Jones and he hired Shenero. Because even Safe Home Environmental didn't find anything when they should have.

"Bob Jones spread mold all over our house and we saw it growing everywhere, and Dr. Shenero couldn't even see it and told us he didn't find anything wrong, but Burke Remediation found lots of mold after they came in."

Jeff pondered her response. She sued Burke because they did find mold. Why did they find it? Given a separate leak had occurred, *Stachybotrys* will be inside the walls, unless things are very nasty, but

Burke's own report notes only water staining on the ceiling of the bedroom. They had sent their samples to an independent lab in New Jersey that reported an inordinate amount of mold in the air of Karl's bedroom, with some *Stachybotrys* present. Something wasn't right.

McKinney spoke slowly, deliberately. He liked his words to carry impact. He disliked histrionics. "I would like you to read to the court the report issued by Burke Remediation and signed by the owner of the company, Mr. James Burke. The section I would like you to read is highlighted at the very end of the report. Could you please read this portion?"

He handed her a booklet open to the page in question. She began reading: "Limitations: This report is based on information supplied by others including, but not limited to, laboratory data. This report reflects data collected at a particular date and time only."

"Do you understand what you read? If so, could you please explain it to the court?"

"Ummm, not really." Mary Sue grabbed another tissue from the box on the witness stand, dabbed her eyes and then blew her nose, softly, delicately. A honker would have been a distraction, subtracting from the mood she was trying to create.

"No? Then, let me help you. It means, first, they are going by what you told them to do as far as water damage and health are concerned. It also means that the measurements they took were conducted several months after Bob Jones and Dr. Shenero had been hired. So these measurements apply only to when Burke's people did their tests. This is standard procedure, Mrs. Tamsen, and is universally accepted not only in this country, but internationally."

The defense attorneys, as well as the single prosecuting attorney, could see Mary Sue had trouble grasping the concept of reverse time interpolation. No doubt, decades of alcohol and cigarette abuse did not help her clarity of thought. McKinney didn't care whether she got it or not. He'd said it for the judge's sake, not for the sake of the witness.

"Incidentally, Mrs. Tamsen, All American paid you good money, which included funds for Bob Jones and Dr. Shenero. Why didn't you pay them for their work?"

McKinney caught Mary Sue with her pants down, again, on that one. She struggled for an answer. "Because we were going to pay them when we got the house fixed, but we never got it fixed," she responded, weakly.

She thought for hard second or two and came back with, "Because we had to put the money toward a doctor who would help us."

"We'll come back to that later," replied McKinney.

Jeff reflected, Nothing counts anymore, not signatures or promises, not disclaimers, not sworn oaths, nothing. Welcome to the Twenty-First Century. Hey, everybody has a right to make an honest living in a free enterprise economy, even Mary Sue and her flock. People should try to succeed at what they can do best.

McKinney drilled deeper, "Mrs. Tamsen, if you were so concerned with mold affecting your health, why did you follow Dr. Shenero inside the containments when he asked you not to do it? They were there to protect you."

This caught her off guard. She responded by breaking out in tears, again. McKinney really didn't give a damn. He wanted to let her know he was on to her.

"Please answer the question, Mrs. Tamsen," McKinney directed.

"I wasn't thinking. I mean, the whole thing made me and my family off-kilter."

"Mrs. Tamsen, what did you say to Burke Remediation when you first called them?"

"I asked to speak with Mr. Burke personally."

"Yes. What did you tell him? Remember, you are under oath."

"I told him that my whole house had mold all over it and my family got sick from it and I got sick from it."

"How did you know the entire home was bad?"

"I felt it was bad and so did my children and so did my husband. I lost my husband," she sobbed.

Now he's gone?

McKinney ignored her grandstanding and thumbed through a sheaf of papers. "Mrs. Tamsen, what did Burke Remediation tell you to do with all the contents in your home?"

"They said to destroy them."

"They told you destroy them after they ran their tests, am I correct?"

"Yes, when they first came into the home, the owner of the company, Mr. Burke, took one look at the back bedroom and went outside and he and his crew put on heavy respirators to run the tests, things were so bad. They even gave me a mask to wear."

"The back bedroom?"

"Karl's room. And Mr. Burke was so nice. He sat down with me for six hours straight and explained everything we needed to know about his work and our home. That's more than other people did."

"He was so nice that you sued him." McKinney made a little show of scratching his head. "Let me understand this. Burke spent six hours with you explaining things?"

"Yes, at least."

"Is it okay if I ask him how long he personally visited with you? Remember, you are under oath, under penalty of law, and under penalty of perjury, for willingly providing false information."

"Of course. Maybe it a little less than six hours, now that I think of it."

"Your husband wasn't there?"

"No, the man worked so hard trying to support the family and his boss wouldn't let him get away for the meeting with Mr. Burke, I think he said."

Jeff guessed that Burke spent no more than fifteen minutes in discussion with Mary Sue, and that would be off and on, anxious to escape the insanity of her overtures.

"By Karl's room, you are referring to the room that had water damage to a ceiling. Am I correct?" asked McKinney.

The witness nodded.

"We need a 'yes' or 'no' answer so the court reporter can record a response."

"Yes," replied Mary Sue."

"Mrs. Tamsen, you claim a lot of medical problems resulted from your exposure to mold in your home."

"Yes."

"I know you told us a few of the problems you incurred. Could you name a few more of these problems for the court?"

"Well, my kids and I have Attention Deficit Disorder and they also have Attention Deficit Hyperactivity Disorder and had to go into special education classes because they couldn't concentrate, and all of us lost our short-term memories and a lot of other things. I have an eye twitch that won't go away and my ears ring all the time, too. According to medical reports, all of our kidneys and livers are out of line, also."

"Out of line?"

"Yes, out of line. I think my back might be, too."

"How's your spleen?" McKinney had to ask.

"That's probably out of line, too, since you mention it," she answered, soulfully.

"Sorry to hear that," McKinney stated flatly, trying to avoid sarcasm, which would draw the ire of the judge.

NINETEEN

McKinney looked thoughtful, obviously trying to figure out what the witness had told him. He slowly walked over to the clerk's desk and found an item marked "Plaintiff's 3." He picked this up and sauntered back to his table, situated in front of the where the jurors would seat, if they were present.

"In my hands is a list of items in your home which you discarded as a result of the advice given by Burke Remediation. There are hundreds of items listed for a total of close to fourteen thousand dollars, yet you had enough memory to list the value of each. Your short-term memory didn't seem to be affected when it came to listing these items? How do you respond to this?"

"We did the best we could. A lot of those things were guesses," the witness stated meekly, her mouth turned downward.

Frank recalled his discussion with Matt about her list. They surmised that, in addition to being complicit in the scheme, Bud may have compiled it. This suggested the man had an organizational mind. To them, this brought forth an interesting factoid.

"Let's see, here. You note a loss of eight thousand dollars' worth of men's socks and underwear. Excuse me, ma'am, I'm an attorney and make a decent living, but I sure don't own eight thousand dollars' worth of socks and underwear."

Mary Sue slid along as smooth as silk. "I worked for a company that sold these things and I kept a stock of them at home so I could distribute them in the local market."

"Do you recall the name of that company?"

"I'm dreadfully sorry, sir. I can't remember the name. I think it is out of business."

"How about glasses and dishware? Did you throw them away, too, or did you think you might be able to wash them in the dishwasher?"

Mary Sue began to cry. "I didn't want to lose any of my family's possessions, but Mr. Burke told us to throw away everything, so we did. We were following his directions."

"Do you recall why he told you to do that?" asked McKinney.

"Because he found deadly toxic mold in our home," she stated proudly and sat up straighter.

"So, by this time, there was nothing left of the master bathroom but the studs, a portion of the adjoining wall to the master bedroom was cut, the bath was under containment, Burke opened the ceiling of Karl's bedroom, and he sealed that room in plastic.

In other words, say goodbye to Karl's room. They opened a portion of the wall near that leak, and so forth and so on." McKinney gently shook the papers in his hand. Is that essentially correct?"

"Yes."

"So really, Mrs. Tamsen, for a period of what amounts to a several months, your family lived in a portion of your home before you moved to a motel. Yet, you were paid on three separate occasions to have the areas repaired after the remediation, but you never did. Is that correct?"

"Yes."

"I'm curious what you did with all that money, if you didn't use it to repair your family's dream home. Can you answer that?"

Even the judge looked attentive, curious about what answer the witness would give.

Kressler looked down at McKinney's mention of the words "dream home," a term he himself coined; a term McKinney now used with abandon. Kressler could make no objection to the statement.

Mary Sue stammered, clearly out of her league and trying to come up with any plausible answer. "Uh, because...Bud and I were always arguing about who to hire to do the work, because we didn't trust anyone anymore and we were sick all the time..."

"I'm confused. Didn't you and your husband move out of the home at some point?"

"Uh, yes, sir, but we were all suffering from all the mold in our home..."

McKinney barreled onward without giving the

witness time to construct a serious answer. "Not only did that occur, but you never repaired any part of the home, not after the first leak and not after the second leak; nor did you pay your bills even though you had the money to do so. I've never heard of anybody who has ever called in this many experts into their home on a mold lawsuit and eventually trashed the home and filed suit against them all, including your insurance company who already paid you several times, and four other defendants. Never. Why you?"

"I already told you. Because Bob Jones and Dr. Shenero caused all our problems."

"That's not a good answer."

"Objection!" Kressler shot to his feet. "Asked and answered. Counsel is badgering the witness."

"Sustained."

McKinney turned to Mary Sue with a direct look. "Mrs. Tamsen, how much money do you want?"

"What?" She instantly sobered up and gave him an innocent look.

"How much money do you want? That's the reason you're here, isn't it? Please answer the question."

Mary Sue covered her face with her hands and began to sob once again. She took a tissue and another cup of water and blubbered, "You can't put a price on what we went through. My family's health is ruined, we're all going to die soon, we're no longer together as a family, and you insult me because we lost everything..."

Then Mary Sue looked up and said, "We haven't quite worked that out yet."

She knew. She was saving it for Kressler to provide the answer to the question.

"Mrs. Tamsen," McKinney said, "I am going to read to you a portion from a page from a deposition you gave dated April ninth. This deposition was taken several months after Bob Jones Restoration, Safe Home Environmental, Burke Restoration, and Dr. Shenero entered your home."

He cleared his throat and read from the paper in his hand, his voice filling the courtroom. "Jeffrey Shenero and Bob Jones have destroyed my family and our lives. I fear for my children and for children everywhere if these two are free to do their rapine and their evil. They are lying scum that are no better than dirt, they are monsters and may yet be killers of my family. They have poisoned us as surely as if they put arsenic in our food. Somebody has to do something to stop them."

McKinney put down the sheet of paper and said, "That's quite poetic, Mrs. Tamsen—almost as though the words were written for a soap opera. The question is, do you still feel the same way?"

"Even more so, sir, except that Dr. Shenero is to blame the most because he didn't find what he was supposed to find."

"What was that, Mrs. Tamsen?"

"You know what. Deadly toxic black mold and other kinds of deadly toxic mold."

"Do you watch soap Operas, Mrs. Tamsen?"

McKinney asked.

Kressler stood. "Objection. Relevance."

"Do you have a point to make, counselor?" asked the judge.

"I do. Please permit the plaintiff to answer the question."

The judge turned to the plaintiff. "Please answer the question."

"Uh, sometimes," Mary Sue said.

"Do you ever watch Ruined Lives?"

"Uh, I guess so."

"Well, one of my workers is a stay-at-home mom and she does like that soap opera. She told me the words you just used to describe two of the three defendants are almost the exact words used in an episode of that drama only two days before you gave your deposition. How do you respond to that?"

"Uh, maybe, I don't remember," Mary Sue meekly responded.

At this point in her testimony Jeff felt as though he was recipient of an award from the "No good deed gets unpunished," club.

"Have you ever sought a second medical opinion in your case or in the case of your family?" continued McKinney.

"No. Why should I? I mean, we? I'm not going to get better. Dr. Campbell told me so. He also told me there are few people who do get better, except for maybe once in a while, after they leave their home they might feel better, but when they come home they get sick again."

Frank looked at his friend who was earning a college degree in courtroom drama. Spending money, getting belittled and insulted, and wasting time were only a few of the perks that came along with this education.

The clerk of the court sorted forty-five documents in front of her, ninety percent of which were at the behest of Kressler. This judge might read them all, but probably not. She would probably think about what she needed in order to answer questions of her own that she might have of the witnesses later in the trial, and then turn to those documents as reference.

"Thank you, Mrs. Tamsen. No further questions," said McKinney.

Just like that, Mary Sue got off McKinney's barbecue spit and onto Matt's. Somewhere down the line, Jeff's turn would come to rotate on the grill.

"All right," said Judge Craycroft. She looked up at the wall clock. "After the break, Mr. Collins, you may cross-examine."

TWENTY

Here's how to use a cell phone as a weapon. Find out the opposing attorney's cell phone number. Simple stuff. Then program the number into your phone in your speed dial list and wait until he is examining a witness. At the right time, you surreptitiously, push the "Send" button on your phone. The judge blows a gasket when the attorney's cell phone goes off, and your side gains points indirectly, given that the man neglected to turn off his phone. It does happen.

Frank, hidden from view from the judge behind the defense table and the barricade, pushed a speed dial button and Kressler's phone rang. He'd done it on a flier because all those present in the courtroom, especially witnesses and attorneys or directed to turn off their phones. Kressler had neglected this simple rule and got caught.

Frank figured that even if Kressler had switched his phone to vibrate, at the least it would distract him and give him a bad case of right-hand-fumbling-for-the-phone-to-shut-it-up-itis.

It took the big man a good five seconds to reach into his pocket and fumble with the off-button. Judge Craycroft was livid and demanded that he give her his phone. He did and she turned it off. "You'll get it back at the break," she declared. "After the break you will give it back to me. Is that clear?"

"Yes, Your Honor," Kressler declared, sheepishly, without having the opportunity to see who called.

Matt chanced a quick glance at Frank who gave the faintest twitch of a smile.

Kressler picked up the glance and he turned to look at Frank. At the same instant, Frank closed his eyes as if asleep.

So far Matt hadn't asked a single question of the witness.

Matt walked from the judge's bench to the front of the table labeled Defendant, ambling to the far left. He sat down in the end seat of one of the nine juror chairs.

"Mrs. Tamsen, have you ever undergone psychiatric evaluation?"

"Huh, well, no."

"Mrs. Tamsen, you testified about Jeffrey Shenero causing the problems incurred by you and your family. What did you mean? You must have a reason to think that mold caused these problems."

"Because television showed a special about mold and since then, I've learned a lot about it by talking with friends and reading about it and looking it up on the Internet. I educated myself," she replied proudly.

"Again, how do you know your symptoms can be related to mold?"

"Well, Dr. Campbell told me they were."

"Ah, yes, Dr. Campbell. Well, if you know, which molds caused your problems?"

"I do know about one of them, Stacch... staky ..., the deadly toxic black mold. Mr. Burke sent me information about this mold, too."

Both Jeff and Frank knew Campbell because their profession exposed them to a lot of tangential sciences and persons associated with them. Also, one more than one occasion, Jeff and Frank discussed the practices of this man and others like him. A few were well meaning and did good honest work with the client's best interest at heart; others like Campbell were dangerous.

Jeff expressed a diametrically opposite viewpoint than did Campbell. Campbell believed, or professed to believe, that most molds possess a toxic component and by inhaling their spores, one would be exposed to the toxins on their surface. On the other hand, Jeff didn't believe any mold spores possessed a component toxic enough to cause harm to humans when inhaled, for the simple reason that the number of spores required to cause toxicity would be so astronomical that the person would die of suffocation first.

To Frank, this legal case exemplified every fear generated by the media, and it brought out both great researchers along with the lower life forms to testify in this fantasy theory about toxicity.

Matt paced about, turned toward one table, and then the next, and finally spun about and faced the witness. "Mrs. Tamsen, did you buy a motorcycle?"

"Hmm, yes."

"What kind of motorcycle did you buy?"

"A Harley Davidson."

"How much did you pay for this motorcycle?"

"I found a used one for about fourteen thousand dollars. It was something I always wanted, and anyway, I only drove the bike a couple of hundred miles."

"If your joints ached so much, how did you start the motorcycle?"

"Oh, it has an electric starter."

"And the vibration of the bike didn't bother you?"

"The bike rode smoothly"

"Did you stop driving the bike because your joints hurt or because your attorney advised you not to show off?" Instantly, Matt pulled back. "I'll withdraw the question."

"I'm wondering where you got the money from, Mrs. Tamsen. I'm thinking you used the insurance money earmarked for home repair and to pay the people who worked on your home."

Kressler stood to object and then sat down again. Matt had not asked a question. He was only making an observation.

"Mrs. Tamsen, a good many experts entered your home through your periods of complaint. Is that correct?"

"I don't know exactly how many came in," she

said.

Matt proceeded to name them off and the dates they came into the home. "Does that sound about right?" he asked again.

"I guess so."

"And All American Insurance paid for each and every one of them, either directly or through you. Is that right?"

"Yes."

"And your home got torn apart several times because you wanted people to look for mold, is that correct?"

"Yes, but they did find mold and Mr. Shenero missed a lot. He should have found the mold in the beginning. The man is lower than dirt and he should have reported to us what he found instead of hiding it."

"Mrs. Tamsen, do you know who that is?" he asked, pointing at Jeff.

Jeff excelled as a natural born teacher and had trained for years under many of the classical mycologists. Frank could tell that he was embarrassed. He'd received local, national, and even international attention on so many occasions he couldn't remember them all. Whatever he accomplished, he did for the sake of imparting information to others; information that might be of help to them, never for himself.

Frank felt for him. Seventeenth-century Salem witch hunters had returned, attempting to fell a mighty tree with a cheap plastic sword.

"Do you know what this man has done in his lifetime?" Matt asked.

"Well," here she stumbled. Kressler failed to prepare her to answer this question. Indeed, Frank thought that Kressler himself failed to investigate Jeff thoroughly enough.

"I think he has a big degree in art and has a side job running some gadgets inside houses."

Vindication, at last. In one fell swoop, Frank's best friend had been elevated from guttersnipe and mass murderer to art dealer and gadget operator.

Matt began to pace back and forth, then stopped and addressed the witness. "When did you first begin to see Dr. Campbell?"

Mary Sue poured still another full cup of water.

"We saw Dr. Campbell after we got the report from Burke Remediation that said deadly toxic mold covered all our walls and possessions in our dream home," responded the almost runner-up beauty queen of her small high school.

"All over?"

"Yes."

The reports typically prepared by Burke Remediation were second in length only to a religious tome. But instead of holding substance, their weighty reports were notorious in presenting five percent substance and ninety-five percent fluff—information about how molds affect allergies, pages and pages about detailed mycotoxin research from laboratories and experimental animals, but mostly about the wonderful company employees.

Burke pulled pieces from Internet junk hype, numerous pages about a dozen molds, as well as esoteric details about how deadly their toxins were. If you ate or drank the purified toxins, then, okay. If you inhaled them, no. Burke Remediation mailed their literature to the Tamsens as a scare tactic, without ever having looked through a microscope in his life.

Jeff and Matt could only bide their time and build upon the plaintiff's mistakes until the trial's proceedings delivered Jeff to the witness stand.

"No further questions, Your Honor."

The judge looked up at the clock on the wall and noted the time, which now exceeded the time for the afternoon break. For her own reasons, Craycroft decided to dismiss the court for the day. Perhaps she, too, needed to pick up some party favors. Working this trial might give her the urge to pick up a bottle of Oklahoma moonshine, Frank considered.

The men reconnoitered at a coffee shop across the street from the courthouse. Jeff sat on a booth seat opposite the two attorneys. He appeared dazed. "I don't know how much more of this fantasy I can stand," he said. "I'm serious. Does the judge realize the extent of the crapola she's being force-fed?"

"If it makes you feel any better, Jeff, Craycroft has presided over a number of malpractice cases and served as a former defense attorney," Matt tried to mollify his client.

Frank said, "I know Craycroft. "She's fair and takes her role as judge very seriously. You could do a lot worse than having her preside."

"I need to testify," said Jeff. "At least to refute Burke's and Campbell's statements."

"You don't need to get into a fight with Campbell," said Matt. "You are not a medical doctor. I know, except for the letters after his name, he isn't either, but your fight is not his fight. Choose your battles. We know you have the knowledge to refute him, but so what? Don't forget our mission statement, Jeff. What were you hired to do? Can anybody present evidence that finds fault with what you did? The rest of it is a problem for All American Insurance and George McKinney, not us."

TWENTY-ONE

Sandra Hudson instantly became fascinated by the story of the courtroom story featuring her old friend—captivated, in fact. She considered it an omen. Unknowingly, Mary Sue had provided her with the solution to her own problem——how to slowly bring organized society to its knees.

All of Sandra's years of study, preparation and positioning had not borne fruit because she still needed the trigger for her master plan. How many times had she been ready to launch and how many times had she aborted the mission because it didn't feel right?

Is this perfect, or what? How about we make this a dual effort.

It would take her but a few days to rehearse and prep.

It didn't take long to get herself up to speed on mold. You could claim anything, and as long as it's in the realm of reason, they'd have to prove you wrong.

A quick study, she continually rehearsed her lines, as an athlete runs through virtually every moment of his or her performance in their mind—all this without casting suspicion upon herself while she taught her class.

On the following Monday, two days prior to the first day of the trial, Sandra checked herself in the mirror one last time, grabbed her small briefcase and purse, and left her apartment. She really wouldn't need to bring a lunch today, but she brought one anyway in order to maintain a normal demeanor for another average workday.

Sandra wore her usual smile when she arrived at the school where she had lovingly taught for eight years. She greeted the staff and the principal, Jim Hughes.

A thin, balding, pale man of average height, Hughes radiated sincerity and always welcomed Sandra and his other teachers whenever they entered his school.

They shook hands briefly. Sandra felt the warmth of the touch, not the cold, clammy feeling of many other handshakes. She viewed him as a nice guy with marriage problems trying to survive in a typical top-heavy school district.

For her part, Sandra re-entered the world that constituted her dreams, the world in which she must operate deliberately and flawlessly, given the spark from Mary Sue.

The background references failed to mention Sandra Hudson's burning desire to cause as much pain and suffering as possible. Years of planning were about to come to fruition. She'd even changed her name to Hudson, the name of her foster family, after her testosterone-laden father was sent to prison, where he died.

Hudson thrilled at the thought of herself as a pressurized canister filled with poison gas, but not one to quickly explode, but one that would release the gas a little at a time, until all its surrounds choked from the poison.

Of all the psychology-related subjects in which Sandra had immersed herself while in college, the subject of psychogenic illness held her spellbound. Because children in virtually any society evoked the most empathy, they would be the mechanism of choice for payback. But how to link the two? She'd considered beginning false rumors of a serious disease, but that could be quickly disproved and would make her look foolish. Also, claims of asbestos inhalation could also be easily disproved, so could literally a dozen other claims.

Sandra only needed a simple firing pin. It could be something everybody feared and something which could be exploited—something that tied everything together neatly into one bundle—something that could not be disproved.

She finally gave it up, certain that one day the solution would come to her. Now, all of the events were falling in sequence.

Mold. The thought of it excited her. And Hughes looked like he might make a nice little sex toy. It might be time for that. A true convergence of space and time for events. And what is it they say about payback?

"I'll walk you to your classroom," offered Hughes.

Over the years, Sandra Hudson worked ardently at being the best teacher in the school. Long ago, she joined the largest church in the community, joined the teacher's union, represented the school at PTA meetings, and started a school committee to support the removal of soda machines from the school grounds.

One hour later, Sandra stood at the whiteboard and followed the text as students took turns reading various paragraphs. Two minutes after a student named Brian began to read, she lowered the hand holding the book, dropped the book onto the floor, and walked to her desk, sat down and began to massage her temples, short black hair spilling over her fingers and hands.

"What's the matter, Miss Hudson? Don't you feel well?" asked a short blond-haired lad named Jamie Gordon, the school chess champion.

She wanted to say, "No, you little prick, I feel great because you have no idea what move is coming next."

Instead, she replied weakly, "I smelled some mold, Jamie, and now I have a bad headache. I'll be all right in a minute or two. I don't want to get sick and miss school."

Sandra looked up at the class, who were all staring at her. "Brian, it's your turn. Keep reading. I don't ever want any of you to quit reading as long as you live. Promise?"

"We promise, Miss Hudson," said the class together.

"Do you promise?" she said loudly. "I want a strong answer."

"We promise, Miss Hudson," the thirty-two voices chimed in such perfect unison that, in an older school, might have caused the room to vibrate.

"My mother tells me that when I get a headache," said Jamie, "I should drink lots of water and rub my head and lay down."

"Thanks, Jamie," said the teacher. She appeared to search for words to say during this well-rehearsed moment. "I think it's more than a headache. I smelled something funny like gasoline or mothballs and I feel like throwing up, and I feel all nervous and kind of spacey."

"Gee, Miss Hudson, do you want me to call for the principal?" asked Carla, a stringy-haired girl seated in the fifth row, who popped to get a better look.

"Oh, no Carla. Let's show some personal strength and get on with it." Sandra pushed her hair back on both sides of her head. She stood again with apparent courage and faced the roomful of students who were watching the drama unfold in perverse fascination.

In the last few seconds, Sandra had programmed thirty-two students in the fashion of Pavlov and his dogs. Sandra knew that no school nurse would be in attendance today. Cost-saving measures mandated that the registered nurses retained by the school district rotate their duties among its 25 K-12 schools—a cost-saving measure, all of which bought Sandra the time she needed.

"Miss Hudson says she has mold and has a headache and is nervous and feels like throwing up and is all spacey," Jamie announced to the class.

"My mom says she gets spacey a lot, too," volunteered one boy in the first row.

Other contributions came from numerous other students regarding the state of affairs of their parents and their relationships with one another, as well as with their extracurricular activities.

Hudson stood up from her desk and took a deep breath, giving the obvious appearance of being in pain. Beads of sweat on her brow caused her hair to cling there in a random pattern.

The students looked at her curiously. "I'm so sorry," she apologized, smiling weakly. "I don't know what happened to me."

In fact, she did know: nothing happened. Some might attribute her problems to menopausal symptoms. Let them say something about that. She passed a complete physical only two weeks before beginning work.

Sandra said, "Let's see. Where were we? Oh, it's Carla's turn."

"No, Miss Hudson," Carla said, "it's still Brian's turn."

Sandra appeared to be the only confused person in the room as the others agreed with Carla.

After a couple of minutes, Sandra took over and began reading from the book at the point where Brian left off. A few moments later, she paused in her presentation, her voice becoming weak. To the class, her symptoms began anew and Sandra Hudson openly repeated them to the classroom, as she had done a few minutes earlier. The stricken teacher put her elbows on the desk and massaged her temples once more, then moving her hands to the back of her neck after several seconds.

TWENTY-TWO

"What happened, Sandra?" inquired Hughes, honestly confused. The battery-operated digital wall clock read 9:15 a.m.

"I don't know, Jim," she said, who then recounted a detailed report of her activities and symptoms in the classroom, timing her explanation as she had rehearsed it numerous times the weekend before. Timing in an act of drama held equal importance with delivery of well-written lines.

"Well, gees, I can get one of our administrators to cover your class," responded Hughes, sympathetically, and went out to speak with his office staff for a moment. One of the women stood and spoke with him. She had retired from teaching, opting for administrative work. She volunteered to take Sandra's class.

During her studies, Sandra read papers published in the New England Journal of Medicine, Journal of the American Medical Association, Psychology

Today, and numerous other professional journals. These reports dealt with the subject of mass hysteria, clinically known as Mass Psychogenic Illness or MPI.

The subject had captivated her from the moment she first read about it. After that, she couldn't read enough. Under what circumstances did MPI occur, why did it occur, and why did it self-feed? Sandra found the subject so fascinating that it became her private area of expertise. She never spoke of it to anyone, except in the most casual of academic discussions. She could introduce a new term to the literature, one that she proudly coined: *Mass Psychogenic Programming.*

Hughes called in Jackie Longley, one of the district nurses, from her posted school of the day. A confident woman, the experienced stout nurse arrived within twenty minutes. The clock read 9:55 a.m. From the time she reported her illness to Hughes until Longley arrived, enough time passed for her to compose herself and to not cast undue suspicion on herself by appearing overwrought before the experienced nurse.

Sandra rested in Hughes' office with a glass of water in her hand and recounted her story to Longley, apologetic during its entire telling. "I really feel so badly," she said. She refrained from crying and kept it straight for the moment. "This has never happened to me before."

A dubious person by nature, Longley was clearly puzzled. Nothing in Sandra's record suggested that she possessed a propensity to exaggerate injury, even under duress. To make matters worse, only a few minutes after Hudson's exit from the classroom, three of her students reported to the office with many of the same symptoms she had noted. A few new symptoms were mentioned including disorientation and stomach cramps.

Once again, Sandra complained about the smell coming from air registers to Hughes. He told her he couldn't turn off the air handler throughout the school during this warm period of time outdoors. He offered a comromise by offering to have maintenance close the them in her room. Would she return to the class then?

She consented to the experiment and after the mid-morning snack break, returned to her normal self to finish out her teaching day without further incident.

TWENTY-THREE

The men shook hands and Hughes led Jeff to Sandra's classroom, at Dunham Elementary describing her symptoms to him. Jeff's mother had taught at Dunham years before. Hughes' pro-active approach immediately impressed Jeff. You can't let these things go too far.

Still, Jeff didn't need this. He had to prep for a trial, yet the call to duty could not be denied.

"Does she have asthma? The odor of mold can trigger an asthma attack in some people," Jeff told the principal. He slow-walked the periphery of the room, looking at its contents in detail, thankful to be on a case rather than the case being on him.

"Not that I'm aware of, doctor. She said that a moldy odor was coming from the air register. Do you want me to turn it on the A/C? It went off automatically at 3:00 p.m. when classes let out."

"Go ahead," Jeff directed.

Hughes left the room and a few moments later,

cool air began to flow out of the air register, located above Jeff's head. Hughes reappeared.

"I don't smell anything. Sometimes, when the air handling system is contaminated, you can have mold growth on the cooling coils which might give you an odor, or if the drain line is clogged, you can have on overflow in the unit or a drain pipe leak might give you water and mold between the walls. But you'd probably be smelling it all the time. You can also get water precipitation in the ducts followed by microbial growth. There are other causes; however, the smell will be present. There are lots of cases where there can be odor without the presence of spores, but your teacher's symptoms don't fit into any of the typical categories."

"Can you run some tests?" asked Hughes.

"Sure. I'll go to my car and get my equipment. The first thing we can do is to see if there are any spores in the air and where they might have come from. If the unit is contaminated, chances are the spores will be different in appearance from those outdoors. When do you want the results?"

"As soon as possible, if you don't mind."

"Normally, I'd do them myself and save you a few bucks, but things have been pretty busy for me lately, so I'll put a same-day-rush on them and FedEx them to the lab in the city. They'll fax me the results and then I'll let you know. Will that work?"

"Thank you, doctor. You're as efficient as they say you are," said Hughes.

Jeff slept poorly, concerned about the trial all. Finally, at 8:00 a.m., he placed phone call to Billy Kirk at Oklahoma City's KOKO television. Kirk hosted the prime time news during evening broadcasts and wouldn't be at the station until 4:00 p.m. Jeff decided to call the newscaster at home.

Jeff knew the press. If they smelled a fish, they wouldn't touch it with a ten-foot pole; if the story looked ripe, they would be there in a flash. He was taking the chance that Billy would recognize this as a hot story; either that, or the man would try to sell a stinking fish.

Isn't that what friends were for?

Jeff placed the call.

Billy answered.

TWENTY-FOUR

Charles Campbell, M.D. was disliked equally in both the scientific and legal communities, except when he could serve the purposes of a plaintiff's attorneys, never for the defense.

Reputed to own and manage a solid family practice established a generation back, Campbell suckered onto the mold issue like a rubber suction cup onto a glass surface. He made millions peddling his philosophy, understood by nobody—-possibly not even by himself.

Jeff explained to Matt that he, Frank, and Campbell had presented seminars at air quality forums at one period in time. The three would eat lunch together before the good doctor had "gone south."

In court, Campbell appeared so casual that he wore loose-fitting gray trousers and an unbuttoned vest with multiple pockets over a short sleeve white shirt with no tie. As lover of fishing, Frank considered that the fishing flies must be there somewhere.

If not, he could recommend a place where the good doctor could store them. But when you're paid ten grand to show up and testify, win or lose, who cares? Other than those qualities, Frank supposed that Campbell's resume could hold its own. Just ask him.

Jeff came dressed in a new white shirt and traditional Brooks Brother's tie, khaki trousers, and black loafers. He and his representatives believed in the law and believed in dressing for an occasion.

After the swearing in, Campbell took the stand.

"Please state your name for the record," asked Anthony Kressler.

"Charles Waylan Campbell."

"Dr. Campbell, you are the practicing physician for the Tamsen family, are you not?"

"I'm not their primary physician. They were referred to me because of their mold exposure, my area of expertise, my specialty in practice for quite a few years, particularly in the field of toxic mold exposure, which can affect various areas of the body including the skin, respiratory tract and nervous system, causing a wide variety of symptoms including the cracking of skin on the hands and feet and sore knees..."

Before Campbell could come up for air, Kressler asked, "What symptoms did Mrs. Tamsen purport to have when she filled out your questionnaire and when you interviewed her?"

Craycroft said, "Mr. Kressler, please permit the witness to finish answering the question before you ask your next question. The court reporter cannot record both of you simultaneously. You may continue, Dr. Campbell."

"Yes, Your Honor." Decorum be damned. Nobody wanted Campbell to talk for long, including Kressler.

Jeff smirked. Campbell had bad diarrhea of the mouth and would never ever end a sentence unless someone ended it for him. Trying to get him off the podium at a conference was frequently an entertaining sight, if he were even permitted to speak in the first place. But to the prosecution, Campbell was crucial to the case and needed to be led on a leash toward any fire hydrant which needed to be pissed on.

Matt stood. "Your Honor, I might suggest that the witness answer the question without innuendo."

"Yes. Dr. Campbell, please keep your answers brief," responded the judge.

Although Kressler had cut off Campbell's answer, Matt didn't really care. None of it applied to Jeff's case, which revolved around what Jeff didn't find, his expertise and his use of completely acceptable procedures.

Campbell continued, "...and possible loss of ability to become pregnant, backache and loss of bladder control. There are numerous other symptoms, which could include loss of short-term memory, pre-cancerous vaginal dysplasia, dissolution of a portion of the myelin sheath covering the nerves of the central nervous system, along with liver and kidney dysfunction."

He ignored the judge's admonition to keep it

brief, but he actually did finish a sentence, noted by everyone in the courtroom.

Over time, Campbell rambled so much and so many objections and admonitions were given that it soon became time for the mid-morning break.

A quarter-hour later, on the witness stand, Campbell pulled a thick file toward him and began to read. "She presented typical symptoms of toxic mold exposure including severe dermatitis from putting on moldy stockings in which mold grew only on the inside and not the outside, and from touching moldy faucets and the moldy toilet seat in her bathroom. Her behavioral signs are suggestive of, if not consistent with..."

Campbell launched into an incredibly detailed explanation of detailed nothingness; so much so that only Jeff had an inclination of what he might be referring to.

Jeff leaned toward Matt. "I know he doesn't have a clue as to what he's talking about. I know this guy. You will never get a 'yes' or 'no' answer out of him. Look at the judge. Even Craycroft looks like she's falling asleep."

"She's not, she's tuning him out," Matt whispered back.

"...symptoms of lower back pain, both acute and chronic, as I say, bladder and bowel dysfunction, loss of sexual drive, sleepiness, insomnia, muscle cramps, itching skin, loss of attention, loss of short-term memory, loss of appetite, dyslexia, anxiety, coughing, dry mouth, vaginal candidiasis, which are all consistent with toxic mold syndrome and poisoning, resulting primarily from the inhalation of spores from her home."

"You can say that for certain?"

"Yes, I can make those statements within a scientific level of certainty denoting problems caused by her exposure to multiple mold species, many of which are toxigenic which include numerous species belonging to the *Aspergillus* genus along with the well-documented black mold *Stachybotrys* indeed there are other species that ..."

"Can you say whether your findings relate back to the time when Dr. Shenero did his testing?" Kressler needed to get somewhere with this witness. He chanced an interruption from the judge to let his own interruption pass.

"Yes, my diagnosis of the patients and their case histories reflects a past exposure to toxic mold and this experience can be traced back to their exposure during the time when Dr. Shenero did his work. You see..."

Kressler and Campbell went through the lengthy laundry list of problems exhibited by the different members of the Tamsen family, although Craycroft intervened several times to warn Campbell about keeping his statements brief. In the end the good doctor attributed all symptoms to Jeff's apparent lack of findings.

Jeff grudgingly admitted to himself that Campbell's declarations offered him a certain perverse amusement. After all, never in the modern recorded history of mankind had anyone else attributed such a wide range of symptoms caused by the inhalation of no mold spores. The noon hour rapidly approached.

"Dr. Campbell, you see before you a copy of Dr. Shenero's raw notes on the Tamsen home," continued Kressler. "Can you tell us what these notes say—the parts you can read?"

Kressler handed Campbell two pages of Jeff Shenero's personalized shorthand chicken scratches.

Jeff watched the proceedings, knowing that nobody really knew details about Jeff's equipment and standard procedures. It reminded him of the old game of telephone, where one person tells something to another who passes the message along to somebody else. By the time the tale gets passed to several people in a row, the original message is totally lost.

"Do you know what these symbols mean?" asked Kressler.

"Not much, except to say whoever took these notes wrote about green mold growing all over the inside of the house," responded the witness.

"I also read those words. Thank you, Dr. Campbell. I have no other questions."

Glancing at the clock, and probably disappointed that Campbell would ramble more before completing his testimony, Judge Craycroft excused the court for lunch break.

Frank rose from his front row seat and caught Jeff and Matt as they exited the swinging door from the court to the audience—an audience that had grown considerably in size since the beginning of the trial the day before. "Jeff, think of it as a cartoon. Nothing more than that. I mean, you can't make it up."

The three men began to file out of the courtroom.

Campbell, because he served as a witness for the plaintiff and wasn't being sued, in his turn, served as an expert witness. As such, he didn't require a personal attorney. He collected his documents, began speaking with Kressler in private, and they walked toward the exit of the courtroom.

Jeff stopped outside Room 272. He told Matt and Frank to wait a moment. At last, the last of the stragglers, Campbell and Kressler walked by.

As Campbell passed by, Jeff looked him up and down and said, in full view of Kressler, said, "Asshole."

Jeff kept himself trim and athletic. His almond shaped eyes and features reminiscent of a Mongolian background enhanced the glare he gave Campbell. For an instant, Frank and Matt thought he might create another lawsuit for himself as a karate Black Belt attacking an unarmed man to end up in jail with criminal charges against him, thus blowing the case and doing time.

For the first time in Frank's life, he saw his friend in a different manner. Years ago, he'd heard that Jeff had even shaken the hand of an attorney who represented Jeff's ex-wife. No such handshake on this occasion. In fact, Frank reflected, back in the old days of the bar fight, Jeff slugged the guy while Frank had been the backup. He surmised that one single event

served to defined the differences between their per-
sonalities—Jeff acted, Frank reacted.

Campbell pulled back. Frank thought maybe he
might to pull out an expando-marlin spike from one
of his pockets and go after Shenero. "You should
watch your mouth, Jeff."

"Get a new life, Charles," Jeff whispered loudly,
with a sinister tone. He bit his tongue to prevent it
from inflicting further harm and watched Campbell
become a single dust mote floating in the stale air of
the courthouse that swept it into the handicap-only
elevator to take the doctor down a single floor.

"I can't lie back and watch people kick me
around and not be able to fight back until time and
court proceedings dictate that I defend myself," Jeff
complained. "I teach this subject to seniors masters,
and doctoral candidates and this a-hole freakazoid
makes it up as he goes along."

The pressure boggled Jeff's mind with scenari-
os too hideous to describe, most of which revolved
around teaming up with Frank to break apart certain
dirt-bags in a graphic and definitely illegal Army
Ranger scenario.

In his own fashion and in front of Kressler, Matt
and Frank, Jeff held his right low down, palm up.
When Kressler looked down at the hand, Jeff closed
his hand tightly into a fist. When Kressler look up,
Jeff showed his teeth as he smiled.

TWENTY-FIVE

Judge Linda Craycroft spoke into her microphone. "Mr. Collins, you may cross-examine."

"Dr. Campbell, how much did you charge the Tamsen family for their initial visit?" Matt asked, after inquiring about the man's credentials.

"Approximately eight thousand dollars, in keeping with standard procedures in concert with my policies which dictate the amount to be charged to each person who enters the clinic for consultation procedures..."

"Your Honor," pleaded Matt, "The man is not answering the question."

"Permit the witness to finish his statement." The judge looked at the witness, not without frustration. "You may continue, but make it brief."

Campbell, the living skeleton, opened his lips again. He looked as though he had been trying to grow the same mustache since his teen years, but it never quite came in. "Much of the money goes to corporate fees and a certain percentage goes toward laboratory charges, which include blood testing and sonograms."

"Sonograms for what?

"Sonograms for mold toxicity."

"I never heard of that. Could you please tell us about that procedure?"

"It's something I developed and we use it on all our patients to tell what kind of mold they have been exposed to and when they got that exposure and what effect it is having on their bodies."

"That's amazing," responded Matt. "Is this a published technique?"

"Not yet."

"Is it fair to say that nobody in the medical field is aware of it?"

"Yes, it's fair to say that."

At least Campbell is honest about what he is lying about, so thought the entire defense team.

Matt continued with the cross. "How many patients have you used this technique on, if I may ask?"

"Probably close to two hundred people who have been referred to me regarding their illnesses that relate to mold exposure, although..."

"Don't you attribute about everything to mold exposure according to the symptoms that the Tamsens reported?"

"Yes, that's true. However..."

Here the judge intervened. "Mr. Campbell, please limit your answers to a 'yes' or 'no' when appropriate. If not, then please be as brief as possible."

"Yes, Your honor," Campbell responded.

"How much do you charge for this sonogram reading, doctor?"

"I charge ten thousand dollars per patient in addition to their regular workup which costs another five to six thousand dollars, but in this case, I only charged eight thousand because I didn't feel they could afford more and they were in need."

"So you're saying that you charge what the traffic can bear, is that right?" asked Matt.

"I like to think of it a benevolence on my part," smiled the witness.

"Yes, thank you, Dr. Campbell. I can tell you are a benevolent person," Matt responded, sarcastically.

The judge let the statement go without any objection from Kressler. Perhaps Kressler himself was weary of the good doctor, or perhaps his feet were sore from standing up and objecting.

Frank saw Jeff lean far to his left to attract the attention of Anthony Kressler who sat next to him at the table marked "Plaintiff." Kressler picked up his movement and leaned toward him in turn.

Jeff said, "Anthony, look at all the time you've put into this case and you're not even going to get paid by any of these nuts," said Jeff.

Kressler smiled. "I wouldn't worry about it, Jeff. You're going to be the one who is going to be paying the bills here."

Matt went after Campbell like a bishop baiting a queen. "Dr. Campbell, where did you get your training in mold toxicity?"

At that, Campbell described his medical background and his experiences in studying mold-related illness until the judge stopped him cold, tired of it all.

"Doctor, how many people do you employ?" asked Matt.

Campbell rambled on, again.

"Your Honor, please instruct the witness to provide us with a number."

Craycroft obliged him. "Please answer the question."

"One. That is, myself, along with a nurse and a secretary," answered the witness.

At least the man did exhibit the capability of speaking in monosyllables.

Frank watched Craycroft's demeanor. Nothing there. She continued to look down to take occasional notes.

"Thank you. Dr. Campbell, how much would it take to support Mrs. Tamsen for medical expenses as a result of her illness from their mold exposure as a result of this problem for say, the next twenty years? What I want here is a simple statement in terms of dollars per year."

"Ten thousand dollars, but..."

"Thank you. And for the rest of the family?"

"Well, depending upon..."

"Give us a number, please."

"Mr. Collins," Judge Craycroft interjected, "let the witness answer the question. As I've said before, the court reporter cannot transcribe efficiently when two people talk over one another."

"Sorry, Your Honor," said Matt.

Frank reflected that Craycroft herself seemed to be confused as to whether to let the witness ramble or give a curt reply. She did have a point about the stenographer.

"I would say about ten thousand dollars each," the witness answered, that is, except for Mary Sue who would take twenty thousand a year."

"Thank you, doctor. So what I'm hearing," said Matt, "is fifty thousand dollars a year would be paid to you, which is one and the same as your corporation, will be necessary to provide them with the health care they need. Am I correct?"

"Basically correct, since I am the only one in the world capable of treating them properly; but we must look at the overall degradation of Mrs. Tamsen's health, since mycotoxicosis is severely debilitating, and once a person is exposed, can only cause a degeneration of the mental and physical makeup of the patient. In her case, it is quite severe with proper treatment from my staff, we can lessen her pain and suffering although all the family members are destined to die at an age earlier than can be expected if they had not been so severely exposed to these toxigenic mold species."

Jeff couldn't help but shake his head slowly from side to side as he stared at this charlatan who posed as a medical doctor. At that moment, he didn't care whether the judge saw him or not. If eyes projected shafts of contempt, Jeff speared him through and through.

Frank, in turn, suddenly thought of cartoon characters. Campbell appeared to him as one named Elmer, who might be expected to say something like, "I would wuv to wisit warious areas in Awaska" or another one who chomped carrots.

He also thought that Campbell might be so imaginative, so versatile, that he might check to see if a client might have an allergy to a certain color.

Matt asked the esteemed doctor, "Dr. Campbell, do you know what a snake oil salesman is?"

"Pardon?"

"Never mind." Then Matt went on to test the doctor's knowledge of the details about mold itself, which turned out to be a wasted effort. One after another he asked questions followed by Campbell's vague answers.

"One more question, sir. How do you know anything at all about the toxic effects of mold on the human body?" Matt was definitely curious, as was his own client, Jeff.

Campbell looked at Matt simplistically. "We're taught about it in medical school."

Jeff knew better. He warned Matt to expect Campbell to answer in lengthy replies. Matt glared at the doctor. "That's interesting, because Dr. Shenero, the defendant, teaches at a medical school and if the subject comes up at all he points out that it is speculative.

"In fact, when you went to medical school, sir, back in the sixties, I'm fairly certain that the association between inhalation of spores and clinical symptoms that might have to do with toxicity of spores wasn't even known. Even today, we know very little about the association. But you know so much. That subject is what this trial is about, isn't it?"

"Yes," responded Campbell, caught off-base and desperately trying to redeem himself. "That's what this trial is about; however, I've read about it and taught myself and developed new techniques for measurements that transcend the knowledge of other doctors and scientists in the field—on the cutting edge..."

"Thank you, Doctor Campbell," said Matt.

"Please permit the witness to finish his response," requested the judge, not for the first time.

The garrulous Campbell droned on and on, perhaps practicing to be an auctioneer in his next life, a person who could speak seemingly forever without having to come up for air. Minutes passed. At last Craycroft herself stopped the man.

"But I was about to explain..." Campbell responded.

"That will be fine," affirmed the judge.

Matt moved on."Now, Dr. Campbell, if a mold is growing on damp gypsum board in a home, when does it produce its spores?"

"Spores are produced when the mold begins to die. It's called 'going to seed' and seeds are reproductive units." Campbell gave a rare short answer.

Jeff almost laughed out loud, despite the possibility of expulsion from the courtroom by the bailiff.

Jeff felt certain of one thing: Life is not structured for reproduction to occur when death is imminent, but instead, when the life form is young and viable. Seeds are produced when a flower begins to die, yes. But a flower is part of a regular cycle of a plant. Just because the flower dies doesn't mean the plant dies. Indeed, everything has exceptions, but the formation of a flower means the plant is healthy.

Mold in a home releases its spores through air currents or physical contact. Outdoors, wind, ultraviolet light, temperature and humidity changes are release-triggering factors.

Matt walked over to Jeff. "I don't know what else to ask him, Jeff."

"It's okay, Matt," replied Jeff. "The guy knows how to play the game. He's small fry and I'm going to beat him and show him up for what he is. He's already told me all I need to hear to expose him. We'll talk later." Jeff said this loud enough to reach the ears of Anthony Kressler.

Matt nodded, then turned toward the witness. "My expert will take exception to your last statement, sir.

Then he turned to Craycroft, "No further questions, Your Honor."

Craycroft pounded her gavel. "We'll take our break now."

Immediately prior to the start of court, Craycroft called Matt and McKinney into her chambers for a conversation to report that Kressler would be late. She had received a call from him. Apparently, during the break, he had gone to his office to retrieve some important papers for the case, and was presently receiving a traffic citation for speeding on his way back to court.

Some twenty minutes later, Kressler returned, sweating and flustered. He apologized and court continued.

Matt looked into the audience and turned back to the judge. "We would like to call Julie Robinette, Your Honor."

The owner and founder of Safe Home Environmental was sworn in and took the stand.

Julie married an owner of a successful firearms store, with two children. Jeff knew her to be a tri-athlete. Jeff had always held her in high esteem because of her self-discipline and professionalism. Like every company that did business in their line of work, the state required her to carry a minimum of a ten thousand dollar deductible and a million dollars in liability insurance, the same insurance Jeff other investigators maintained.

Matt's questioning of Julie lasted perhaps twenty minutes. She described her role in testing the same two rooms mitigated by Bob Jones and reported she could find no mold present in either of them. As expected, Kressler took a pass on her.

Kressler then stood. "We could like to call James Burke, Your Honor."

Burke stood and walked to take his seat at the witness stand.

Frank looked around the courtroom. Still no Bob Jones. One would think he'd want to be present to hear Burke's testimony.

When Jeff looked at Burke and then at Campbell, he saw a very tall, thin man standing next to a short thin man. His guess was that snake oil salesmen came in all shapes and sizes.

This day Burke wore a basic brown corduroy coat, tan slacks, and plain brown tie. He was clean shaven with a full head of brown hair parted down the middle. His flat and somewhat squashed nose suggested to Frank that he might have blocked someone's punch with his face on more than one occasion. This feature contrasted starkly with his thin face. The man spoke in a pitch bordering on falsetto.

Frank's term for persons such as Burke was "expert witless."

Frank considered the group: Mary Sue Tamsen, Charles Campbell, James Burke, and Anthony Kressler. They made up as sleazy a team as ever strutted into the ring of showmen. Like peacocks fluttering in unison flashing their colorful tail feathers, the birds of a feather were cut from the same cloth. Frank thought they sported too much glitter and overconfidence, characteristics reserved for world class movie actors and actresses.

After the swearing in of Burke, Kressler began his questioning with the standard request to state Burke's qualifications and work experience. Burke did so. The man possessed an average background. His integrity stood alone—at the bottom. To Jeff,

Burke appeared to be a self-proclaimed expert, misguided by the doctrines of one or two associations to which he belonged, one of which he was the only member.

"Mr. Burke, if you would, please tell us what you found when you entered the Tamsen home."

"I saw mold growing on some of the areas of the home, and well..." Burke wiggled his fingers in the air like a fairy sprinkling magic dust, or perhaps, delicately strumming a spider's web. "I sensed something wrong in my nose, so I went out to the truck and got my mask. I also directed my team to take out masks and suits. I gave one to Mrs. Tamsen.

Kressler asked, "Because she already lived in the house and had been exposed, if that is the right word, why did you think it necessary for her to wear a mask?"

"Simple, sir. She needed to be protected," Burke replied with great compassion and confidence.

"Mr. Burke, I hold here a copy of your report and refer you to Appendix A, which contains the laboratory data for your live culture samples."

Burke turned to the page already marked.

"Could you please tell the court in more detail about Appendix A, if you would?"

"These are laboratory results from air samples we took in the Tamsen home."

Judge Craycroft spoke to the court. "Unfortunately, our delay this afternoon will necessitate our completion of this day's testimony.

"Court is adjourned," declared Craycroft, slamming the gavel and rising to her feet at the same time.

Billy Kirk, wildly popular anchor reporter for KOKO-TV in Oklahoma City, sat at the rear of the audience section in the courtroom and took notes. Wearing casual clothing, a baseball cap and sunglasses, he sat far behind Jeff, Matt and Frank, in order to avoid any association with them or to be recognized.

Outside, the television cameras captured Campbell exiting the front doors. Clearly agitated, he mumbled a few statements and kept rambling on with his speech, eventually breaking free to shoulder his way past the crowd of reporters.

At six o'clock, Kirk presented the evening news with a focus on the ongoing trial, highlighted by the attempted interview with Campbell. The video of this appeared in a special report with the Norman courthouse in the background.

"This is Billy Kirk reporting from Norman, where a trial is in progress that has all the makings of insurance fraud, malpractice, poor science and millions in payoff. Or is it a legitimate claim? The trial involves the Tamsen family, who claimed several remediation companies, along with a nationally renowned mold expert, to be the cause of their problems which they claim, were all caused by mold.

"The footage you see is our camera crew being rebuffed by Dr. Charles Campbell, treating physician for the Tamsen family. Dr. Campbell refused to make any comments to us. We will remain at the doctor's mansion in Oklahoma City in our efforts to get his opinion of the trial to date. Today, Dr. Campbell reported that he needed fifty thousand dollars a year from the Tamsen family to keep them healthy, and that nobody else in the world is qualified to do it. Is he right?

"We will be covering this trial for you and we will update this case as it unfolds."

TWENTY-SIX

There are no pathognomonic indicators of mass psychogenic illness. Establishing the diagnosis often entails ruling out a long list of potential, sometimes far-fetched, causes. It is a social phenomenon, often occurring among otherwise healthy people who suddenly believe they have been made ill by some external factor. (The New England Journal of Medicine, January 13, 2000)

The words played through Sandra's head. The reports in numerous prestigious journals were in general concurrence. In her own estimation, Sandra could do no wrong, a belief which she fervently held. She sat entrenched at the other end of the spectrum from a politician who promised them everything and gave them nothing. In her case, the opposite declared: Go them one better. Promise them nothing and take something away.

The next morning, Tuesday, the day before the

trial and after classes started for the day, Sandra repeated her performance and waved at the air handling register for all the students to see, "Something's coming out of there," she declared.

Hughes called Longley, who soon arrived to find Sandra laying on a cot in the nurse's office, a small room behind the front office, where the teacher lay on a cot. She claimed nausea and barely got her head over the edge of the cot before she managed to vomit out her breakfast of sausage, eggs, toast, and orange juice. The latter had soured sufficiently by this time to provide an odious scent to the mixture...a little added touch.

The teacher sipped some water and reported, "Jackie, it seems every time I'm in the classroom, I get sick, and when I leave I get better. What should I do?"

By this time, another half-dozen of her students reported ill. A few children from other classes heard about the arrival of the district nurse, all because Miss Hudson got sick for the second time. Students who requested passes to see the nurse obtained those passes.

A short school-wide break served to spread the word throughout the school that the Third and Fourth Grade teacher, the wonderful Miss Hudson, had some illness that she probably caught in her classroom. One of the science teachers, an ardent conspiracy theorist, knew that only the female mosquito sucked blood, but decided not to advertise his opinion.

By 10:20 a.m. the paramedics arrived and took Sandra to the hospital where she lay on a bed, attended by a doctor and two nurses who took her vital signs and in their turn, drew her blood.

By noon she recovered enough to return to school, at her insistence, where she continued to teach, albeit slowly and weakly.

By mid-afternoon, twenty-eight students and six staff members reported various ailments that tended to match those of Miss Hudson. Somebody said they overheard Sandra used the word "mold," soon destined to evolve into the unspeakable "M" word in the school. Paramedics had already been assigned to the school and soon found themselves making occasional ambulance runs to the hospital.

Once home, Sandra waited until 7:00 p.m. and called district headquarters to report that she didn't think she would be able to make it to school the next day.

That same Tuesday, Jeff completed lunch with Matt and placed a call to his office to check in with his secretary. "What's up Carmen? Anything going on?"

"Yes, boss. Lots. You got a call from an apartment complex that wants you to inspect and air test before they rent.

"Then you got a call from Jim Hughes who sounded desperate and said that the problem at his school is worse and wants you to call him the minute the lab results are in. Then you got a call from the lab and they said you will receive the faxed results of the samples you collected from the school by three this afternoon."

"Thanks, Carmen." Jeff hung up. *Nothing like a hail storm,* he thought.

TWENTY-SEVEN

"I already told you on the phone, Jim, you've got nothing going on. I mean zilch, nada, clean. The labs confirm it. My home should be as clean in the air of your school," Jeff told Hughes.

"She insists it's the smell of mold that is giving her problems, doctor." Jim Hughes walked the school building with Jeff.

Jeff was definitive. "Jim, there's no wet dirt or dirty socks or anything to suggest that mold is her problem. The air quality tests came back negative. The air ducts in her room did not have spores coming from them and neither did the other three in other classrooms I checked. There were only background mold spores in the rooms and in the hallways. The halls have more spores simply because they are directly influenced by the outdoors. That's it.

"Nothing personal, Jim, but how well do you really know this person. Every once in a while a run into a case where all is not as it seems," said Jeff, trying to cast a broad net.

"Very well, doctor. She is our most trustworthy and reliable teacher." Hughes stated, adamantly.

To Jeff, it appeared as though Hughes actually believed his own statement. There appeared to be no room for doubt in the man's mind.

Jeff tried his best to summarize by going back to the facts. "Fine. I will add this: I consider your general air quality to be very good to excellent. Your total dust level is low in six different size ranges, the amount of carbon from car and school bus exhaust is minimal and the amount of pollen that has entered the building is negligible. So is the concentration of microscopic lawn cuttings. These are allergenic, too. I took duplicate samples to check my data against what the lab came up with and we are in agreement. In fact, I check for a lot more than they do. Your night cleaning crew should be commended.

"Granted, odors are more difficult to track. Since the human nose is probably many times more sensitive than most instruments. I can tell you with confidence there is nothing to smell that concerns me."

"Maybe it's something you can't smell," contributed Hughes, shrugging.

Jeff considered Hughes's statement, which could have some truth to it. Hughes continued. "Look, all I know is that she swears it's mold, doctor. In fact, she had another episode today. That's why I was so concerned when I called your office.

"As you may heard, a lot of her students and some from other classes got sick, too. Watch the news tonight. There are enough self-styled and real experts out there to choke a horse."

"Jim, I don't have a lot of time to pay attention to the news."

Hughes stopped walking the hallway. "Doctor, I'm afraid I gave your name to the press when they were here?"

Jeff stopped and looked at Hughes with narrowed eyes. "For what?"

"I wanted them to know we were doing everything we could to find out the problem and that you were working with us."

"But I haven't found out anything. At least not yet."

"We're confident you will, doctor," Hughes assured him.

"Well, let's check the specs on your air conditioners and take a look at your mechanical room. Could be you're pulling in something from outside on an intermittent basis, such as air flow from the dumpsters. So far, my intuition tells me there is nothing wrong. Do you think that is a possibility?"

"Then why is Sandra getting sick everyday" asked Hughes..

"I don't know, Jim, why don't you ask her, or better yet, why don't you put her in another classroom and see what happens?"

"Two things wrong with that, doctor. First, the health department is talking about closing down the school until they investigate why so many children are getting sick; and second, and second, we could be liable for using Sandra as a human guinea pig," explained the principal.

Clearly puzzled by what Hughes told him, Jeff reluctantly responded, "Unfortunately, I'll have to admit, you are correct in both regards."

TWENTY-EIGHT

"I got flooded out last night," Jeff said, in a low voice, minutes before the start of court.

"Huh? How so?" Frank asked.

"Somebody broke a corner out of a window on my house, shoved the garden hose through the window and turned the water on."

"When did you find it?"

"About four in the morning when I got up to take a leak. I called emergency services and they came over within the hour and spent a couple of hours sucking up the water and making holes in the lower portions of the walls to get them dry. From the looks of things, I'd say we got lucky and for what it's worth, we shouldn't get any mold."

"Damn, Jeff, did you fail any students lately?"

"No. I teach seniors, masters and doctoral candidates. They're 'A' students. The failures get sifted out long before they get to me."

They were both thinking the same thing.

Although Sandra Hudson did not come to work the next day, numerous parents called in to report that their son or daughter would not be coming to school due to various medical issues. Then the media arrived. Television and radio newscasters began to report about a mysterious epidemic hitting Dunham Elementary.

Sandra's decision to remain home was a crucial one. Her absence served to reinforce her reputation as a reliable and stable teacher. This helped direct attention toward a legitimate illness, thus deflecting attention away from herself. MPI would play a role soon enough, but still too early in the logarithmic growth phase of the reproductive, self-generating cycle to make big moves.

Although the school remained open for the day, Hughes consulted with the district supervisor who advised against reopening. A daunting task lay in front of them: the need to contact the media and making hundreds of phone calls to inform parents of the school's closure.

Anthony Kressler recalled James Burke to the stand to complete his direct examination. "Mr. Burke, as you might recall, you were going to explain to the court the results of the lab tests you sent them from the Tamsen home. What do those results tell us?" asked Kressler.

Burke nodded all knowingly. "There are a lot of mold spores in the air of various rooms of the home.

These spores include members of the *Aspergillus* grouping."

"Is this important?" asked Kressler.

"Very. This grouping contains species known to produce the most potent mycotoxins known. Since these spores are present in the air, they get inhaled."

Jeff leaned back and Frank leaned forward. "This man's interpretation is so stupid as to boggle the imagination. He doesn't even mention the outdoor spore count. I'll bet he has more spores on his shirt than he found in the entire house."

Kressler moved on. "And what does the information on the following pages tell us?"

Burke pursed his lips in preparation to provide the court with some bad tidings. He stared almost straight up in the air, as though he were sitting in the dentist chair counting holes in the ceiling, or preparing to recite a line from a Shakespearean play.

"These are lab results of total air spore counts we measured. That includes live and dead spores."

"What information is present on this page?"

"Again it demonstrates the presence of Cladosporium, another mold known to produce fungal toxins, known as mycotoxins. This is in addition to the *Aspergillus* and *Penicillium* spores along with *Stachybotrys*.

"Thank you, Mr. Burke. I have no other questions."

Craycroft declared a break.

After the break, the judge declared, "Mr. Collins, you may begin cross-examination."

Matt walked up to the witness and asked, "Mr. Burke, how long does it take mold to develop in a home after water damage has occurred?"

"Probably within forty-eight to seventy-two hours, give or take," the witness responded.

Right on that one. Like they say, put a monkey at a typewriter long enough...thought Jeff.

"Mr. Burke, you stated earlier that there are a number of mold species capable of producing mycotoxins. In terms of *Aspergillus*, what might they be, if you know?"

Burke spent the next several minutes reciting a memorized list of mycotoxins produced by various members of the *Aspergillus* group.

Matt said, "And these toxins are carried on the spores themselves, is that correct?"

"Yes, they are inhaled."

"Are you aware of a paper published way back in 1987 by Dr. Shenero in which he demonstrated that a well-known fungal toxin produced by *Stachybotrys* can cure a terminal disease?"

"No, I'm not aware of that paper," answered Burke.

"Do you ever read any scientific papers?" asked Matt.

"Of course."

"Let me ask you this, Mr. Burke. If a fungal toxin can cure a disease, wouldn't that make it an antibiotic?" Matt asked.

"Uh, I guess so."

"You did find *Stachybotrys*, is that right?"

"Yes, it's right there in the lab report."

"I'm curious. Dr. Shenero didn't find it. Neither did Safe Home Environmental," countered Matt. "How do you account for that?"

"They must have missed it."

"Ah, so Dr. Shenero missed it when he looked through the microscope, and the lab Safe Home sent their samples to missed it as well, is that right"

Burke gave no answer.

"Please answer the question."

"Uh, I guess."

Wrong thing to say.

"You guess?"

"I guess they must have."

"If one highly skilled expert and one experienced laboratory miss something, maybe it's because that something is not there. In fact, you told the Tamsens to destroy all their belongings and their personal memorabilia because of something nobody found. Is that right?"

"If you put it that way," Burke smugly responded. "But we did find it."

"Yes," Matt slammed back. "Months later. Please answer the question, Mr. Burke."

"No, I told them to move out and destroy their belongings because we tested the air and the lab identified it," Burke defiantly proclaimed.

"You found it because you caused it to be there," accused Matt. "But we'll get to that."

"Mr. Burke," Matt spoke slowly and deliberately, "you failed to mention that the toxicity of any mold identified in culture had yet to be proven. That is to say, whether the exactly specific mold that was identified by you produced any toxins at all and if so, would they cause noticeable harm? "In other words, Mr. Burke, did you have any toxicity tests run on any mold you found in the Tamsen household?"

"No."

To Jeff, Burke came across as a high school baseball player competing in the World Series. Jeff became intrigued, fascinated by how such a web of deceit could be spun from absolutely nothing.

Matt continued his attack, "Then, why is it, Mr. Burke, you never requested the lab, who identified the general groups of molds on this page, to define the species—I believe the term is 'speciate' them, or to conduct toxicity tests once that is done; or maybe you didn't want to know. On the other hand, it probably wouldn't matter because you're getting sued along with a lot of other people here."

"Your Honor," Kressler stood. "Is there a question here somewhere? May you ask counsel not to provide speeches, but to ask questions."

"Objection sustained," decreed Craycroft.

"All right, here's the question," stated Matt. "Why didn't you direct the lab to speciate the spores? I mean, they did identify *Aspergillus*, but only some are toxic."

"That could have taken a couple of weeks to do," Burke shot back. "We needed to make a fast decision. The home was contaminated."

"Really. Why did you assume the spores were

toxic when no toxicity tests were run on those that were identified?" repeated the attorney.

"Because we always assume they are toxic," Burke responded, now on firmer ground. "We like to err on the side of caution."

"Let me ask you this, Mr. Burke, what evidence do you actually possess that the inhalation of such a few number of mold spores can have such an influence on health, which is what this trial is all about."

"That's up to the medical doctor," Burke answered

"But you made that decision, Mr. Burke."

Burke looked like a man who knew he'd screwed up; caught with his pants down. His answer also dribbled out a little more slowly than the preceding confident responses. "Because many of us believe any *Aspergillus* has the potential of being harmful."

"Sure, when it grows on cooked rice left out in the sun in Uganda or grows on damp hay or nuts and it is eaten. I'm wondering how people who live in rainy climes throughout the world breathe in tens of thousands to hundreds of thousands of these spores every day. Surely they live with many more toxic spores than we have here and nobody there has toxic poisoning from inhaling them. How does that work?"

Just before Kressler stood to object about Matt's speeches again, Burke, back in his comfort zone, smugly responded, "That we know of.""Not that anybody on the planet knows of' might be a better answer. In fact, Mr. Burke, you don't really know, do you? You supposed and wrote this report on what you supposed."

"I wrote the report on what we found."

"No. You wrote the report on what you didn't find, like this entire case is about there not being anything present in the air or on the surfaces when my client went in there to conduct his testing. Indeed, you opened the walls and let things into the air that weren't there in the first place. The evidence is clear."

Kressler rose quickly. "Objection! Your Honor, counsel is badgering the witness. And counsel has not established any evidence to point to his claim."

"Sustained."

Calmly without missing a beat, Matt asked, "All right. Let's get to the evidence. Mr. Burke, what is the meaning of 'excessive debris present' listed at the top of the column for the single indoor room you tested?"

"I'm not sure what it means," replied the witness

"Perhaps it means that you opened up the walls in the home before collecting the samples and the debris refers to drywall dust."

"I'm not sure what the lab statement means."

Burke might not have been sure, but Jeff knew.

Kressler jumped to his feet. "Objection, Your Honor! Asked and answered."

Before Craycroft could respond, Matt said, "I will rephrase the question.

"Mr. Burke, did you or any member of your work crew do remediation work before you conducted air tests? Did you cut into any walls before you took any air tests?"

"Yes. That is our normal procedure. We performed our duties as we normally would."

"Thank you. Matt looked directly at Kressler. "To me, a confession serves as evidence." Turning back to the witness, he continued, "That would certainly explain the fact that you unloosed mold growing inside the walls, and it would also explain the high level of debris noted by the lab to whom you yourself sent the samples. Therefore, the spore count and types of mold in the air might have been a lot lower, if you conducted your tests before you opened up the walls. Is that right?"

"It might have been," Burke squeaked.

"Oh, one more thing. Who interprets the laboratory data when the lab results are returned; I mean, for data analysis and report preparation?"

"I do," said Burke.

"What gives you the qualifications to review the data?"

"There are no mandated qualifications."

"Exactly what I thought." Matt knew the question didn't have a lot of merit and while it took a fair amount of skill and knowledge to make a proper assessment, he meant his statement to demean the witness. "Did you tell the Tamsen family all of their possessions had to be destroyed?"

"Yes."

"Why?"

Burke sat up straight. "Because they were all

contaminated with toxigenic fungi."

"On Mr. Tamsens' bowling trophies from years before?" asked Matt, incredulously.

"Absolutely, I don't remember exactly, but if those trophies were garnished with ribbons, then the toxins would be present on the ribbons and handling them could have posed a serious health hazard."

"And glass shot glasses?"

"Yes"

"Ashtrays?"

"Yes."

"Plastic cups?"

Burke's voice raised a notch, in an attempt to become more authoritative, to no avail. He sounded squeaky. "Look, the cost of decontaminating those items could've exceeded their value."

Matt pounded on Burke. "What about their family photos and the pictures taken in their dream home? Did you tell them that they were all contaminated with toxic mold and had to be destroyed?"

"Of course."

"Of course? And their furniture and their souvenirs they had collected from their travels over the years and, for God's sake, their wedding photos?"

"Of course," squeaked Burke. "They were toxic."

"How do you know that, Mr. Burke?"

Where's my baseball bat when I need it? Frank thought. Then he remembered an old rhyme his father once taught him. Although he had been speaking about the life of a salmon, it fit Campbell and Burke perfectly. "In my heart I know they're smart.

In my guts I know they're nuts."

"We're past time for a lunch break. Court will reconvene at one o'clock," proclaimed the judge, probably feeling the need to take a long hot soapy shower herself. But some kinds of scum can't wash out quickly.

"I only have a few more questions of this witness, Your Honor," said Matt.

Craycroft pounded her gavel once, and arose from the bench.

Matt wanted the man to stew during the break. Frank's brain flip-flopped between a scandalous verdict in favor of the plaintiffs that would result in the ruination of Jeff, or one that allowed his friend to walk away relatively unscathed.

Frank watched Kressler clap Burke on the shoulder as the man stepped down from the witness stand and they began the walk through the court toward the exit. Kressler obviously congratulated Burke on another job well done, thus maintaining Burke's reputation as a teller of truth, justice and the Salem Witch Hunt way.

For Frank and Matt, the morning drama represented pretty much of an average courtroom session.

TWENTY-NINE

Court began at 1:00 p.m. sharp.

Matt recalled Burke to the stand and reminded him that he was still under oath. "Mr. Burke, I have in my hands the medical journal called Medical Opinion. Are you familiar with that journal?"

"Of course."

"I am looking at an editorial in the issue from January of last year where the editor explains the policy statement of the journal and the medical community at large. He states that there is no scientific evidence to support toxicity due to mold exposure. Do you agree with the editor's statement?"

"It's garbage," said Burke.

"How about the policy statements made by at least a dozen various allergy, lung, medical and pediatric associations both foreign and domestic. They all say the same thing. Are they garbage as well?"

"I would say their opinions are politically motivated and they haven't done the research that I've done," Burke parried.

"How about this paper, also published in a medical journal, where the medical doctor reviewed every *Stachybotrys* article ever written over the previous thirty years and found no basis for ascribing toxic poisoning as a result of inhaling the spores of this mold. Is that garbage as well?"

"Yes."

"And the policy statements from both bodies of the United States Congress and the Centers for Disease Control? Are they wrong as well?"

"I would say they are obviously not versed in the current findings."

"But you are?"

"Yes."

"And do you believe that fungal toxins can be inhaled—that is, would you put them a list along with other volatile organic compounds like, say, formaldehyde, or acetone?

"Absolutely," responded the witness.

"Because I hold here in my hand a document by the American Chemical Institute in which they state the opposite: that is, the molecular weight of fungal toxins is so large, compared with say acetone or formaldehyde, that they cannot fly around in the air on their own. "What do you say to this report?"

"It is in error."

"How is it, Mr. Burke, that everybody in the world is wrong and you are the only one who is right?"

"It just works out that way."

Jeff wondered if a person's brain hurt when they were as cerebral as Burke. If he had known years ago that Burke would be in his future, Jeff could have avoided college altogether and asked Burke anything he needed to know. Because Jeff didn't know a lot about a lot of things, he definitely needed somebody who knew everything about everything to help with his business and his personal affairs. Burke could serve as his aide, his personal consultant on all matters—well paid, of course.

"Your Honor, I have no further questions of this witness," said Matt.

Matt did not try to hide his disgust of this man who claimed to be a professional, and who, according to his own reports, earned over a half-million dollars a year. Burke could not hide his complete and overt love with himself. Despite a lawsuit filed against him, he refused to hire an attorney.

Burke had made a series of mistakes. He didn't plan ahead. He thought this trial would be another run-of-the-mill rip-off job powered by BS fuel. Once pretentious, now reduced to rubble on the witness stand, Matt exposed him, naked for the world to see.

A world that included Billy Kirk.

The news that evening garnered a very large viewing audience at home and in the bars, in Norman, OKC, Tulsa, points between and points beyond.

"This is Billy Kirk reporting from Norman. I'm

standing in front of the courthouse. Today, in this building, a lengthy trial continues.

"James Burke of Burke Remediation testified in the ongoing trial regarding the Tamsen family, who claim severe injuries from mold in their home. Burke testified on their behalf saying in effect that toxic mold caused their problems. Today, Mr. Burke testified that he has more knowledge of this topic than any major medical association and all the published literature regarding toxicity of molds. KOKO is trying to locate the Surgeon General of the United States for his opinion on this topic.

"Dr. Jeffrey Shenero is expected to testify in a couple of days and directly refute Mr. Burke's assertions. As a follow-up to yesterday's testimony by the controversial Dr. Charles Campbell, KOKO attempted to interview Dr. Campbell at his office and at his home. Dr. Campbell has refused interviews, citing patient confidentiality.

Also, Bob Jones of Bob Jones Remediation continues to be absent, even though he is named as a defendant, citing personal family matters."

The television then cut from Kirk to a female reporter who stood in front of what appeared to be a medical office.

"This is Karen Reed of GNN. An ongoing trial in Norman, Oklahoma, has caught the nation's interest. The specter of what may be insurance fraud has been raised. "Dr. Charles Campbell of Oklahoma City is being investigated for 'snake oil salesmanship' and the charging of tens of thousands of dollars to hundreds of patients. We will remain on-site at his home and office in an ongoing attempt to interview him.

"We will keep you updated as news develops in this story."

Once home, Sandra slipped into her robe and relaxed on the sofa with a good book.

At four-thirty that afternoon, she puttered in the kitchen of her apartment and munched on Cheetos. She sipped a Coke and felt the desire for a serious drink, preferably vodka and orange juice. This would not be a good time to engage in personal weaknesses. It would be similar a drug runner driving a car with a tail light out. One stupid slip-up and the game would be over; it could mean the destruction of years of planning. Right now her internal barometer read stable, but there was no reason not to keep a watchful eye on it.

This one's for Daddy, she thought.

Sandra turned on the TV and then pushed the mute button, deep in thought. The system put him away and took me away. If I directly kill one person, I'd get sent to prison. Therefore, I would trade my life for theirs. Not a good trade. A better way is to deliver misery to the masses and walk away completely free. Gee, she pondered, with great facetiousness, which shall I choose?

The age of 'eye for an eye' had come to a close. Planning, training, and education had allowed her grand scheme to unfold. Thank you, Mary Sue. Oh, yes, let's not forget to thank Daddy and our lost baby. And the other man who beat me half to death. They all taught me so much. Tears came to her eyes.

Over years past, while living alone and going to school, she had developed the habit of disconnecting the phone line for privacy purposes and shunned the cell phone, keeping it on only to receive text messages. This eliminated calls from wrong numbers, hang-up calls, salespersons, and limited friends, which left a lot of room for privacy. However, she ensured that Jim Hughes, one her most trusted friends, had been given her very private number. It turned out to be a near perfect system for isolation combined with communication.

At noon she checked her cell phone and did find a text from Hughes. School had been closed for the day and would remain so for an indefinite period of time.

Sandra waited until early evening before turning on the phone. Once she accomplished that simple act, she expected things to become interesting very quickly. She could give the press small morsels to feed upon regarding her worsening symptoms in time for the five o'clock news. Later in the evening, she would call in to district headquarters to offer her services for the next day. The gesture would count in her favor and offer conflicting reports at the same time, thus bringing more controversy into play.

The early salvo had been fired. This included paramedic involvement, ambulances, the hospitals, parents, and the blessed media spin. The local story would be picked up by the wire services and social media. Next would come the offer from experts around the state and the country, the involvement of the parents, the lawyers, the lawsuits, and above all, the rebellion against the establishment. How many items in the long list of media spin topics were invented and promoted by a single person?

There always had to be some sort of newsworthy event going on with the media. Ergo, let's add one more. How about an unknown factor in our nation's schools that is affecting our children's health? We'll call it Sandra's Disease.

The five o'clock news came on. She turned off the mute button at the sight of her school where a favorite local reporter Angela Scott, stood in front of its entry where the words DUNHAM ELEMEN-TARY stood out emblazoned in red into the stone of the building's structure.

The scene shifted to the school's interior where Angela Scott is seen walking along a corridor with the school principal. To the reporter, Hughes is filmed giving Sandra Hudson great credit for being a wonderful person and even a better teacher.

The scene flashed back to the front of the school where Scott gave a wrap-up of events and closed her segment with the words, "Would you feel your child is safe at this school?"

If they had ever been un-united, the trial had apparently re-united the Tamsen family. They had completed a dinner at the Golden Corral buffet restaurant next door to the Comfort Inn where they enjoyed a nice split bedroom unit. They had lost all their possessions thanks to Burke. As a result of this, they had purchased a limited number of items for the interim with their newfound wealth.

Mary Sue had decided to put motorcycle in storage, for the sake hanging onto her husband until the trial had concluded. She could go after half of his money, along with child support, for Karl and spousal maintenance at a later date.

Upon entering the room, Wendy pulled out her phone while Karl began to play his Game Boy.

Bud had just turned on the TV news. The reporter, Angela Scott, was talking about the school closure and had used the word "mold."

Mary Sue had heard about the closure and assumed it had something to do with the flu or the mumps. She saw something that caught her attention.

"Turn it up," said Mary Sue.

"I was going to look..." Bud began.

"Turn it up!" his wife almost screamed.

Bud turned up the volume and stepped away from the set with his palms open and facing his wife, as if to say, "Okay, fine."

Mary Sue watched Angela Scott walk the hallways with the principal and then a picture of Sandra Hudson came on the screen.

"Oh, my God, she's here in Norman and I didn't even know it," Mary Sue declared.

"Who?" asked Bud.

"Never mind," Mary Sue said sharply. Apparently the brief conversation been concluded. Some things are better left unsaid. She poured herself a stiff drink and went outside to smoke a cigarette and to think.

At that same time, Sandra Hudson sat glued to the TV, watching the face of Mary Sue come up in one report and her own in another. She went on the Internet and tried to learn everything she could about this Shenero scientist. That pain of a man was involved in both the trial and her school. It wouldn't be long before Hughes called on him to interview her. Maybe she could find a way to go after him, too. If Mary Sue could do it, so could she.

Sandra basked in the sights and sounds of the television, as a lizard without predators might lie in the sun, almost as a being made of chlorophyll, absorbing warmth and rays of the electromagnetic spectrum.

Minutes after plugging in her land line, it rang. Expecting the caller to be a reporter, she took a breath and picked up the receiver after the fourth ring.

"Hello," she said quite weakly.

"Miss Hudson?"

"Yes."

"This is Jim Hughes. I'm sorry to disturb you. I tried to call you earlier, but your phones didn't work."

"Oh, Jim, hi. What a pleasant surprise. Oh, the phones. I turn them off when I take a nap. Sorry."

"I hope I'm not disturbing you. I wanted to see how you are. I mean, you did give me your private cell number."

"Of course. You caught me in my robe, trying to unwind. My neck and shoulders are killing me from the stress, you know. It's so great to hear from a friend."

After a slight pause, Hughes asked, softly, "Is there's anything I can do?"

Sandra managed not to chuckle. In her most seductive voice, she responded, "Not unless you know how to rub necks?"

Another pause ensued. "Actually, I consider myself a neck and shoulder expert."

"Oh, my. Well, if you can spare the time, you might come over. Do you know where I live?"

"Yes. Half-an-hour?"

Hudson showered, shaved, used no fragrances, and left her hair alone. She wanted to be clean and raw at the same time. Then she put on her robe, no undergarments permitted, and picked up her apartment. She turned off all but the essential back lights.

Hughes arrived three minutes early. Sandra delayed answering the door after the second knock.

She unhinged the door. "Oh, Jim. I was falling asleep. Please come in."

Hughes did so and Sandra closed and double locked the door behind him. They went through the usual platitudes until Hughes finally refreshed her memory regarding her neck and shoulder problems.

"Oh, Jim, I have some lotion in the bath. Could

you get it please?" she requested with a weak voice.

Hughes went into the single bath of the one room apartment and returned with the lotion that had been conveniently set on the vanity beneath the mirror.

Sandra seated herself on an office chair which afforded Hughes access to her upper body.

Sandra loosened her robe such that her breasts were amply exposed while her masseuse worked on her neck, then her shoulders and began on her upper chest. She leaned forward as he did so, exposing herself even further.

"Oh, Jim, don't stop, please, don't stop. Don't ever stop," she whispered, holding onto both of his hands with hers, then drew them down to her breasts and held them there. "Oh, Jim, I need you so much."

Apparently, he needed her, too. Hughes did not pull back and vowed to provide to her all the support he could, albeit moral support was discounted to immoral support.

Before Hughes left two hours later, Sandra told him he had made her feel absolutely wonderful—a man among men in her eyes. She described to him in lurid detail why he made her feel that way. "Please don't make this a one night stand, Jim?" she pleaded. That was the first of several biweekly visits that Jim Hughes made to the small apartment.

The next time he came, she would ask him if he enjoyed pain. She was hoping he would say yes.

THIRTY

Despite the trial, the closure of the school gave Jeff a chance to become more deeply involved with the case and the strange illness of Sandra Hudson. He'd performed every test he could think of and had even operated a robot camera in the duct work of the school to look for breaks where odors might enter the air space. He found a trace of airborne fire ash that had probably blown in on air currents from a large forest fire in Mexico, a normal event. His instruments could collect ash particles from every fire on the planet, thanks to various upper and lower level wind currents circling the globe.

All to no avail. In his eyes, Sandra Hudson had no case. Whatever might be causing her problem, mold could be ruled out. If somebody wanted to call in other specialists, they had his blessing.

Jeff recalled a riddle Frank had told him not long ago. He had asked, "What's the difference between a great white shark and a cruise ship passenger? Answer: One of them regularly becomes engaged in an uncontrollable feeding frenzy that can last for days and the other one is a fish."

Jeff related the story to his present circumstance in which the press fed on him like a piranhas after a piece of meat, and they were not going to finish until all the meat had been chewed off the bone.

The following day, Sandra received a phone call on her landline from a number she did not recognize. However, the caller ID said Norman Gazette. She had prepared herself for this call.

"Miss Hudson, this is Mark Bradshaw of the Norman Gazette. I'm sorry to disturb you, but could I prevail upon you to answer a few questions about what happened at Dunham Elementary School earlier this week? If you want me to hang up, I will. I don't want to be a bother," said the reporter.

"I don't want to get my district or my school in trouble, Mr. Bradshaw. You understand, don't you? I want to teach. That's all I ever wanted. The children come first." She had a problem with using the word "kids" versus "children." She discerned a pause at his end while he wrote down her response.

"Perfectly, Miss Hudson. I'm on your side. Now, if I could ask a few questions?"

Sandra knew a veteran reporter when she heard one. Bradshaw's stories were front page. This had to be a grade "A" performance. "Go ahead, sir."

"Thank you, ma'am. Could you please recount what happened to you on those days?"

Hudson pulled a notepad toward her. She recounted her case history, up until the time she had been released from the hospital. As an aside, she casually mentioned her vomiting episode.

"What did the hospital find wrong?" asked Bradshaw.

"I don't know, really. They said it would be awhile 'till they ran the lab screening."

"Do you think it is a problem with the school?" Bradshaw queried. "Do you think it might be something the janitorial staff or school maintenance might have down wrong?"

"I don't know anything right now, Mr. Bradshaw. I'm pretty confused."

Bradshaw started to get pushy. Sandra could have read him his own script.

"Do you exonerate your school from any wrongdoing?" asked Bradshaw.

"Sir, I haven't thought about anything like that," she replied, in her softest and most convincing voice, ensuring that she did not entirely discount any problem with the school. "Mr. Bradshaw, if you don't mind, I need to get some rest. I want to go to see my...children. I know the school is closed. I hope the problem is resolved quickly." She could have told Bradshaw how much she loved the school and teaching her children, but she kept herself from being too gushy.

"What do you think about the reports on TV?" asked the reporter.

"Sir, I rarely watch television. I don't think it's

good for a person to watch TV too much, do you? Give me a good book, any day. Mr. Bradshaw, please excuse me, but I really have to go." she said, with a slight trace of urgency in her voice. At that, she softly hung up the phone. Finished with Bradshaw, she reached behind the phone to pull out the land line when it rang again. Startled, she automatically picked up the receiver, not checking the caller ID, thinking Bradshaw had thought of a follow-up question.

"Ms. Hudson?"

"Yes," she replied, cautiously.

"Ms. Hudson, this is Jeffrey Shenero. I don't know if you know me. I've been working on your case and wonder if you could help me understand a little better what you smelled and when you smelled it and your exact symptoms. I wanted to hear it from you directly. You know how the press doesn't give the complete story. There's something I might be missing."

Shit. Shenero. The last person in the world she needed in her life. Well, she asked for it when she started the whole business about knowing mold when she smelled it. Why couldn't she have left it non-specific? She weighed whether it might be better to back off the mold aspect, but decided not to appear to be wishy washy in the face of pressure, a move that might damage her credibility.

"I'll try," she said. She couldn't change her story now.

Somehow she did her best to answer his questions, keeping things as vague as possible and citing loss of short term memory as one of her problems, one of the same problems she'd heard Mary Sue had complained about.

Two minutes after the start of the conversation, Shenero knew he had landed a lemon. Did she want media exposure, money, or was she simply your run-of-the-mill whack job. He needed to start paying attention to the news so he wouldn't get blindsided by the media every time he stepped outside and get microphones shoved in his face. He certainly didn't need this Hudson business and the exposure it brought him, especially during this trial. Would he be considered negligent in this case, as well, because he didn't find anything? Why not? The trial was kicking his emotional butt, he had run out of patience, and the most difficult part lay ahead.

Well, at least this Hudson business had ended. It rankled him that the school where his mother had taught was being dragged through the mud by this woman. He would complete his report on her school tonight and turn it in tomorrow. That would be the end of it.

Finally, Sandra Hudson, academician, turned politician, elementary school teacher, and lover of good drama, unclipped the line from the back of the phone and reached beneath the kitchen sink for a bottle of Tennessee Whiskey.

She watched some news about the incident. Fully

half of the school's children and staff had reported symptoms of dizziness, disorientation, inability to concentrate, and occasional rashes. These latter, she knew, could probably be attributed to people scratching an imaginary itch on their arms, as reported by the scientific papers she had read on the subject of MPI.

According to the news reports, many parents who came to pick up their children had described symptoms similar those reported by their sons and daughters. Perfectly scripted mass hysteria. Contagious to the core.

Sandra felt quite exuberant from the whiskey. With school to be closed again the following day, she could have some days off. What the heck, a few drinks might make her look even more haggard. She wondered: *How long would it take for the system to go bankrupt when it had to deal with non-existent issues?*

I lost my Daddy's baby. That's reality.

THIRTY-ONE

At seven o'clock the next morning Sandra turned off the television after having watched it off and on all night. She felt good about her bed session with Hughes wherein she led him to believe he was in complete control.

Of the three, the sex with Hughes had bothered her more deeply than she thought it would. First, the came across as being so desperate that he didn't know faking when he saw it. Second, while she needed to use him, she was disgusted with herself for needing to have sex for any reason at all. But she needed him to feel wanted so he could provide his total support—to protect her as much as possible.

Sandra took a long cold shower, but did not shampoo her hair. She let the water flow on her head to ease the pain of a hangover. She scrubbed her teeth and washed out her mouth thoroughly, then drank coffee along with a glass of orange juice, ate a slice of toast and peanut butter for breakfast. Then she plugged in the phone. Today could be busy.

At nine a.m. the phone rang. Sandra let it ring five times, then picked up the receiver. The caller ID showed Bradshaw's number. "Miss Hudson, I'm sorry to disturb you so early, but I wanted to inquire as to your health."

"Thank you for asking, Mister Bradshaw," she continued, apologizing, but not too much. "That's nice of you. Actually, I spent a pretty sleepless night," she responded groggily. I'm still trying to figure out how I feel this morning."

"I don't know if you've seen the news yet, Miss Hudson," Bradshaw stated. "I wanted to inform you of the fact that many of your students and staff, some two hundred and fifty all together, have reported school–related illness.

"Oh, dear, that's terrible news," she murmured. She could smell Bradshaw searching for something he could hang his hat on. "I certainly hope no other schools are involved, Mr. Bradshaw." The train had left the station. He would print her words.

As luck would have it, events were slow in general—no wars, no serial murders, no political scandals. She went online and found her story in the state media, which included the cities of Tulsa, OKC, and numerous smaller communities. She had even made the news in Kansas City to the North and Dallas, Texas to the south. The name of Sandra Hudson was the centerpiece along with the ongoing investigation into the mysterious illness that ravaged the school. Parents of students and friends of parents also reported symptoms, according to the stories. She saw Shenero's name mentioned and got a sudden sinking feeling, from which she quickly recovered.

Despite the fact that her symptoms would not abate, Sandra consented to a television interview. Standing in front of the school, she appeared haggard. Her hair looked half-groomed, her skin sallow, and a sleepless night gave her eyes a darkened, sunken appearance with puffy upper and lower lids. One could tell she had been crying.

"I feel so badly for the children," said the teacher. "They caught whatever I have and it's spreading."

The carried the front page story about how an epidemic had closed the school. The story quoted a television reported who had said, "Unnamed sources have suggested the epidemic might be starting at other schools in the city. These same sources suggested that in a few days the entire state could be affected. Health officials caution the public to remain calm, even though they cannot rule out the possibility of biological or chemical terrorism. When questioned, Cleveland County Health Commissioner, Richard Redding, flatly denied such an accusation. The strength of his denial helped to fuel the suspicion among the public at large that proved a cover-up was definitely in progress.

Mass psychogenic illness should be considered in any outbreak of acute illness thought to be caused by exposure to a toxic substance or biological agent. The two may go hand in hand. Many times, health authorities will suspect the occurrence of mass hysteria, without the discovery of a biological cause, yet will feel obliged to explore an accident to a deeper level in order to placate the community at large.

(The New England Journal of Medicine, January 13, 2000)

Dunham Elementary had closed for the semester and would remain closed until further notice. Presumably. The school would open for the fall semester.

An investigation began, which was coordinated by the Environmental Protection Agency with assistance from the Agency for Toxic Substances and Disease Registry, the Centers for Disease Control and Prevention in Atlanta (CDC), the National Institutes for Occupational Safety and Health (NIOSH), the Occupational Safety and Health Administration (OSHA), the Oklahoma State Department of Health, the State Department of Agriculture, private contractors hired by the school district to maintain the integrity of the schools, and local emergency personnel. Aerial surveys of the area near the school began, taking note of wind direction. Had there been any caves in the vicinity, they would have been explored. Persons working and living in the neighborhood were interviewed and all complaints of illness were logged.

Scores of water samples were taken from fresh water, ground water, drinking water, stagnant ponds, and collected rainwater. Mosquitoes were captured and examined for the presence of bacterial and protozoan pathogens harmful to humans.

Core samples were drilled into the earth for various laboratory analyses. Twenty-seven different testing techniques were utilized to search for volatile and semi-volatile organic compounds, pesticides, ethylene glycol, radon gas, asbestos, fiberglass, pollen, and of course, mold.

Air samples were tested for carbon monoxide, carbon dioxide, diesel exhaust fumes, hydrogen sulfide, and poly-chlorinated biphenyls. Geiger counters were employed in and around the school.

Retribution, time to get even, ten eyes for one, destiny, kill before you are killed, take before being taken from, Sandra Hudson began to spin it all. By her calculations, it could eventually cost the nation tens of millions of dollars. Not a bad start, she thought. In her mind's jaundiced eye, she envisioned a world-wide pandemic. So far, her baton waved front of the orchestra that played at her tempo.

Sandra took a long drive southward on I35 toward Dallas and began to feel much better away from her project. She hadn't realized how constricted she'd been. Still a heroine, she and the other teachers at the school were on paid sick leave. They felt grateful to be a part of a system that took such good care of its employees.

Beginning a few days after the school closing, two other schools near Dunham Elementary reported similar symptoms. These included respiratory problems suggestive of allergenic or asthmagenic particles or irritant gases. Those schools were also closed. Parents and relatives of affected students complained of various ailments that might be associated with "Hudson's disease," a name coined by Mark Bradshaw himself.

Media attention heightened as more schools in the district began reporting illnesses. Office workers and city and county employees began to report various ailments. These ranged from simple allergic sneezing to loss of concentration and stomach cramps.

Final clearance reports began to come in and newscasters renewed the speculation that terrorism was directly responsible for the ongoing wave of illnesses currently sweeping the state. In a way, they were correct in their thinking. These reports sparked a second round of activity. Network and cable news channels and numerous talk show hosts attempted to schedule appearances with Sandra, as book and movie offers began to come in to her.

At last, Sandra Hudson found herself the center of attention in the national press. She had not calculated a potential for influx of money, only an outflow of venom. With that in mind, she practiced her lines in front of the mirror at home and stayed off the booze.

"They say it's contagious and I feel so badly that I'm the cause of it all," she would respond to inquiries, a little shaky in voice, and perhaps would require a sip of water from a glass set aside at her request.

"Do you think your problems might have had to do with what you ate? How did you feel when you went to school in the morning? Can you comment on the school lunch program, the administration, terrorists, mold...?"

"No, I haven't had occasion to and...well, I'd like to wait until everything is cleared up."

No specific answers. Let it percolate on its own.

THIRTY-TWO

Jeff stood in the doorway of his office, rubbing his bald pate. The contents from sixteen drawers of file cabinets were randomly strewn over the floor; they included decades of scientific papers numbering in the hundreds, student files and records, reports, government grants, works in progress. They were scattered so widely that walking in the room without stepping on them was impossible.

Even the drawers of his desk had been emptied.

The security guard shifted uncomfortably. "I'm sorry, doctor, I really am."

"How'd they get a key, Rick?"

"They didn't need one. They forced the door." The security guard pointed to the splintered door jamb. "Somebody took a crowbar to it."

"So, what good is it to have a lock and key?" Jeff didn't care whether he sounded as bad as he felt. "What good is it to have building security, Rick? It's three goddamn o'clock in the morning and I don't need this. Isn't the outside door locked at night?"

"Yes sir, it is. I don't think they came in at night. The outer doors are definitely locked and I make regular rounds through the three floors and around the perimeter and parking lot. Usually, we catch 'em. Not today. He must have come in during the day, hid somewhere and waited."

"Then how did he get out?"

"We're still working on that, but he probably pushed the latch and walked out a minute or two after I left the building for my outdoor rounds. Leaving's the easy part."

"Why me?"

"I don't know, sir, is somebody mad..."

"Rick, the lab."

Jeff turned on his heels and ran down the hall to the stairwell. He bounded up two flights to the third floor where the laboratories were housed. Once on the third floor he made a hard left, feet slipping on the freshly polished floor, with Rick in close pursuit. Jeff pulled a set of keys from his pocket and unlocked the door to his laboratory. With great apprehension, he pushed the door open, prepared to flick on the full dozen neon ceiling lights. He found them already on in the splendorous room.

Bespectacled Emily Whitcomb, wearing her lab coat, stood at the scintillation counter, recording radioactive emissions from tagged DNA molecules. Notebook in hand, she turned to face him. The brilliant twenty-eight year old doctoral candidate looked puzzled. "Dr. Shenero, what brings you here at this hour?"

"Pulling an all-nighter, Emily?"

"Honest research waits for no one," the student responded, smiling.

Emily's work involved a unique approach in that she and her mentor believed low doses of mycotoxins could be used in combination with other antibiotics in the cure of cancer and terminal bacterial diseases.

Jeff ignored her words and looked past her at the lab. Deep concern clouded his face. The laboratory consisted of twenty-five feet of marble-top counters running the length of the room on either side with eight feet of floor between them. Small desks were situated at the far end of each counter where four graduate students set up shop. All the equipment appeared to be intact and in place. Expensive equipment sat along virtually the entire length of each counter. Located below the counters were wood-enclosed cabinets with glass-enclosed cabinets above them.

Jeff inspected the equipment, each piece in its turn. All appeared to be operational and undamaged.

"What's the matter, Dr. Shenero, why is Rick here?" asked Emily. "Should I be worried about something?"

"Somebody trashed my office, Emily. We don't know exactly when it happened, but it happened tonight," Jeff replied. "You haven't seen anybody strange running around here, have you?"

"All graduate students are strange, as far as that

goes," gibed Emily, known for her wit, "But no, sir, nobody here who didn't belong. I've been in here for the last eighteen hours with another six to go. Except for a brief potty break or two, I've been joined at the hip with the scintillation counter."

"Okay, thanks anyway. I'll let you get back to work." He left the lab with Rick and they headed back to the stairway and to Jeff's office.

"All right, I'll allow that my name is on my office, but why did they leave the lab alone, Rick? I doubt they knew Emily was working, it's so quiet. Not even a radio is on."

"The labs are unmarked." Rick paused. "If I can ask, do you trust her? Does she have anything against you? I'm sorry, it's my job to ask."

Jeff tried to pull his wits together. "Well, Emily and I had a disagreement about her commitment to work on this project at one time, but that has all been resolved. I'm sure she's gotten over it."

"Do you want us to get a crew to clean up your office?" asked Rick.

"Yeah, thanks. I think Room 110 is empty. Have them stack the papers neatly onto carts, and move the file cabinets in there, too. I'll have my students tend to it tomorrow, or, I should say, today." Jeff stopped himself. "Wait. On second thought, you'd better call the police first."

"I already did, doctor, right before I called you."

"Then where are they?"

"Guess they figured the mess would still be there when they got around to showing up."

Jeff shook his head. *What next?*

Later that same morning Matt picked up Frank and Jeff in his new Cadillac Escalade. As a lover of big American cars, he bought a new one every two or three years. He had once told Frank that he wouldn't be caught dead in one of those little foreign jobs. Frank called him on it when he purchased a Porsche as a second car and then declared that it wasn't a little foreign job, but a Porsche.

Jeff sat next to Matt in the front seat. Frank sat behind Jeff. Frank had never seen Matt so mad. Matt didn't like the press at all and certainly not in a courtroom. Meeting in Jeff's office a number of days ago, he casually expressed this view. Now he went after both men before he even started the car.

"How the hell did Billy Kirk, of all people, get involved in the trial is what I want to know? Answer me that, either of you," Matt snapped.

"It's called self-defense," replied Jeff, calmly. "Going on the offensive can't hurt me."

Matt glared at him. "Damn it, Jeff, this isn't an athletic contest. This is a court of law, and it can hurt you. You think Craycroft is happy about drawing this much attention to herself and to one of her cases? And what's this crap about mold in a school with your name plastered all over the front pages from here to Tim-buk-fucking-tu? And not only a school thing, but a school scandal. And Billy Kirk, again. Didn't I tell you to lay low?"

Matt wasn't finished. "In the end, the whole thing

could come back to blow up in your face when she rules against you. She's human and may exhibit prejudice in your case, not legal prejudice, but personal prejudice."

Matt's word stung. Jeff said, "Matt, nobody can stop this if they wanted to, just like nobody can stop the nation from grabbing on to television scare tactic designed to help their ratings. Even the original Superman in the comics couldn't fly. Now look at all of his super powers.

"I could present at least a hundred false ideas we have from astrology, to vitamins, to organic foods. Matt, I lecture about false concepts in science and everyday life."

Frank laughed from the back seat. "I get it. So, is the lion the king of the jungle? Last I heard lions live on grasslands. Maybe Tarzan knows differently."

"Exactly," said Jeff. "How about the tens of millions of swimmers who were told by the Red Cross over a hundred years ago to wait an hour after eating before getting into the water. These days they serve food at swim meets for the competitors themselves.

"Matt, half our world is fact and half is fiction and most of the time we can't tell one from the other. Some misbeliefs take a little time to develop, others are widely accepted almost overnight.

"My point is, this concern for mold occurred about as fast as they get."

"At least you could have consulted with me first," replied Matt, not yet mollified.

"Damn it, I didn't know the whole school thing

would turn into a train wreck. It just happened."

Matt glared at Jeff. "What I want to know is, are you the one who called Kirk into it? And when did you call him?"

Jeff had the strong urge to say something like, "Objections. Multiple questions asked of the witness." Instead, he answered simply, "I did."

"And you knew about it?" Matt turned to Frank.

If a person can nod sheepishly, Frank did.

"Why Kirk of all people? Why couldn't it be Miss Jane Doe reporter?" Matt demanded.

"Billy, Frank and I used to live together when we went to school here back in the old days," confessed Jeff, with a certain amount of smug satisfaction. "We've been best friends for years."

After Jeff spoke, Matt swiveled his head quickly and looked at Frank questioningly, as if to say, "Is that right?"

Frank shrugged in agreement, but, try as he might, he couldn't keep a smile off his lips.

THIRTY-THREE

In contrast to Frank's character, Jeff opinions were not intractable. New discoveries could change his mind. He could tolerate cowards and human mistakes, but not those guilty of seditious or traitorous acts. He had a vindictive streak a mile long. This trait had been there ever since Frank could remember.

Jeff's biggest personal problem, in Frank's estimation, lay in the fact that he didn't have any ass to hold up his pants. He kept hitching them up, tighten his belt. Recently, he had purchased a ratchet belt, which helped this condition enormously. Furthermore, Jeff disliked suspender. Jeff had once checked into getting an ass transplant, but all they had available at the moment was one belonging to a 400 hundred pound lady from Uganda they were keeping on ice. Jeff passed on the deal and opted to tough it out.

In March, nine months after his initial visit to the Tamsen household, Jeff signed for a thick envelope that read Law Offices Kressler and Associates, located in Oklahoma City.

Mystified, he drove to his office and opened the thick envelope. He found that Kressler and Associates and the Tamsens had named Dr. Jeffrey Shenero in the lawsuit as a party at fault and negligent in his duty to the client. It also named All American Insurance, Bob Jones, Remediation, Safe Home Environmental, and Burke Remediation.

The suit against Jeff alleged that he should have inspected the entire home, and that he exhibited gross negligence in his work because he failed to find several species of deadly toxic mold, including the notorious black mold, which had been later discovered. This failure led to the severe illness of four family members. No dollar amount was specified.

Jeff felt like a traffic cop who heard an original story from a speeding motorist–a story he could tell at the station. He showed it to Carmen who shook her head slowly, wordlessly.

Jeff called Frank, who had already planned to be in Norman the following day, and gave him the document to read when he arrived at Jeff's office.

Frank slowly and carefully read it over and explained it to him. Then he set it down and said, "I thought you told me you didn't find anything."

Totally confused, Jeff replied, "The containment was one of the cleanest I've seen in a long time. Hell, man, you were here when I got the call from Bob. I did what I always do. I got hired to check out their master suite and that's what I did."

"Says here they are filing suit against you because you didn't find anything," said Frank.

"The gal's a left-threaded wing nut from the get go." Jeff retorted, emphatically.

Frank picked up Jeff's landline phone. "Let's see if we can get you out of this. I'm going to call a friend of mine, another attorney. His name is Matthew Collins. He's got impeccable character and as good an attorney as I know."

Frank spoke for a few moments, then hung up the phone. "He couldn't get away until after work hours, so how's about we meet him at six-thirty in his office."

"Tell me about this guy," said Jeff.

"Sure. Matt's a great detective and a master prosecuting attorney. In court, he's eccentric enough to pace and slouch, he picks at papers on various tables, then might spin around and ask the person on the stand if he or she might be gay to throw them off balance. He's about your height and very laid back. He's got a full head of graying hair, well-groomed and long. He fast walks five miles every morning, rain or shine.

"He's a meticulous researcher and can find details that escape even my own eagle eye. If he takes the case, it would probably be his first mold job, similar to your being a defendant for the first time. He's old school and undoubtedly knows things about winning a case that I won't know for another twenty years.

Matt's office consisted of a renovated three bedroom house with a well-manicured lawn with flower beds abutting the home, and a picture window that opened onto a small forest directly across the street. The forest consisted of London Plane Tree, Bald Cypress and Southern Magnolia trees.

Frank made the introductions and the men shook hands.

"So you're the famous doctor Shenero. I'll have to get your autograph for my collection."

"It'll cost you," responded Jeff, chuckling. He suddenly realized the irony of his statement and closed his mouth wondering how much he would be paying, instead.

"Let's see what you got there, Frank," said Matt, as he returned to his desk chair while the two others sat in comfortable arm chairs across from him.

While Matt read the documents, occasionally going back and forth, Frank looked over at Jeff, wondering how he was going to handle this possible stain on his reputation, or if he even had a clue about what the future held.

Matt finally put down the papers on his desk top and asked, "What happened, Jeff?"

Jeff explained the case again, his memory improving the more he got into the story. He summarized by stating that "No goddamn bastard freeloading deadbeats are going to get a cent of my money." The way he figured it, putting all his money into himself painted a lot better picture than pissing away the money to pay off the Tamsens. "Fuck 'em," soon become a regular part of his vocabulary whenever he referenced this case. If he decided to take the case, Matt needed to keep Jeff from saying it in the courtroom.

Then Frank spoke with Matt in technical legal terms about the situation from his perspective, as one familiar with the area of Jeff's expertise.

Matt said, "I'm going to need you to help me on this one, Frank, because of your experience in the field. I'll do the courtroom, you do the observation and consultation.

"Also, I need you to find out what you can about the Tamsens. These people smell like they make a career out of this sort of thing. My guess is to start with a call to All American Insurance, because they're also named in the suit, I'm certain they will be happy to share their information with you. You might try speaking with Steve Hirshfield. He's not only the Tamsens' agent with the company, he's also mine."

"Jeff, my fee to you will be $15,000 dollars. I expect the trial to last close to a week and there will be pre-and-post-trial hearings and meetings. I'll file for hourly fees with the court after the trial is completed, which the Tamsens will have to pay, if we win, that is."

Jeff agreed and the men shook hands.

Matt was in new and old territory at the same time. He had a fair-to-good feeling about his chances in the case. In this instance, winning meant not losing. He didn't know mold, but he did know human idiosyncrasies. Jeff would help educate him on the medical aspects of mold and the different types of indoor contaminants while Frank would help him link normal versus abnormal findings along with existing standards. Jeff would serve as his own expert witness, so they didn't need to spend good money to acquire another one.

Then, Matt filed a counterclaim against the Tamsens for $20,000 to cover Jeff's projected upcoming expenses, which included attorney's fees and lost wages from his company. He also filed a motion for the judge to state *absolutely* why they had lost the case, if testimony warranted a finding against the good doctor. That would be necessary before sending the case on to appeal, if it came to that. To Matt, there appeared to be more 'ifs' in this case than most.

Like many trials, this one, initially scheduled for early April of that year, but got postponed until late in the month. The first judge recused himself from the case for personal reasons. The attorney representing Bob Jones Restoration refused to accept the second judge in line, citing prejudice on the part of the judge against him in a previous case.

Unlike over ninety-nine percent of the similar cases, this one did go to trial. For some reason, Kressler had called Matt at his office and asked him if he wanted to waive the jury and to have the judge decide the case in what is known as a bench trial.

"Hell, yes," responded Matt, without a moment's hesitation.

When Jeff inquired about why Kressler decided to do this Matt explained that everyone knew about Jeff's national reputation. Because the job occurred in Norman, the trial would occur in Norman. Kressler feared that the jury would be biased in his favor because of this—a plus in their favor. A jury could be swayed by theatrics. A judge would be more inclined to be swayed by facts.

The two attorneys argued over the phone. Matt argued strenuously from the beginning that his client's responsible pertained only to what he had been hired to do. Kressler and Associates argued that the Tamsens medical began the day Jeff was there and that Mrs. Tamsen had told him about her concerns, but Jeff had ignored her, and that she had actually first noticed them several days prior when Bob Jones Restoration performed their work, according to the records she kept. She didn't mention the problems at that time because she thought they might go away. But the problems worsened.

In addition, Kressler noted that, like Dr. Shenero, Safe Home Environmental failed to find the real problem, which Burke Remediation finally identified.

All American Insurance would be represented by George McKinney. He would also represent Bob Jones and Safe Home, both hired by All American.

THIRTY-FOUR

Bud Tamsen—Dead Man Walking, plain and simple. When he ambled over to the clerk to be sworn in, Frank half expected him to move like a zombie with arms outstretched, similar to what he did in the middle of a pitch black night in the house. Then the thought occurred to him that Superman flew around with his arms held in front so everybody would think he was cool, but the Man of Steel might be doing it to keep from cracking his head into things.

It seemed to Frank the judge handled the whole proceeding wrong. She should have ordered everyone to stay at home and watch the teenage bowling championships, or a design a new board game called Clueless. How about hiring cartoon characters to come to court to represent their human counterparts. Burke, instead of being long and thin, would be short and pudgy and would talk in a froggy voice about wabbits. Kressler could be a very big talking wabbit. Then we could get into the Tamsens where

Daisy Duck was already spoken for by Mary Sue.

Frank had checked out Bud Tamsen through his own sources. Now fifty-two, going on seventy-two, he had entered the United States from Canada, for some reason settled in North Dakota, where he had gotten married and divorced. Apparently he became tired of the open prairies and moved to Norman after a short stay in Cleveland, where, curiously, he had worked in a bank as a loan officer. Documents indicated he was forced to resign due to some questionable loan practices. All this occurred before he met his current wife.

Bud had a received a couple of DUIs since their marriage which resulted in a short stint in jail and he underwent anger management counseling. Basically pretty average stuff these days; nothing there that Matt or Frank could bring into evidence relating to the present case. To find out how somebody as bland as Bud Tamsen expressed anger would be like trying to teach a rock how to laugh. Maybe he burned ants with a magnifying glass or poured salt onto snails and got off watching them bubble.

Bud slouched and had a noticeable paunch, which threatened to override his belt. Even if he shaved off his sloppy gray mustache and had surgery on his drooping eyelids and removed his comb-over, Frank doubted if he could improve his appearance. In fact, he suspected Bud maintained these features exactly because they did improve his appearance. Did it matter? The man started with a good hunk of insurance money and if he wasn't near bottom already, he would soon be, if the devil woman had anything to do with it. Frank had no doubt she'd go after his money and then some regardless of how the case turned out.

On the other hand, Frank conjectured that Bud could look like hell and act worse; he could do what he wanted without a care in the world. The money did not come to him from the commission of a crime. It came to him tax free and within the limits of the law.

In a packed courtroom, under direct examination by Kressler, Bud Tamsen told of his struggling marriage pushed to the breaking point by the presence of mold in the home and the lengthy list of symptoms Dr. Campbell had recounted in earlier testimony, including kidney and liver failure. He told of the loss of their perfect home, where he and his soon-to-be former wife spent many wonderful years together, raising the two children and holding parties for the neighbors, only to see their house become degraded, wallboard by wallboard. They were forced to destroy thousands of dollars of personal belongings along with their furnishings.

During most of his testimony, the witness seemed to parrot the rehearsed lines Mary Sue and his counsel had prepared for him.

On cross-examination, McKinney tore into him like a chainsaw cutting through a dying branch that refused to sprout leaves. "Mr. Tamsen, I am reading from the medical report prepared by Dr. Campbell. It states, 'As the operator of a diesel powered front end loader and dump truck, Bud Tamsen is exposed on a daily basis to diesel exhaust particles and gases, pollen, mold, ash, sub-micron particulates, microscopic plant debris, volatile organic compounds, dust, fibers, and a variety of other respiratory irritants.' Is that correct?"

"Yes."

"Speak up, please," requested McKinney.

"Yes."

"Aren't you in an enclosed air conditioned cab most of your work time?"

"Yes."

"So how do you get exposed to them?" asked McKinney.

"Sometimes I get out of the cab," replied the witness.

"Do you recollect having any symptoms at all from your work exposure?"

"An occasional cough, I think," said Bud.

"An occasional cough?"

"Yes."

"And then when I went home, sometimes I got nausified," contributed the witness.

"I beg your pardon?" asked McKinney.

"You know, like you want to throw up," answered Bud.

McKinney forged onward. "Your marriage failed, and supposedly, all your bad health occurred after Bob Jones remediated your home from a roof leak during a thunderstorm. According to an insurance report, the leak didn't happen by accident. We can safely assume mold developed from that point on. After all, according to Mr. Burke, mold can develop within forty-eight to seventy-two hours after water damage has occurred. Your wife reported that your symptoms appeared only after Bob Jones actually fixed your problem. Is that right?"

"Because he caused the mold to spread throughout the house," Bud answered.

"Is that your opinion, Mr. Tamsen, or your wife's?"

"Well, my wife noticed it first."

"Noticed what?"

"The mold all over the house."

"I'm confused. Please help me with this, sir. You received a lot of money on three different occasions from All American Insurance, but you never repaired the home.

"Two times you received money for repairs, the third time you received a large settlement, which you divided up between yourselves and your attorney, but your financial records state that you have nothing left of that, either. Why didn't you put any of the money back into your home and get it thoroughly cleaned and repaired? That's what most people do."

"Because the home had been reduced to studs and framing by then and if we put it back together we wouldn't be able to get mold insurance on it anymore."

"I'm at a loss as to the logic of that," stated McKinney, flatly.

Jeff dropped his head, trying desperately not to scream. *The Tamsens wouldn't be able to get mold insurance, anymore? This man had the arrogance to place himself among the millions of persons who could no longer obtain mold insurance in their homes and businesses. The man and his wife were one of the causes, along with Campbell, Burke and Kressler, and yet Tamsen had the nerve to call himself a victim.*

Jeff's self-destructive thoughts ceased the moment when he heard McKinney ask, "Mr. Tamsen, it is my understanding the home is up for sale. Is that correct," striding over toward Jeff, whose obvious display of disgust might be an annoying speed bump in his path to slowly strangle, and then to hang Bud Tamsen. "Weren't you concerned about the health of the new owners?"

"That's not my problem," said Bud.

McKinney stopped in his tracks and stared at Tamsen, agape. "That's not your problem?"

"Look, I got tired all the time with skin problems and personal problems caused by mold. So we paid Dr. Campbell to evaluate us."

"You didn't go to any other doctors, did you?"

"No, he was the best."

"I don't get it, really I don't," said McKinney. "You weren't even living at the home. You and your wife were separated during the latter stages of this affair, weren't you?"

"For some of it."

"In your own words, tell the court how you got so

sick that you couldn't operate your garbage truck?"

Tamsen operated a front-end loader and dump truck, not a garbage truck. Everyone in the court knew it, but George McKinney could dig a little when he became annoyed.

"Objection," said Kressler. "Counsel misstates the testimony as to Mr. Tamsen's profession."

"Sustained," said Craycroft, who appeared to struggle in her effort to maintain a straight face at McKinney's statements and his line of questioning.

McKinney made a show of looking through his notes and then apologized to the court for his mis-stated facts regarding the man's profession. He resumed. "Mr. Tamsen, let's back up. You were about to tell the court why you never went to any other doctors for a second opinion, I mean, with Campbell costing so much. Please continue."

"Because none of them understood mold like Dr. Campbell did," responded a very pasty looking Bud Tamsen.

"How do you know that?"

"Dr. Campbell told us. So did Mr. Kressler."

"I have no further questions, Your Honor."

When Frank listened to Bud Tamsen, something about the man rankled him. He thought of the old movie, *Invasion of the Body Snatchers* in which pods from outer space replaced humans to become emotionless beings. Yet, while Bud exhibited the basic nervousness of a person unaccustomed to being on the witness stand, the words he used bespoke of a larger vocabulary underneath it all, almost as though he were playing with McKinney.

He made a mental note to have his own investigative service run a more thorough check on William Sidney Tamsen. This time, he would ask that Tamsen's prints be run through the international database.

Frank reasoned that Mary Sue wasn't going to marry a dullard like Bud because of his job; certainly not out of love. It didn't add up. In some manner she planned to marry and exploit him. But where had Bud's money come from and how much did he have to begin with? How he had lost it was a foregone conclusion.

Another question came to Frank's mind. Why did Bud settle for a dump yard job when he could return to banking any time? If Bud were to be recalled to the stand, more background information on the man would needed.

Kressler next brought up the Tamsens' daughter, Wendy, even though she came home infrequently during, and even after, the time the leak was first reported. According to what Campbell had told her, the intermittent visits she made were long enough for her to get sick from the toxic mold that ostensibly ran rampant throughout the entire residence.

This day, Wendy's sported a light curl to her long brown hair. She wore a light blue loose-fitting sheath. She recited a list of symptoms that ravaged her body along with those she would probably develop, unless she received proper medical care from a qualified doctor who understood these things.

"I'm also worried I might not be able to get pregnant," she concluded, sadly.

"Did Dr. Campbell tell you that?"

"Yes, it really scared me."

Frank looked at the witness and felt a jolt of irritation course through him. The girl was old enough to go to war and risk her life for her country, as so many at her age made the choice to do. This girl chose to receive free money on a series of insurance scams, well on her way to following in her mother's footsteps.

Unquestionably, Mary Sue loved her, as she loved Karl. Whenever Frank glanced at her, she sat between her children in the courtroom holding both of their hands. They had whispered in each other's ears. Frank hadn't known she possessed that capability. Whether they loved her in return was irrelevant.

Then Frank looked at Kressler and wondered if he wore reversible ties so the grease that accumulated during part of the day could be flipped over and hidden for the rest of the day. That would set him up for a large plate of spaghetti and meatballs. He could slurp the spaghetti all he wanted and nobody would be able to tell. "Would you like another napkin?" a waitress might ask. "No, thanks, I've got my reversible tie," Kressler might reply.

Wendy continued without being asked a question. "Well, my mom has candidiasis, and vaginal dysplasia and pre-cancerous uterine damage all caused by deadly toxic mold, and Dr. Campbell said this problem will probably occur with me, too, due to my exposure to all the mold in the home."

As Frank watched the witness, he failed to notice any lack of emotion in her face. Perhaps Bud's Rushmore syndrome had rubbed off on her or perhaps there was something else, such as, she and the lie were one and the same?

"Do you believe him?" asked Kressler.

"Oh, yes, Dr. Campbell is the best thing that could have happened to us under the circumstances."

"I have no further questions, Your Honor."

"Mr. Collins," your cross.

"Thank you, Your Honor."

Matt stood from his seat next to Jeff. He walked up to the witness, no documents in hand and stood back from her, slightly to one side, not blocking her view from the entire court, filled to capacity. A sheriff's deputy stood on each side of the gallery to maintain order, should it be necessary.

"Wendy, you testified that Dr. Campbell told you that your exposure to mold would probably affect your ability to get pregnant. Is that correct?"

"Yes."

"Then let me ask you this, and remember you must tell the truth. If you don't you will be sent to jail. You are eighteen years of age, considered an adult, and a charge of perjury will hang over your head the rest of your life, if you don't. That is a very heavy burden to bear, especially if you ever plan to work again."

The court held its collective breath.

"Are you pregnant now?"

"What?" Wendy was truly shocked by the question. Her face turned a vivid scarlet. Even Kressler looked up from his fingernails in surprise at the question. Then he stood. "Your honor, please, what kind of question is that?"

"Mr. Collins?" asked the judge.

"Your Honor, I'm simply trying to establish the veracity of Dr. Cambell's claim that she couldn't get pregnant because of the mold in her home."

"The witness may answer the question," directed Judge Craycroft.

"Answer the question, please, Ms. Tamsen," Matt reiterated.

Wendy looked lost and forlorn. Her eyes darted to the judge, to the audience, to her mother and brother. The fear shown in Wendy's face made her look like Bob Jones might hit her with one of the sledge hammers he carried around with him. She looked around at everybody wondering what to do. The courtroom became deadly quiet for a long period.

"Yes," she said weakly.

"Louder please, so it can be entered into the record," Matt directed.

"Yes."

"Campbell told you that you couldn't get pregnant, but you are. Is that right?"

"Yes," she cried.

Background noise could be heard throughout the court as the watchers of the soap opera reacted to the unfolding drama. Craycroft slammed her gavel several times once again and demanded quiet in the courtroom.

Matt continued to drive home his point. "So, ostensibly, your exposure to toxic mold occurred right after the water damage started, during the brief periods you actually came to the home; that is according to Dr. Campbell. Is that right?"

"Yes," she answered, her voice weak.

At first Jeff, Frank, George McKinney, and Kressler thought the question the question absurdly left-field, destined to go nowhere. Obviously, Matt had retained it as a surprise.

"So you were really being disingenuous when you said that Dr. Campbell told you that you might not be able to become pregnant. Is that right?"

"No, that's still what he told me," she cried, defensively, loudly enough for sixty people in the room to hear.

"Your Honor, I have no further questions of this witness," said Matt.

"You may step down," said the judge.

Wendy, sobbing and torn apart by Matt, returned to her seat. Everyone felt for her, and at the same time, wondered what or who had gotten into her head to make her say such statements about her ill health in the first place.

Mary Sue and Bud appeared to be equally shocked at Wendy's revelation. Mary Sue felt deeply hurt and felt the deep sting of betrayal brought about by her flesh and blood. She had trusted Wendy to be honest with her about all things. She was going to be a grandmother and her own daughter hadn't said a word about her pregnancy, well hidden beneath her baggy clothing.

THIRTY-FIVE

In addition to the misadventures in court, Mary Sue followed Sandra's case during her free evenings. She quickly discovered that she herself contracted Hudson's Disease.

Sandra became her new idol with whom she desperately need to talk. God, how she had missed that woman over the years. They both emerged from their cocoons at the same time, where they had been maturing. She decided to attempt to locate her old friend through the school where she taught. Perhaps the principal would know. She would use her old name of Megan Moore. Only Frank and Sandra knew those names and hopefully, Sandra was following the trial and would answer a call from her.

Karl Tamsen was another piece of work. He maintained a D average in high school, had fallen on his head, and possessed a bad back. He expressed no ambitions with no plans to do anything other than to keep working as a part time office cleaner at the No Tel Whoretel, as locals called it.

"So, Karl, do you think your mold exposure hurt your career opportunities?" asked a sympathetic Kressler.

"Uh..."

"Your job potential, your ability to make money."

"I get it. See, I wasn't doing very good," he answered truthfully, "but getting near that toxic mold made things worse."

"You lost out on a soccer scholarship, didn't you, Karl?" Kressler could identify with another athlete who lost his future because of injury.

"Yes," replied the boy truthfully, at least the truth as he viewed it.

"Tell us about your lost golden opportunity, if you would," the attorney prompted.

"Well, in high school I played ball, except my knees got sore so I had to stop. The doctor told me that happened from touching all the moldy stuff in my house. Then I heard a college wanted me to play ball for them."

Karl pulled out a piece of paper from his pocket and handed it to Kressler to read for him.

Kressler read from the paper, "Eastern Kentucky Christian College of the New Life in Southeastern Lexington. Is that the school?"

"Yes, that's the one, I think. Whatever it says there. My mother said she went online and thought they might take me as a student once I got out of high school. She said they also play soccer."

Kressler sped over the speed bump. "But you told them you couldn't take their college scholarship to do the thing you loved most in life because of the problems with your knees?"

"Yes."

"No further questions."

Frank shook his head to rescue himself from the cartoon web of animated characters. Kressler and his attendant cronies were the big spiders that owned the web and anybody who got near to them got their blood sucked out of them, especially green blood. Why had Kressler put the boy on the stand? It made no sense. Maybe he was trying to play the sympathy card by showing how Shenero's incompetence left the family in ruins.

Frank's imagination kept him from grabbing onto the edge of the cliff and keep from falling into the abyss of insanity. He figured his last act before they hauled him off would be to get a plate of spaghetti and meatballs with extra sauce and throw it all onto the tie of Anthony Kressler. Unfortunately, nobody would notice.

McKinney took a pass on Karl.

An unsympathetic Jeff wanted Matt to bury the kid alive, but both men suspected that Karl had already done that to himself, with Kressler's help. Karl's own attorney used him by putting him on the hot seat. The gloves were off. Matt felt obligated to ask the boy a few questions.

"Karl," Matt began, moving to the front of the defendant's table, "the records in my hand say you were always a marginal student. In fact you barely make a 'D' average under the best of circumstances. Isn't that right?"

"Yes."

"And you were close to failing out of high school even before this problem started, weren't you?"

"Pretty much."

"When did you get a concussion?"

"Uh, in junior high school, when I fell off a swing or something."

"Is that the same time you also hurt your back?"

"No, I hurt my back a couple of years later when a horse threw me."

"Did you ever hear of the great Pélé?"

"No."

"Can you name any professional soccer players and the teams they play for?

"I don't know. I think there are a lot of teams in Europe. That's where I want to go."

"I thought you were a soccer fan, Karl," Matt didn't ask, but only made the statement. Craycroft let it go.

"I just like to play it—mostly on video games. I like to play it in school, too. I don't learn about all of the players and stuff."

"Thank you. No further questions."

The judge adjourned court for the remainder of the day, citing another pressing matter.

THIRTY-SIX

"This is Karen Reed of GNN. I'm standing in front of the Superior courthouse in Norman where we are covering the ongoing mold trial. Mary Sue Tamsen claims to have Hudson's Disease and tells us that it is a struggle for her to get up each morning and come to court."

The camera cut away to Mary Sue who said directly into the camera: "We're suing everyone we can because toxic mold caused all of our problems."

"According to Billy Kirk, anchorman for KOKO television in Oklahoma City, the Tamsen family has already been awarded over one hundred thousand dollars for mold issues with their home claiming bad faith on the part of their insurance carrier, All American Insurance. And, as we reported earlier, authorities, including Dr. Jeffrey Shenero, a defendant in the case, called the opinions of Dr. Charles Campbell and James Burke outrageous.

"An ongoing investigation of Dr. Campbell of

Oklahoma City, the treating physician for the Tamsens, has not yet found evidence of malpractice. However, several lawyers we consulted on this matter say Dr. Campbell may be guilty of negligence and fraud, which is de facto malpractice. Dr. Campbell was unavailable for comment."

Next, the camera focused on the wildly popular blue-eyed and black haired Billy Kirk, seated at the reporter's desk in the television studio. The background showed the Norman Superior Court building. He looked up from his papers to face the camera.

"This is Billy Kirk reporting on the mold trial in Norman. Dr. Charles Campbell of Oklahoma City, treating physician for the Tamsens, has apparently left his home. An investigation of his activities conducted by this station has discovered that Dr. Campbell has earned million of dollars for the practice of bogus medicine, according to many local doctors.

Tomorrow, Dr. Jeffrey Shenero, Associate Professor of Microbiology, will take the stand. Dr. Shenero has taken a leave of absence from his teaching position at the University of Oklahoma here in Norman to defend himself in a case where he is being sued because he did not find mold in the Tamsens' home.

"Dr. Shenero has been in the news lately as the lead investigator in the Dunham Elementary School environmental problem. We obtained a copy of his report, anonymously. This report stated that, like the ongoing trial, there is no evidence of mold contamination in any area of the school. This is especially true for the classroom in which Sandra Hudson taught. As you may recall, Ms. Hudson claimed her symptoms were due to mold exposure. She has not ruled out the possibility of filing a lawsuit againt the school and the district."

"This is Billy Kirk, reporting."

THIRTY-SEVEN

Jeff's enjoyed running a six-mile circuit, a small portion of which contained his immediate neighborhood. The majority of his early morning jog consisted of running on a poorly paved two-lane road framed by well-forested terrain, which increased and decreased in elevation. Only a slight shoulder on the roadway and a ditch separated each side of the pavement from the forest.

On this cool morning, the sky glowed other-worldly, with the sun turning the clouded half-dome of sky into a blood-red planet. Jeff ran through the surreal backdrop sucking in the colors.

Three miles out from his home, he came to the half-way point and made the turn to begin the run back. He moved over to the narrow shoulder that bordered the ditch and continued to jog. He waited for a vehicle to pass him. He heard the vehicle accelerate to a high rate of speed.

When Jeff glanced back he saw a dark colored

pickup truck traveling at the far right of its lane almost directly behind him and not down the center of the roadway.

The truck sped past. With a cloud of roadway debris in its wake, it left a rooster-tail of dust and gravel causing Jeff to stop and stare after the vehicle. A moment later and the truck disappeared out of sight. His suspicious mind began to link this event with the flooding of his home and the damage to his office. Jeff began to run again, this time faster. He still a trial to attend—his own.

Sandra checked the wall clock at the sound of a knock at the door. Jim would not arrive until later, and besides, he always knocked five times very politely, while these were four raps that sounded somewhat demanding.

She turned off the TV and rose from her chair. Sandra checked herself in the wall mirror next to the door to ensure she appeared sufficiently disheveled, and cautiously opened the door. No telling who might be on the other side.

Sandra stared at Mary Sue for a moment until recognition set in for both of them.

"Come in, please. Oh, my." Sandra dragged Mary Sue by hand and closed the door behind them. The women hugged.

"What can I get you to drink?" asked the hostess. Then, "Oh, I must look a mess. Let me get you something. Rum, wasn't it? Sit here." She pointed to the end of the sofa where a coffee table stood.

"Rum, actually. Yes. You remembered," answered the visitor.

Sandra poured her friend a tall ice-filled glass of her requested drink and excused herself for a while she went into the bathroom. She returned moments later looking somewhat refreshed with her hair combed, then poured herself a tumbler of Jack Daniels and took a seat next to her friend, folding one leg beneath the other.

"I saw you on TV and absolutely had to get in touch. Where have you been?" began Mary Sue.

"Same here. I absolutely couldn't believe it," said Sandra emphatically. "I've been right here in Norman for years. And to think, we're both stricken with the same disease."

"Yeah, Hudson's disease," replied Mary Sue, as seriously as she could and twitched her head a few times.

Both women burst out laughing, clinked their glasses together. Each took a long swallow.

"Sandra, do you mind if I smoke?" Mary Sue asked. "I mean, I don't remember whether you did and ..."

"Oh, stop it.Not at all. Blow a little my way, okay?" Sandra responded and got up to get a plastic cup which she filled with water and brought back to the coffee table.

Mary Sue lit a cigarette and blew the smoke over toward her friend. "Want a drag?" she asked.

"Hell, just give me the whole damn thing," Sandra responded and took the cigarette from Mary Sue.

Sandra took a drag and began coughing.

Mary Sue laughed and lit another one for herself. "Didn't think you smoked," she said.

"I didn't. You're a bad influence on me," Sandra stated.

The women talked and drank and laughed as the time passed, each sharing her own mold story and the current state of affairs, comparing notes about Jeff Shenero and his potential for sexual exploitation. In this aspect of the conversation Sandra felt uncomfortable. At least this time she was the exploiter, not the exploitee.

Five knocks occurred at the door. "Oh, shit, it's Jim," Sandra slurred, looking at the wall clock. "I totally forgot."

"Who's Jim?" replied Mary Sue.

"My school principal," said Sandra.

"Interesting. I spoke to him and got your address. I told him you would be totally pissed if we missed seeing each other after so long a separation. You were like a sister to me. Why is he here?"

"He likes to make sure I'm all right," Sandra added.

"And are you?" Mary Sue smirked.

"He thinks I am," concluded Sandra, quickly raising and lowering both eyebrows in return. She got up and supported herself by leaning on the table. Unsteady, she made it to the door and opened it.

"Hi, honey, come in," Sandra greeted Hughes. "I want to introduce you to my very dearest oldest friend, Megan, I mean Mary Sue." Sandra hiccuped slightly.

Hughes entered the smoky living room, unsure of the circumstances. He walked up to Mary Sue and stared at her.

"Are you Megan? I mean, the one who called me?" he asked, trying to sound pleasantly innocent, but his insides reeled. He saw the mold lady from TV, the one Dr. Shenero was defending himself against, now in the company of his own dear sick Sandra Hudson, his secret lover and teacher at his school embroiled in her own mold issues with the same Shenero crawling all over his school. And he stood here with them both. His face flushed a deep scarlet.

He saw two liquor glasses on coasters, which were set onto the coffee table. He smelled alcohol and tobacco on Sandra's breath. He saw two smoldering cigarettes in an ash tray. He could hear her slurred speech and saw brightness in her eyes. There didn't appear to be a damn thing wrong with her tonight, nor any other night he'd been with her for that matter. Furthermore, she'd told him early in their relationship that drinking made her condition worse and that she never smoked.

Hughes felt used and abused, sinking without a life jacket. He saw the future, with his name in lights and the media and his wife wanting to know about his late night visits to Sandra's apartment.

"Look," he tried not to stammer. "You guys go ahead and visit and catch up on old times. You don't need me here for that."

"Oh, do stay and visit with us for a while, Jimmy," said Sandra, putting her arm through his.

"No, I'd better go. It's been a pleasure meeting you," he said to Mary Sue, smiling weakly without ever shaking hands with, or even slightly bowing, to the seated woman.

Hughes backed toward the door, turned and exited, closing the door a little harder than he intended.

"Do you think he recognized you?" asked Sandra after Hughes left and she had locked the door behind him.

"I only talked to him on the phone, and so what if he did. Do you give a shit? Because I don't," was Mary Sue's response.

"I'll drink to that," proclaimed the hostess, as the two friends continued their visit long into the night.

At 2:00 a.m. the women said their goodbyes. They held hands by the door. "I'm sorry. I didn't mean to keep you so late. You've got court tomorrow, don't you?" Sandra asked.

"Only as an observer," responded Mary Sue. "I already testified.

"Hey, wait, why don't you come down to the courthouse tomorrow; I mean today. She looked at her watch. If you get in early you can get a good seat. No charge for the show," offered Mary Sue.

"And guess what? Our favorite Dr. Shenero is going to testify," Mary Sue proclaimed.

"Great idea," agreed Sandra. "I'll be there. I missed all the trailers, but I'll be in time for the main feature. How great is that? I know you told me your man, Kressler, thinks your case is going great. Do you think he'd want to take mine?"

"I can speak with him," Mary Sue said with confidence. But who would you file suit against?"

Without missing a beat, Sandra said, "Well, Shenero for one. The district for two. I'll bet Kressler might have some others in mind."

"Do you need the money? Maybe we can work a deal," contributed Mary Sue.

Sandra hiccuped. "A deal is fine, but I'm not after money. I want to give this project a little kick in the seat of the pants. Wait, actually, I might try another lawyer first. I found him online. He's supposed to be very good."

"Oh? What's his name?" hiccuped Mary Sue.

"Frank Bennett. He's an environmental attorney. He'll be perfect for my case."

Mary Sue froze, as though she had been dipped into a vat of liquid nitrogen. Her face drained of all color.

"What did I say?" asked Sandra, concerned for her friend.

"I know him," Mary Sue whispered.

"That's wonderful. Will you talk to him first? Tell him to expect a call from me?"

"I can't, Sandra."

"You can't? Why not?"

"I can't. I'll tell you some other time. Okay? See you in court later."

At that, Mary Sue left the apartment of an extremely puzzled Sandra Hudson, got into her car, and very carefully negotiated her way back to the motel. She unsuccessfully attempted a noiseless entry. Awakened by her clumsiness at trying to unlock the door, Bud did not express surprise at the aroma of tobacco and alcohol surrounding his wife—only by the lateness of the hour.

"Where have you been?" he asked.

"Visiting a friend," she replied.

"Yeah, I'll bet," he concluded and rolled over to get back to sleep.

THIRTY-EIGHT

At last came Jeff's time to sit on the witness stand in defense of his own case. Thrill seekers and journalists filled every seat in the courtroom, most of them to see if Jeff would testify. He had become the flash story, the man who appeared everywhere at once, a man who needed to escape, a man trapped behind the bars of events, notoriety, and the media.

Frank looked over to see if Mary Sue was present. He saw her sitting alone among the spectators. She looked especially haggard, possibly partying all night; doubtless without Bud.

He surmised that the others in her family, already having testified, must have returned to their duties, earning a living, each in their own fashion. He also surmised that Mary Sue wanted nothing less than to watch each of the defendants hang by the neck until dead, although, making a few dollars off the deal couldn't be counted out of the equation.

After his initial visit to the court, Billy Kirk sent

Orlando Reyes to cover the trial. The pair made up the strongest TV broadcast team in Oklahoma and surrounding states. Reyes, born in Puerto Rico, suave, dark-skinned and unmarried Hispanic, had won broadcasting awards in Florida. A popular addition to the KOKO station, Reyes would take over the broadcasting reins at the station if Kirk got promoted, which looked like a strong possibility.

Reyes entered the courtroom, silently sliding next to Frank several minutes before proceedings were to begin, having been clued by Kirk about Frank's appearance. Frank, in his turn, moved one seat from the end with the knowledge that Reyes would be arriving to sit next to him, having dismissed others with the statement that the seat was saved.

Matt turned his head, saw Reyes take a seat and gave Frank a penetrating eye.

Frank quietly spoke to Reyes about what Jeff and Matt were trying to do, no long longer caring whether he and the reporter would be seen together.

Frank originally thought the case might be jeopardized if anybody on the team visited with the press. Never mind that Matt hated the public media when it became involved in his business. Frank believed the opposite; that the press could be helpful, in large part because Kirk and his people were already onboard, thanks to Jeff's call to the broadcaster. Besides, many attorneys were vocal about supporting their clients. As Frank spoke with Reyes, the reporter wrote a few notes, each a salient point to be aired later in the broadcast.

This day the packed courtroom smacked of too much aftershave, perfume, deodorant, and garlic. Jeff regretted not wearing a string of garlic around himself for the day's proceedings. No, he needed to be here, to rip pieces out of Kressler and his client.

Frank looked around the audience. His eyes stopped abruptly. He couldn't believe it. Sandra Hudson herself sat in the audience behind him to his right, across the courtroom from Mary Sue, yet present nonetheless fussing with something in her lap. Although, she wore sunglasses and a baseball hat, there was no doubt. She looked up at the court and missed Frank's eyes on her.

Frank turned back from his survey of the audience and spoke a few quiet words to Reyes who said in return, "Think I'll get a sip of water before things start. Hold my seat."

Reyes got up and walked out the door, past where Sandra sat and returned a minute later without comment.

Jeff wore a new dark blue herringbone suit, well-tailored, but not showy, and a blue and red cross-striped Brooks Brothers tie. Black well-polished lace-up shoes completed his wardrobe.

After swearing in, McKinney stood and asked him to provide the court with his background and qualifications. Jeff's told of the multiple governmental agencies he'd contracted with and the numerous awards he'd received.

"Dr. Shenero, why didn't you test for the presence of toxigenic mold?" asked McKinney.

"Because I believe the concept of toxigenic mold is bogus. At least, at the present time."

"What does that mean, 'at least at the present time'?"

"We always think we know more with each discovery. In fact, we know less. With each, more questions are raised. What is false today is true tomorrow."

"Objection!" Anthony Kressler rose from his seat. "Not called for and unresponsive."

Kressler's ill-tailored suit needed a serious overhaul. So did Kressler. Everybody knew about him. The man endured several years of drug abuse after being released as a pro football player due to insurmountable injuries. Disbarred from the legal profession for possession of so much cocaine the law surmised it must have been intended for distribution, Kressler got readmitted to the Bar Association after providing several hundred hours of community service. Subsequent to his return to professional life, he served time for DUI.

"Objection sustained. Please answer the question," said the judge.

"Your Honor, I don't know what he means by 'toxigenic'," Jeff replied. "If he's asking me if mold can produce toxins that harm people when it grows on food, the answer is absolutely yes. If he's asking me if mold can produce toxins to the extent they can harm a person through inhalation, the answer is emphatically no. Some people even believe that spores can be swallowed to cause intestinal harm. It's all a made up fantasy. Plain talk. I challenge anyone to prove me wrong."

Frank understood it would be difficult for Jeff to control his irritation at the incredible display of ignorance he'd seen in the courtroom. The entire case revolved around experts who focused their attention on nothing existent and built it into a mountain. They had already cashiered on nothing, wanting more of nothing. *Nothing is selling to the highest bidder*, he thought.

Frank signaled Jeff from the visitor's section with hand signs: palms down, pushing gently: *Everything's okay, stay calm and don't be too verbal.*

McKinney liked to pace back and forth, his signature courtroom procedure over the years. In this particular trial, fast pacing coupled with a sudden stop helped keep the witnesses off-balance. With his own witness, he paced slowly to offer an element of steadiness.

As Frank watched McKinney, his mind spun-off once again. *What are the similarities between a courtroom and a jail cell? Let's see. You can pace in both, they are both restrictive, you are under the direct command of others, both have plenty of rules and regulations and both take up a lot of your time. All we need here is an open toilet and a couple of bunks.*

McKinney and Jeff played Q-and-A for a while. At some point, Jeff would be asked to explain himself. The moment would probably occur when the attorney for the plaintiff cross-examined him. For the moment, they laid groundwork, storing their ammunition for later use. To be sure, Frank didn't know if anybody in the other party was even listening to what the witness said, or even cared what he said.

"Dr. Shenero, before we discuss the issues of this case, could you please tell the court a little about mold. What is it? Where does it come from? Where does it live? That sort of thing."

Frank surmised that McKinney had two reasons to ask about mold. First, he wanted to give the judge an education and demonstrate that Jeff's knowledge on the subject far exceeded that of the other expert witnesses. Second, he wanted Jeff to feel relaxed and in his element.

Jeff began, being forewarned by both Matt and Frank, to be as brief as possible, yet, so far, his discussions were right on. Still, nobody wanted to hear a college lecture on microbiology. What they came for was drama and suspense. To Matt and Frank, all Jeff needed to do was to establish his credibility.

"There are a number of groups of micro-organisms. The four that most people are most familiar with are the viruses, bacteria, algae, and fungi.

"Viruses can infect every life form we know of including, bacteria, fungi, algae, plants, humans, pigs, chickens—everything. Viruses cannot reproduce on their own.

"Bacteria are living in that they can reproduce by splitting in two or by transferring their genetic code to another bacterium. That's how antibiotic resistant bacteria transfer their information.

"Algae are not readily airborne. Many are photosynthetic and will turn a lake or swimming pool green.

"Fungi include molds we are all familiar with, such as bread and cheese mold. Also, there are yeasts such as brewer's and baker's yeast; and there are mushrooms. There is ringworm. There is *Candida albicans*, which commonly infects women. There are also soil-borne types along with many exotic species in the more tropical parts of the world.

"When mold grows on something such as drywall, wood or other cellulose products, it produces runners as it produces spores. The spores are the seeds.

"People always ask me where the spores come from. The answer is that they are already present in the air, dirt, or in construction material itself. All you have to do is to water them to see them sprout.

"When drywall or personal contents get wet, the seeds sprout. If the drywall is not wet, you may get surface spores blown in from somewhere else, but there is not enough moisture to make them grow—unless, of course, the air is already damp."

Jeff stopped his presentation and looked at Matt, his expression indicating, "Say the word, counselor, and we'll do a year-course right here."

McKinney, leaning against back his table, smiled and nodded, as if to say, "You're doing fine." He continued, "Dr. Shenero, you teach medical mycology at a major university, do you not?"

"Yes."

"And you studied the subject for many years as a graduate student?"

"Yes."

"And you published papers in the field?"

"Yes."

"With your educational and experiential background, are you aware of various symptoms caused by molds?"

"Yes."

"What are these symptoms? Let's stick to the common molds that might be in any one of our houses, and not anything too exotic."

"A severe allergy to mold can lead to lung complications, sinus congestion and can result in headaches," Jeff said. "Sneezing can occur along with mucous drainage. In extreme cases, an upset stomach can occur along with diarrhea. This is because there might be an excess of mucous drainage as a result of the allergy, similar to pollen allergy."

"Objection," said Kressler. "The witness is not a medical doctor and cannot testify as to what causes these symptoms. Dr. Campbell is the only qualified witness to answer with any validity."

"Your Honor," responded Matt, from his seat at the defendant's table, "Dr. Shenero has every right to answer the question since he has studied and teaches the subject on a professional level at to future and present doctors at reputable university and at a medical school. He has done so for a number of years. In fact, his qualifications far exceed those of Dr. Campbell in this subject area. That's why he's here, Your Honor. He is serving as his own expert witness."

"Overruled. The witness may answer the question," said the judge.

THIRTY-NINE

Jeff had struggled and studied under great and noble men and women. There was no dilution effect. In Frank's estimation, Jeff could already add his name to the list of great scientists.

Jeff continued, "To say that a few toxic spores cause illness or that your feet will crack and you will fail in school because you are breathing a small amount of mold, or your penis or vagina won't work because of mold exposure is a ridiculous thing to say. I challenge any medical man to cite an honest piece of literature to prove me wrong."

Frank could see Jeff wrestle with his thoughts, debating whether he dared risk expostulating while he sat on the witness stand. Frank half expected Jeff to start talking about Houdini, the magician great magician, who exposed charlatan mediums who claimed to bring back the dead. Jeff despised charlatans.

McKinney, a man of science himself, steered the

court back to the crux of Jeff's case, which revolved around the central element: Did Jeff fall below a standard of care; that is to say, was he negligent in his performance of duty? If so, what was that standard and exactly how was he negligent? None of the rest mattered at all.

The plaintiffs needed to prove that any damages were caused by Jeff—a tough sell, since Bob Jones did the actual work. Jeff only measured the results of Bob's work.

If the other side wanted to show Jeff's negligence, they should have called in their own company to run air tests. Because Jeff knew how to use a microscope, the other side would have to send their samples to an independent lab. No problem there. That lab would confirm what Julie Robinette already confirmed. Case closed. Instead, they relied on the report by Burke, a serious mistake in one sense, a strategic move in another. Confounding an issue is better than accepting a clear cut loss.

McKinney took Jeff back to his original involvement with the Tamsen home, when Bob Jones called him to do the clearance testing.

Jeff said, "Mr. Jones told he took extra steps to clean the house because Mary Sue wouldn't leave him alone. She kept harping on the mold issue and wouldn't let it go."

"Objection. Hearsay," Kressler stood and objected loudly.

"Sustained," responded the judge.

Jeff chose his next words carefully so no claim

of hearsay could be interjected. "Bob asked me to do what I always do and monitor the area he'd remediated and, if anything was wrong, to tell him so he could fix the problem."

That statement established Jeff as a sub-contractor solely responsible to Bob Jones, and not to the Tamsens. It also established what Jones requested hired Jeff to do and exactly where he wanted him to do it.

"Thank you, Dr. Shenero. Your Honor, I have no further questions of the witness," said McKinney.

"Mr. Collins, you may examine the witness," stated Craycroft.

Matt and Frank figured Matt's direct examination would take most of the remaining morning session.

"Dr. Shenero, could you please describe your education to the court?" Matt asked.

Kressler stood. "Your Honor, we are willing to stipulate the witness is an expert."

"And I am not willing to stipulate to anything," retorted Matt. "This is my witness and he is a defendant in this case and serves as his own expert. He has a right to defend himself and explain his background since his credibility directly relates to this case."

"Objection overruled. You may answer the question," said Judge Craycroft.

Jeff went on to explain in detail about his education, his training, and his current positions at the university and the medical center along with his personal consultation business that included contracts with the Department of Defense and the CDC.

"Please tell the court how you were contacted for the Tamsen job and what transpired when you visited the home?"

Jeff proceeded to tell of his call from Bob Jones and his experiences with the Tamsens, including the opinion that he considered the whole thing a rigged set-up to which Kressler strenuously objected. Craycroft sustained the objection and admonished the witness for providing his opinion when none was called for.

Judge Craycroft no longer looked down at her papers. She focused her attention on the witness.

Matt continued. "Mrs. Tamsen claims you missed deadly black mold, *Stachybotrys*, in her home and missed other mold later found by James Burke. Can you explain how you could miss *Stachybotrys*?"

Jeff explained, without going into detail, "Microscopically, it's not possible to miss high spore counts of *Aspergillus* or *Penicillium* or *Stachybotrys*. Either they are in obvious chains, like beads on a string, or they are pitch black and oval like little black footballs.

Frank's mind flashed to the Jeff's ongoing school job, another strange case. He pondered whether that was a coincidence, or might there be a connection?

"In Mrs. Tamsen's deposition, she stated you saw black mold on the tile and on the studs in her bathroom and told her not to worry. Is that correct?" asked Matt.

"No."

"Why not?"

"Because there was nothing left of the bathroom. The shower surround, the tub, the commode, and vanity were pulled. The floor tiles were gone down to the concrete slab. Only two-by-fours separated the bathroom from the hall closet which was also stripped down to the studs. I saw no mold at all."

"What did you see on the studs?"

"Nothing I could even extract a sample from. Even the cracks, the seams between the studs, were sealed with grout along with where the base plate met the floor. I only saw pine pitch on the studs. That came with the framing of the house decades ago."

"Let's back up a second," said Matt. "Could you please describe how these monitors work, if you please?"

"Certainly," replied the defendant. "A small air pump is connected to a hose. On the end of that hose is placed a small cassette maybe an inch-and-a-half in diameter and a little more than an inch thick." He reached into his jacket pocket and pulled out a cassette.

"The hose connects to one side and air is pulled into the other side. The particles in the air adhere to a sticky surface inside the cassette—-actually a glass coverslip, as we call it. This is removed in the lab and placed on a microscope slide for viewing," Jeff concluded.

Matt held up the cassette for everyone in the court to see. "So when you got to the lab, you examined the air samples. What did you find?"

Jeff said, "I found no spores at all in any indoor air

sample compared with several thousand outdoors. I saw nothing to concern me, otherwise I would have reported it. In my estimation, Bob Jones performed his job beyond the recommended standards."

Matt asked, "Dr. Shenero, I direct your attention to the Burke Remediation report." He handed the witness a copy of the report. "Please look in Appendix B and the section entitled, 'Viable Spore Counts.'"

"Yes."

"Can you give us your interpretation of the data you see there?"

The great question at last. Burke, the Jerk, the anointed one, was about to be roasted. Jeff would light the fire. The media would hand crank the spit to rotate the meat that Jeff stuck onto the skewer.

Jeff look directly at Burke, who appeared completely unconcerned. "Burke did the absolute forbidden thing in the professional world and got caught at it red-handed. He opened up the walls and then conducted air tests, releasing spores into a previously uncontaminated room, one of the most ignorant acts I've ever heard of."

Craycroft looked at the clock and called for a mid-morning break without admonishing Jeff for his tirade.

FORTY

After the break, Matt recalled the witness and without asking a question, summarized, "So, once again, Doctor Shenero, in essence, you are getting sued because you didn't find any mold."

The attorney gave the judge and the audience a moment to digest that remark, then he switched gears because he knew Kressler would be asking Jeff about his notes. "Dr. Shenero, I direct your attention to the notes you took on the Tamsen home."

"Yes."

"At the top of these notes it says, 'Green mold all over the home.'"

"Yes."

"Doesn't that mean you concur with the Tamsens? You earlier testified you saw no mold."

"Correct, that is what I wrote. Those are notes to myself and I am basically quoting what Mrs. Tamsen is telling me. Those are her words. I always record statements that are given to me by clients to serve as a reference guide. I can provide hundreds of my raw notes that are a record of the clients' statements. In point of fact, it is not possible for mold to grow all over her home anyway; the circumstances are all wrong. It won't happen."

"Anything is possible," suggested Matt.

"Not that," answered the defendant.

His words were slaps in the faces of the plaintiffs and their attorney who were saving that question as a mainstay for their case against him.

"Let's go to your own mold findings," said Matt. "Looking at your data sheet, can you please tell the court what rooms you tested and the results of your findings?"

"I tested the bathroom and the master bedroom. As I said, I found only a trace level of particles in the air of the room such as skin cells, a low level of dust, or drywall debris—normal findings after a proper repair job and a cleanup.

"In fact, considering the literally hundreds of millions of particles we all breathe in each day, I find it hard to accept that the inhalation of a few spores inhaled indoors can be harmful, even outdoors."

"What do the notes say about Mrs. Tamsen's symptoms?"

"They say she is complaining of itching in her mouth and in her vaginal area and a burning sensation in her left armpit. She states she has rashes and eye irritation, as do other members of her family, and the itching is most severe when they sit on the living room furniture."

"Did you test the furniture?" Matt asked.

"No."

"Why not?"

"Once again, that was not my directive."

"What were you hired to do?"

"To monitor and visually inspect the remediated area for mold. If I see anything unusual, I will take note of it. I tested the air in the master bedroom, the master bath, and ran a comparison test outdoors.

"Bob...Mr. Jones HEPA-vacuumed the furnishings and cleaned the air ducts. He detail-cleaned the areas he was hired to remediate. My task was to simply verify the cleanliness of his work. I felt uncomfortable the entire time I was in the house."

"Why did you feel uncomfortable?" asked Matt.

"Because, as I said, Mrs. Tamsen badgered me relentlessly. She seemed obsessed with mold and illness."

"Objection, Your Honor," said Kressler. "The witness is not a psychiatrist to speak of obsessions."

Matt shot back, "Your Honor, he said she seemed obsessed, not that she was obsessed. The witness only gave an opinion, not a medical fact."

"I'll let the statement stand," said Craycroft. "Overruled."

Matt continued, "I refer you to Mr. Burke's data, from the Burke Remediation report dated August 22nd."

Matt handed Jeff a copy of the twenty-three page document, most of it filled with scare tactics and misinterpretations of Burke's own data.

"Dr. Shenero, I refer you to the lab results of Burke's samples. What do you see of importance, if anything, on the data sheet before you?"

"There are several points of note here. First, the spore counts are extremely low, definitely very much lower than what one would expect to see within an average home. It was almost as if nobody lived there or they went out infrequently.

"I can also see that Burke committed egregious errors. The laboratory notes at the top of the data sheet state that all the samples were difficult to read microscopically because of a high level of debris present. Debris can only occur from two sources: basically, from a high level of natural dust, or dust from sheetrock. I can see from the data sheet that they ran their collectors an appropriate length of time. Therefore, as I said before, it can only mean that they opened the walls before they ran the air tests. That's absolutely forbidden. Mr. Burke himself admitted to the practice.

"Furthermore, the bedroom he worked on and tested was sealed in heavy plastic, but he declared the entire house contaminated. I believe he opened up the walls on purpose to create a bad situation."

"Objection," said Kressler.

"Dr. Shenero. Please refrain from innuendo," said the judge.

Jeff looked directly at Burke, who had been directed and paid for by Kressler in order to refute Jeff's testimony, if called upon to do so, a request probably not to Burke's liking.

Jeff was on a roll. "All the Tamsens' furnishings and belongings were destroyed for nothing. I saw no mold growth in the areas of the home I examined. Burke had destroyed the belongings of the family for no reason, based one room he had contained in plastic. If Burke were one of my students, I'd give him an 'F' for the course. His ability to interpret data and his knowledge is disgusting small and appalling."

Kressler objected to Jeff's innuendo, for which Jeff received another admonishment from the judge.

FORTY-ONE

Frank looked at the Tamsens who appeared not to care. Perhaps this was this another average day in their otherwise dull lives. Did Jeff's statements hurt them in the least? Perhaps the pods from outer space had actually taken over these people, and their corporeal beings were replaced by an alien thing called unreal free dollars. The thought of vast wealth could turn a normal being into an otherworldly creature on a moment's notice. Then Bud could buy himself a new garbage truck and Mary Sue could ride her Harley around and Wendy could continue on with beauty school and have her babies and Karl could wear new clothes while he worked at the only thing he could do—-being a clean-up man.

Frank ached to tell Reyes what he'd learned about Bud, but let it go for the moment. His attention returned to the witness stand.

"Dr. Shenero, do you know what malpractice is?" asked Matt.

Jeff thought for a moment and replied, "I would think that it has to do with a doctor who assists patients under false pretenses for the sake of stealing their money."

Matt smiled at Jeff's answer. He'd answered truthfully. Craycroft gave a fleeting smile.

Then Jeff got it. "Oh, you mean as relating to standard of care?"

"Yes," Matt responded.

"Actually, I don't really know."

"Then I'll make it easy for you. It means you would fall below the standard of care in what you did. Were you less than professional in your actions in the Tamsen home?

"No."

"No further questions, Your Honor."

"All right," said Craycroft. "We'll continue with cross-examination after lunch break."

This time Kressler would be going after Jeff.

FORTY-TWO

Frank recalled Jeff's analogy: Every scientific report on the subject is like a single pixel on a million pixel screen. What investigators were trying to do is to fill in the screen and see what pictures emerged.

Kressler stood and remained at his table, looking as though his feet hurt. "Mrs. Tamsen testified that she got a rash from wearing a sweatshirt with mold growth on the inside. Couldn't that happen?"

Frank read a bad sign in Jeff. He was about to go off. "No. That's what she said. In point of fact, mold will grow through the fabric using its runners, like it does in damp drywall, like grass grows through dirt.

"It's precisely because of cases like this that fewer and fewer people in this country can be covered for mold damage, not Your Honor, not you, Mr. Kressler, and not millions of families. And, insurance for many cases of water damage will soon be cancelled."

"Your Honor, please," Kressler pleaded.

Craycroft said sternly, "The witness will refrain from innuendo."

Reyes write quickly in shorthand. He eased a hand into his shirt pocket to ensure the disguised pen-recorder was in operation.

"The witness will refrain from innuendo," said Judge Craycroft.

"Sorry, Your Honor." Like hell.

"Dr. Shenero, you describe yourself as your own expert witness, so perhaps you can help me with this," Kressler continued. "Dr. Campbell linked toxic mold exposure to the Tamsens' illnesses. Can you explain his findings?"

All the attorneys, including the judge, herself an attorney, knew that particular question should be asked of Campbell, but the good doctor was nowhere to be found. Kressler's demeanor suggested that he thought he had the witness on that one. Unfortunately, he knew as much about science as he knew about Pluto's dark side.

Jeff returned, "First of all, again, that's what he says he found, not necessarily what he actually found. Furthermore, because, in my opinion, Dr. Campbell based his diagnosis and treatment on what Safe Home Environmental and I found in normal air, which, in this case, is virtually nothing. As I said before, I would never have directed any of the Tamsens' furnishings and possessions to be destroyed or even cleaned. That's how uncontaminated the home was, and how clean Bob Jones left it," Jeff reiterated, staring directly at Mary Sue. "There is no such thing as toxic spores and there is no such thing as airborne mycotoxins and I challenge anyone to disprove me."

Jeff's look at Mary Sue prompted Frank to sneak a look over his shoulder at Sandra, but she had gone. Someone else occupied the seat. The clock on the wall read three-forty-five.

"Dr. Shenero, your statement of billing says, 'Inspection and Monitoring of the home of Mr. and Mrs. Tamsen, does it not?" asked Kressler.

"Yes."

"So you inspected the home?"

"Only the rooms Bob Jones hired me to work."

"All that is very interesting," said Kressler, "but what do you mean you weren't hired to inspect the home?"

"This memo is internal between Bob Jones and myself. This is standard stuff. Nothing complicated here. He knew my statement referred to the two areas I was hired to inspect. It's the same thing I write every time I perform a job of this nature."

Matt had coached Jeff to answer a question with only 'yes' or 'no.' He changed his mind when he heard the strength of his client's words.

Jeff made compelling statements. Overwhelming the listener was a time-honored technique as basic in the courtroom as filibustering in the United States Senate. A technique followed by Campbell. Matt wanted Jeff to be as accurate and concise as possible. Jeff's testimony cut down hours and days of lectures into minutes.

Kressler asked about thirty questions in a row. Jeff answered them perfectly by saying yes, no, yes and no, things don't happen that way, depends, not necessarily, and sometimes. Kressler never dug any deeper, knowing he wouldn't be able to relate enough to the answer in order to form an intelligent follow-up question.

Anthony Kressler hung alone in space. He looked up at the clock: The dial read 4:50 p.m. "I have no further questions, Your Honor," he said.

All testimony having been completed, tomorrow would bring the request for money.

FORTY-THREE

They day of Jeff's testimony, one of Frank's staff members had met him outside the courthouse to reveal information they had uncovered about Bud Tamsen. Frank did not have the opportunity to tell his friends during court. He had decided to wait until court adjourned for the day to avoid distracting the two men. The news had remained hidden for so long that a couple of hours more wouldn't matter.

Once the men found their seat in Matt's office for a wind-down summary session Frank said, "Gentlemen, I found out some interesting news a short while ago. It seems Bud Tamsen, aka Burt Hardy, aka William Hardy has an interesting background. Most relevant is his conviction on two counts of extortion and embezzlement nineteen years ago. He worked as an accountant for a big business firm. Add fraud and income tax evasion to the list."

"Holy shit," said Jeff.

"You got that right," Frank said.

"Where did it happen?" asked Matt.

"Canada. Montreal."

"He's Canadian?" asked Jeff.

"Yes," replied Frank. "At least he grew up in Montreal. There's more."

"Damn, man, hit me," Jeff said, as if waiting for the one face card that would make their day.

Frank threw it down. "He's hot. He skipped out of Canada. They've been looking for him for nearly twenty years. Bud Tamsen is a wanted man."

"Twenty-one, spot on," exclaimed Jeff.

"That strongly suggests Mary Sue married him for money," Jeff said, sarcastically, grinning.

"Why am I not surprised?" Frank added, smiling, pleased to see the handoff called The Mary Sue Curse passed to another sucker. Somehow it made him feel better.

Then Frank realized the time frame. Mary Sue had been married to Bud Tamsen when she had blackmailed him twelve years before. She must have taken Bud's money, gambled it away, and wrote to Frank, hoping for a response from him. Frank responded. In spades.

Somehow she always got what she wanted. That's what scared Frank the most.

Frank considered: If junk science were an entity, it might have slithered its way into this courtroom. It would have injected its venom into the mother lode in the closing arguments of this trial. He might also say that this particular pile of junk science measured as deep as a garbage landfill.

For Jeff, getting railroaded was a new experience.

Frank looked over at Mary Sue, the only member of her family in attendance. There was nothing but boredom in the courtroom for the kids. And Bud must have figured he had walked into a gold mine when his wife came up with her scheme out of the clear blue. The last thing he probably expected was to have TV cameras and microphones shoved in his face. Too late.

The media fed and sucked every tiny bit of flesh from the case, fresh or dried. Like mice, reporters flooded into the courthouse in another cartoon version of reality. When Frank looked closely, he thought he could see the building expand with the influx of protoplasm. Outside, satellite feeds and dishes sprung from the neighborhood like black and silver flowers in full bloom. The food establishments and the sidewalk hotdog venders couldn't sell fast enough. One reporter called the trial a three ring circus without the rings.

Judge Craycroft cleared her throat. "Mr. McKinney, do you have a defendant to testify?" she asked.

"No, Your Honor, we do not."

"Mr. Jones is not present?"

"Your Honor, Mr. Jones is not present."

"Then we will proceed," declared the judge.

In his usual seat Frank could see Jeff whisper something to Matt. No doubt he'd asked him about Jones' whereabouts. Jones' testimony would have been critical for Jeff's defense.

Matt represented a number of cases with Craycroft serving as the judge over the years. Each understood the other. Jones had issues that were better left unsaid, which, in all likelihood, were not related to the trial in progress.

Matt gave one of his patented shrugs to Jeff's question. Frank didn't have to hear Matt's answer to know what he said. If a judgment is made against Jones, then All American Insurance is not obligated to pay it. This is because, even though Jones is insured with them, an insured must cooperate with the insurer to maintain coverage in liability cases. So, they have every right to deny his coverage. Why? He never appeared to defend himself.

"What does that mean to Jones?" Jeff would have asked Matt.

Matt would probably have responded, "Jones might have to pay any award out of his pocket, but only for his portion of the award to the plaintiff, and his non-appearance still has nothing to do with your supposed act of negligence. Therefore, it has nothing to do with you. It's his problem, not yours."

Craycroft looked disapprovingly over the top of her glasses as Jeff and Matt talked and whispered. The non-appearance of the man, who supposedly started it all, clearly agitated Kressler, who whipped his head around, looking for Bob Jones. Obviously, Kressler was ready to prepared a blistering attack against the absent defendant.

Through his legal eyes, Frank figured that McKinney and Jones must have decided they stood a better chance with Jones' not in attendance. But for what reason? A fair probability existed that, although Jones followed the book in performing the work on the Tamsen home, something negative in his background might have been disclosed; perhaps a drug habit or a recorded history of belligerence to authority figures such as attorneys or judges. One never knows. The witness stand is not the best place to be when people are firing shots at you—there is no place to duck. It's similar to a new guy in prison getting pissed off at somebody when the other guy is a lifer surrounded by his heavyweight buddies and you can't run home to mama.

"Then, counsel, please present summation arguments," Craycroft softly offered.

"Yes, Your Honor," said Kressler. Today the man dressed as the cartoonish figure of a man who is overweight wearing a poorly fitting double-breasted suit, and an off-yellow tie with red dots, similar to the appearance of bird droppings that one might find on their sidewalk from the little darlings that ate cranberries for sustenance. "We are ready with closing arguments."

"We are as well, Your Honor," responded Matt.

"Then let us proceed.

"Mr. Kressler, please begin."

Cameras were not permitted inside the packed courtroom, but reporters from national networks wrote like mad. Miniature high-tech audio and video recorders undoubtedly abounded.

Kressler stood and turned toward McKinney,

who stood to the left of his own table.

Kressler appeared peeved when he said, sarcastically, "George, in cases of absentia, it is customary to bring a picture of your client so we can all pay homage to it."

"That will be all, Mr. Kressler," said Craycroft.

"Sorry, Your Honor." Kressler began, "Your Honor, the Tamsens were a happy family for nearly twenty years. Sure, they argued, all families do, but they lived in their perfect house. They entertained their neighbors at holiday parties and barbecues. They opened their Christmas presents in the home.

"Mrs. Tamsen, once a healthy woman, welcomed her husband when he came home from work. She raised the fine children we saw here in this very room. Then a catastrophic event occurred in their lives when Bob Jones let loose deadly toxic mold into their homes and Dr. Shenero and Safe home Environmental couldn't find it through their ineptitude. In fact, Your Honor, the company they trusted the most to help them in time of need, All American Insurance, dragged their feet on the loss, even when the Tamsens complained of mold-related injuries.

"The Tamsens lost their home, their health, their employment, and, in the end, their family was torn apart."

Kressler re-spun the tale of injury to his clients, listing their myriad symptoms along with the destruction of their lives and the incredible amount of suffering they'd endured. All of this, he said, would culminate in a slow and painful death according to their trusted doctor, Charles Campbell.

Kressler began to list his demands. These demands were based on medical expenses, loss of income for the rest of their lives and the cost of health insurance for them from here on out, cost of continued medical care to be administered by Dr. Charles Campbell, along with a variety of other costs.

"Because of this damage to their health caused by Bob Jones and Dr. Shenero, Safe Home Environmental and All American Insurance, we are asking for seven million dollars."

FORTY-FOUR

Everyone in the courtroom grimaced, defendants and media alike.

Seven million. Guidelines for payment of paraplegics and quadriplegics typically didn't exceed more than one or two hundred thousand.

Frank's mind computed. Let's see, that's about what the United States of America paid the Russians to buy the entire State of Alaska.

Such pandemonium broke out that Craycroft was forced to pound her gavel several times, calling for a ten-minute break in the proceedings. She immediately arose from the bench and walked out the back door of the courtroom.

Matt left Reyes and immediately walked through the gate to visit with Matt and Jeff. He squatted down and said, "Kressler probably advised his clients to ask for a lot, and even if they didn't get it all, they could expect a sizable portion. What's a few million, give or take?" Knowing Mary Sue, Frank figured she would roll for the lucky seven with all the chips on the table.

Matt replied, "Jeff, you have to learn to relax. First of all, it's all posturing. Kressler wants to tell the press that he's a high roller. If he wins, very serious clientele will be calling his office."

Jeff's eyeballs were so wide, Frank thought they would pop out of his head. He needed to be defused, so he added, cheerily, "I totally agree. On the bright side, Jeff, figure that you will be world famous in having lost one of the dumbest trials in the history of mankind."

"No doubt, that's the good news. You can't make it up, "Jeff quipped, and both men broke out in laughter.

Reyes got up to find a quiet location in the hallway to make a phone call.

FORTY-FIVE

The clerk informed the court that the judge would be a few minutes late. Frank looked over to his left and saw Mary Sue. She caught his eye, then looked down. Like a magnet, he rose from his chair and went around the back of the courtroom, walked down to where she sat and knelt next to her. To him, she didn't look too bad in her blue pantsuit.

"Hello, Megan," Frank said.

She fidgeted with her fingers in her lap. "Can we step outside," she said, softly.

He rose and walked out the door of the courtroom into the hallway, holding the door open for her. He walked over to the nearest bench where she sat next to him. Unlike the courtroom, the hallway was empty.

"Frankie, I don't know what's going to happen to me, so I wanted to see you one last time and tell you that I never ever would have told anyone about... you know, your secret. And I never ever will, either.

I need to know if you trust me on that."

Frank didn't know what her future held, either, but he suspected she might be facing a half-dozen felony charges. She'd thrown craps.

He saw the little girl who kept making wrong choices, a girl turned into a woman whose goals were screwed up. He saw the two of them in their innocence long years before "Yes," I said, "I trust you."

But that was a lie. How could you trust a person hard-wired to win at all costs, and to do to her best friend what she had done to him? He'd known men who would rather die or undergo torture in lieu of turning on a friend.

Frank took a picture from his wallet and handed it to Mary Sue. "Remember this?" he said.

"You kept it all this time?" she asked, surprised, with a sense of profound sadness and curiosity in the mix of her simple question.

He held a laminated picture of a young Frank holding a Chinook Salmon in both arms. Hap and his own dad had taken them stream fishing on a cool overcast day. Frank was eleven years old.

On that day, both children hauled in halibut and pike. Still, stream fishing offered its challenges. The two men and the two children about twenty yards apart on a rocky bottom, each struggling to stabilize themselves against the flow of the river. The fish were swimming upstream in droves to lay their eggs. Frank got a nibble, yanked to set the hook, and yelled, "Fish on!"

Then he held on for his life. He didn't have a bracket into which he could set the pole. He didn't have any place to leverage it into his clothing or body. The fish and Frank fought for supremacy. The three others came around, Hap and his dad giving instructions, Megan yelling at him not to give in. After about ten minutes, he hauled in the salmon onto the round pebbles of the shallows, whereupon the fish freaked and zipped back out into the stream another hundred feet or so. Frank fell on the rocks, but held on. His hip waders filled with water. His back and shoulders burned, his right leg and butt cheeks ached from the fall.

He refused to give up and sloshed backwards onto the shore to haul the fish in closer, slipping again as he did so. "Keep that pole bent," yelled his dad. "You get that any straighter and you'll bust the line."

Frank knew that, but was too busy to answer. He walked forward toward the water again as he'd been taught, reeling in the whole while. Another eternity of battle with the Chinook and he finally hauled the fish within netting distance. Hap scooped it up and his Dad bonked it in the head with a club. The fish lay still.

Megan, came to him and gave him a peck on the cheek. "Good fight, Frankie. Good job!" Then she took his picture.

"Thanks," he muttered, drenched in sweat and stream water, sore and hurting. The fish lay across both his arms.

His dad took the salmon and hooked it on a hand-held scale. "Thirty-six pounds," he announced, proudly. Frank received hugs and claps on the back as a great reward.

The memory completed, Frank took the picture from Mary Sue's hand, got up and re-entered the courtroom, throwing the photo into the trash can next to the door as Kressler began his presentation.

FORTY-SIX

"In round figures, what we are asking for is the following: $3,500,000 for Mrs. Tamsen, $2,500,000 for Mr. Tamsen, and $500,000 for each of the two children. The court can fractionate the amount as it sees fit, of course," said attorney for the Tamsens.

By this, Kressler meant that if the court found Shenero ten percent at fault, he could be liable to pay ten percent of the amount awarded by the court. The court would have to determine to what extent each of four defendants was at fault.

After a quarter-hour of detailing the amount he believed should be paid by each of the defendants, Kressler finished and Matt stood.

Once again, Matt bore into his defendant's main theme regarding job assignment and hammered the court with the credibility of the witnesses. He restated that not a single witness came close to proving Jeff had done anything unprofessional and not up to standards Julie Robinette upheld his findings.

In fact, if he had committed an egregious error in his measurements (unlikely because of his experience), there was no proof of cause and effect upon the health of the Tamsens. In fact, there existed no evidence of a cause.

At the end of the summary statements, Craycroft requested both sides to submit their Findings of Fact and Conclusions of Law, summary pages laid out in ABC format to present the main points of their case and the law as it pertains to those points. She gave the parties seven days to file these documents.

At the conclusion of the official proceedings, Matt contacted Darryl King, the Cleveland County District Attorney, to inform him where he could find Bud Tamsen, a wanted man.

Orlando Reyes (read Billy Kirk) was present with a camera crew when city police arrested Bud at his apartment. The story had already been written by Kirk's staff thanks to information provided by anonymous sources.

Matt and Frank wrestled with the knowledge of a wanted man being free when they knew of his guilt. The alternative would have been that his early arrest might cause there to be bias toward the case and a mistrial might be called. If that were to happen, a jury might be empowered the next go-around which would not bode well for their case. The men decided their chances were better to have him arrested after the trial, especially because the man had no reason to flee at this time.

Money aside, this was still a civil trial and not a

criminal one and the two events—the trial and the arrest—were separate and distinct.

FORTY-SEVEN

From the National Cable Service:

"This is Karen Reed of GNN, reporting from Norman, Oklahoma. We are at the mold trial involving the Tamsen family who claim seven million dollars for damages to their home and their health. The case is under advisement by Judge Linda Craycroft, who will review a veritable mountain of evidence submitted by both sides.

"In an ongoing investigation, our sources inform us that Dr. Charles Waylan Campbell, testifying for the plaintiffs, was paid tent thousand dollars by their, Anthony Kressler attorney for his single appearance, in addition to the eight thousand he received from the Tamsens for his services. Dr. Campbell is under investigation for malpractice by the medical board of the State of Oklahoma. A subpoena has been issued for the records of all his clients and for his income tax statements for the past several years. The FBI informed us that they are unable to make a statement because this is an ongoing investigation. In addition, and we cannot confirm it at this time, a grand jury is being summoned to investigate claims of fraud to be filed against the doctor. According to unnamed sources, a class action suit against him is being prepared. This is Karen Reed. More later."

From your local television service:

"This is Billy Kirk of KOKO television, Oklahoma City. In a bizarre twist to the toxic mold trial taking place in Norman, Anthony Kressler, attorney for the plaintiffs, has asked the court to award the Tamsen family seven million dollars for damages caused by the fact that mold was not found in their home. George McKinney, attorney representing Bob Jones Restoration, as well as All American Insurance, accused Charles Campbell, doctor for the plaintiffs, of quackery. Dr. Campbell could not be reached for comment and may have left Oklahoma. A warrant has been issued for his arrest."

Frank laughed out loud. The broadcast reminded him of the government paying a farmer not to grow a crop. The government agent would say, "We'll pay you three times more if you don't grow soy compared with what we'd give you if you don't grow corn."

The farmer might think for a moment and ask, "What's the most you can give me for not growing something?"

Whereupon the agent might barter with him and say, "How about seven million if you don't have any mold."

FORTY-EGHT

Frank sat in his office in Oklahoma City catching up on a variety of cases when his intercom buzzed.

Frank pushed the button. Yes, Chloe."

"There's a lady here to see you. I told her you were not taking any visitors, but she insisted she see you."

Then he heard Chloe say, "Wait, you can't ..."

A short moment later, a short, frumpy woman appeared in his doorway. Chloe stood behind her. "Frank, I told her she couldn't go in, but she came anyway."

"It's all right, Chloe. Why don't you stay here while I meet with this woman?" He wanted Chloe to serve as a witness, if it came to that. Chloe understood.

Frank didn't invite his visitor into his office. Still, she took a step inside. He stared at Sandra Hudson. She wore a smirk on her face.

"Mr. Bennett. My name is Sandra Hudson. I saw

how great a lawyer you are when I went online. I don't know if you watch the news, but I have having health problems at my school."

Frank stared without saying a word. "Go ahead, Miss. It is Miss and not Missus Hudson?"

"Miss. Well, I have terrible health problems as a result of exposure to various things at my school, including mold and I want to file suit. Can you help me?"

"Who would you sue, Miss Hudson?"

"Well, I don't know if you've heard of a Dr. Shenero. He's a mold expert and he didn't find any mold and I know there's some."

"Shenero. I've heard of him," Frank replied. "Some sort of scientist, isn't he."

Unseen by Sandra, Chloe, standing behind her and six inches taller, did her best to keep from laughing.

"Can we talk?" Sandra asked, trying to be pushy.

"This is not a good time. Chloe will book an appointment for you to come back. Have a nice day." Frank went back to his paperwork while Chloe led Sandra to the front office.

Thirty seconds later the intercom buzzed. "Yes, Chloe."

"She's gone," his secretary said.

"Good. Make sure I am always out when she calls again. Then recommend Anthony Kressler as an attorney."

Frank heard a giggle. "Got it. Will do."

FORTY-NINE

Billy and Frank arrived at Jeff's private office at the same time.

Jeff opened the door and welcomed his friends. While the three men were close to thirty-eight years of age, Kirk looked the youngest. The others surmised it might be due to a little hair coloring combined with good genetics.

Not a minute later, a familiar knock sounded at the door.

"Hello, counselor, what's the password?" Jeff queried.

"Deadly toxic mold," Matt responded."

"Correct, you may enter."

Billy and Frank looked at each other and grinned.

"Hey, Frank, Don't you ever work?" Matt said, shaking his head in feigned disgust.

"No," he answered. "Remember, Matt, my family received millions from a mold litigation case and suddenly my mental and physical health improved so much you can't believe it."

Jeff stood and introduced the notable Billy Kirk, destined for stardom as ever graced a television set. Kirk stood to give Matt a handshake.

"Somehow, Billy, your face seems a little familiar," said Matt, with friendly sarcasm.

Matt flopped into the armchair. Billy and Frank sat on the sofa and Frank put his feet up on the coffee table made from varnished two-by-fours that Jeff created years before. He sat in the desk chair with a computer at his back. The screen ran various images of mushrooms at one minute intervals.

Jeff's coffee table always displayed various curiosities, such as books on the inventions of man, the philosophy of time and time travel, the physics of baseball pitching, and a pictorial history of the English language. Once, Frank brought over a current copy of one of the weekly scandal magazines as an addition to the literature. This issued featured an alien abduction and the latest speculation about co-habitation by actors and actresses on location. Jeff loved it, but Carmen forbade it. Frank accused her of taking it home to read for herself.

"The judge could take weeks before she comes out with a ruling," said Matt. "So, you might as well relax and enjoy the absence of Bud and Mary Sue Tamsen in your lives for the time being. We can celebrate that bit of justice.

"Bud's behind bars. He's trying to plea bargain by pinning the idea on Mary Sue, and if anything happened to him, she was going down with him. The plea bargain wouldn't get him out of charges in Canada, but it might get him out of charges here because the U.S. would have dibs on him after Canada got through with him. He says he's got written records of their conversations, which he made in case she tried a fast one on him. He says she knew of his past and you can add harboring a fugitive to the list of charges she faces." Matt concluded.

Frank took a deep breath. He wanted to tell them about his life with the woman, all of it. But Jeff already knew the story. For some reason, he felt compelled to tell the rest of them, to feel absolution.

Billy asked, "Why didn't you tell us before, Frank?"

Frank gave a quick shrug. "Why? What good would it do? Even if I left out the bad job part, you already knew her for what she was. And besides, what are you going to ask her? Let's see, uh, Mrs. Tamsen, have you ever blackmailed anyone, and if so, please detail the circumstances surrounding that event. In other words, why did you do it, how did you do it, when did you do it..."

"He's got a point, guys," offered Billy.

"A damn good point," said Jeff.

"My concern is more about the job you held for what, six, seven years? Are they still dumping the TCE?" asked Matt.

"Probably, but I don't actually know, anymore," said Frank. "I've been away from it for years."

"And if they are still dumping?" queried Jeff, to no one in particular.

The four remained silent for a moment trying to digest the implications of the question.

"We're all in a bad spot," said Matt. "We know about the issue, to call attention to it will likely dredge up Frank's name and he's married to the wife of the company vice president with two children in a happy marriage..."

"Her father will be president next year," said Frank.

"President. I stand corrected," said Matt.

"And people are getting poisoned," Billy threw in.

"Here's an idea," offered Jeff, holding up a finger. "We may be able to accomplish the same thing, but keep Frank's name out of the picture."

"I am definitely listening," said Frank.

Jeff looked at Billy. "We have here a legitimate news story; I mean about the water aquifer, not only here, but everywhere. Everyone wants unpolluted drinking water. Suppose you run a story...and I don't want to stick my nose into the operations of the press..."

"Yeah, and I'm Santa Claus," laughed Billy

Jeff chuckled, "Maybe if you could do a general story about, say, chemicals found in aquifers around the country without pointing fingers, it might get Frank's old employers to back off."

"Could work," nodded Matt.

"My producers will never go for it." said Billy. "It's a much bigger story if we can actually catch somebody with their hand in the cookie jar."

The men were quiet again.

Matt said, "Frank, does your wife know about what you did on the job?"

"Yes," Frank replied. "And she knows how much it bothered me. She's on my side."

Billy stroked his chin. "You know, Frank, you might want to share with your wife that you heard that Billy might have overheard Karen Reed with GNN say they might be doing a story on chemicals in the aquifer tied to airline companies back east. She might think about maybe sharing that little bit of gossip with her father. But don't quote me on that."

FIFTY

Jeff served coffee all around and took a plain club soda for himself.

"It's all meaningless, anyway," Matt said. "The judge will believe what she wants to believe. Why? Because she is subjected to the same media hype as the rest of us. In one sense, none of it matters because nobody ever addressed the real issue of negligence. Reading back in time cannot be done and it's foolish to pretend otherwise. Look at the disclaimers you and everyone else in the business puts into their reports.

"Don't look so worried, Jeff," continued Matt. "We're set for appeal. It's a detailed and lengthy process, but I'm ready to file. Look at the bright side. No judge likes their case overturned and an appeals court is very likely to overturn this one like they do with almost every one of the others like it.

"And don't forget, if Craycroft cannot show exactly and precisely why you were negligent and absolves you from guilt, then we file the counterclaim against the Tamsens. If you are found at fault, we appeal and when you are cleared on appeal, every other mold issue that makes it to court where money might be awarded to a plaintiff for mold liability will likely be denied."

Billy watched and listened. Like a trained detective, the man didn't miss a thing.

Frank said, "It comes back to tort reform. States usually award plaintiffs in any injury case. Witness this trial. The problem is with over-awarding."

"Yeah, but who is going to vote for tort reform? The members of a state government who are lawyers themselves?" asked Jeff. "It's like asking senators to vote against term limits."

"Okay, granted," Frank conceded, then continued with his point. "Take Campbell, for example. The man has no social conscience. He's a total fraud and does little to hide the fact. Does he believe his own garbage? I doubt it. Does the American Medical Association accept everything the man says? We know they don't. The same thing is true for Burke and people like him across the country who espouse far-fetched nonsense to serve their greed. Does Burke make it up as he goes along? Yes. Will he continue to do business? Same answer."

"Not really," stated Matt. "According to documents Hirshfield got for us, eighty percent of his income comes from insurance-related jobs. That should come to a screeching halt. Burke should be out of business by year's end, lose his medical license and will probably go to prison."

Billy contributed, "Jeff, your mold trial story is national. The media is partly responsible. Our industry accepts truth and prospers on hyperbole.

"You're also national on the school story that is getting close to the boiling point. You're an item."

Jeff said, "People want a safe home. Whether it's clean or not is their business. What they need is some person or an agency to turn to. There is no serious vocal advocate to promote cleaner indoor air. Do you know of any agency on the state or national level to assist the homeowner with better clean air indoors?"

Frank nodded. "I agree. What can the average citizens do? Where can they go? There is no answer at the present time."

Jeff became animated, as the computer screen turned from a single red mushroom to a field of large red-black mushrooms growing between stalactites in what appeared to be a cave.

Always vigilant of the press, Matt asked, "So, Billy,"What's happening at your end?"

"A lot of things I can't control. I can set the stage, steer and direct the press to a certain degree, but at some point, a story either takes off or it dies a quick death. A story like this one has to be fed, and as we all know, this one is self-feeding. The press can't be controlled, except by the Department of Defense, ergo, the federal government."

Billy knew he spoke among friends. "I evaluated what Jeff initially told me over the phone. The story smacked of a good human-interest piece and I really didn't think it would go this far. A lead is a lead and a story is a story, regardless of its source. Well and good. So I decided to attend the trial, and lo and behold, we fell into a live one.

"From there, I spoke with my producer and he directed our news team to conduct a further investigation and we sold rights to GNN. That was good for me and my business, and it good for the story, which, by the way, has gone international. My sources told me that concerns about the entire issue of legitimate television reporting, insurance fraud claims, malpractice suits against doctors, lawyers supporting bogus claims and lack of scientific evidence will soon be brought to light. The down side is that we may get some bad legislation out of it. You never know. So, whether Jeff wins or loses this case, I will do my best to ensure he is vindicated, one way or another."

Somehow, the others didn't like the way Billy said those last words. And nobody believed for a minute that this wonderful expose would make a lick of difference, not even Billy.

Jeff then told Billy about the vandalism to his home and his school office. Jess suspected Bud Tamsen.

Two weeks after the trial ended, Frank received a call from George McKinney. Apparently Jones' conscience bothered him to the extent that he confessed to vandalizing Jeff's home and office and that he tried to "sport" him with the pickup truck while Jeff was out jogging. Jones had been treated for paranoia in the past and was prescribed medication to control it. In this instance, he believed Jeff was in league with the plaintiffs for a piece of the big money.

Jones would soon be the target of criminal prosecution for vandalism. McKinney spoke to Jones and encouraged him to obtain immediate medical treatment for a nervous breakdown, which Jones did—not for the first time.

The admission by Jones explained his absence during the entire trial proceedings and confirmed Frank's own suspicions. On the witness stand the man would have faced torture and dismemberment at the hands of Anthony Kressler.

FIFTY-ONE

"Matt's got the verdict, Jeff," Frank declared. He just called me. He said to meet us in your private office in an hour."

"I'll be here," said Jeff, who asked Carmen to attend the upcoming meeting and take notes. She deserved to be there.

Frank tried to call Billy on his cell phone, but only got voice mail. So he called the station and told them it was an emergency. It turned out Billy was on assignment in the city. The station contacted him on a special line and patched Frank in. After he gave Billy the news, Billy delegated his work to a colleague and headed down to Norman. "Give me about forty-five minutes," he said.

Within the hour, everyone arrived at Jeff's office, where Matt occupied the seat of honor, the single armchair. Jeff took a seat at his backup computer, Billy and Frank sat on the sofa. Carmen, lovely as always, sat a folding chair near the inner office.

Twenty days had passed since the conclusion of the trial. Jeff's name still appeared in the news because Sandra Hudson had indirectly put it there.

After small talk, Matt said, "They're done for. Craycroft ruled Burke's testimony to be not credible, and you, being the Ph.D. are more knowledgeable and experienced about the situation. McKinney and I are awarded attorney's fees; basically an unheard of ruling in cases like these."

"I'm lost," said Jeff. "Did we win or lose?"

"We didn't lose, which in this case is the same as winning," replied Matt, enthusiastically. "They get absolutely nothing."

"Well, I'll be dipped." Jeff grinned ear-to-ear, got up and gave Carmen a big hug. She didn't pull away.

"Good show," Frank said.

Matt continued with his explanation. "As for the rest of it, are you ready for this?" Matt milked the moment. "Judge Craycroft ruled the Tamsen claim frivolous. She threw it out."

"Yes!" Frank exclaimed.

"Congratulations," Billy said.

"Right." Matt expounded, "And Bud Tamsen will be looking at extradition."

"What about the kids?" Billy asked.

"Well, Wendy's eighteen so she's on her own. Karl, unfortunately, will have to go into a foster home until he reaches eighteen."

"And," Frank added, with a certain amount of satisfaction for debt that needed to be paid, "Mary Sue will likely be doing time for numerous charges.

For one, insurance fraud is a felony. So is harboring a fugitive. So are several other charges I could list. "

Frank realized that Mary Sue might have a hidden stash or two. She'd probably taken her father's advice to do so. She'd best leave it alone. On the down side for her, they'd probably find everything she possessed. On the up side, at least he wouldn't have to be involved.

"So Kressler and his crew don't get paid because they took the case on contingency. Is that correct?" Jeff asked.

"Absolutely," said Matt, "and Kressler and his boys are also out hundreds of hours they put into this case. For an attorney, time is money. My guess is that the time he spent on this case to generate five-thousand pages of documents and reviewing them could cost his outfit a good hundred thousand to quarter million or more in lost income from other clients."

"So you get attorney's fees," said Jeff. "Does that mean I get back the fifteen thousand I paid you so far?"

"Yes," said Matt. "Plus what you didn't get paid for the job. I've been in touch with George McKinney, who is more experienced in this area than I am. He figures he put in about a thousand hours on this case and I put in at least half that amount of time. You have to keep track of this stuff. Anyway, multiply that by our hourly rate and it comes to a lot."

"How do you get paid?" Billy asked.

"I submit a detailed bill to the judge. The bill will

have all my time and charges and she awards me the money from the Tamsens. They'll pay me with what they have left and from the sale of the home. McKinney will get paid by the insurance company he represents."

"So the parents, especially the old lady, shopped around and found Kressler, the only one who would take the case?" queried Jeff.

"Correct" said Matt. "Their side made a number of fatal mistakes. For one, they took the case in the first place. They got overconfident after the initial award. Then they joined Jeff with Bob Jones, a stupid move motivated by sheer greed. This brought me into the case. To top it off, they went to a bench trial.

"Furthermore, naming Safe Home Environmental in their suit was also borne out of greed, not common sense because Julie backed up Jeff.

At least Campbell is through in this state."

"I suspect Billy will take care of the losers, looking at his friend.

"No, that's not good reporting, Jeff. I don't have a motive when I cover a story," replied Billy, sharply.

"Oh, spare me," Frank admonished. "You've got an agenda, Billy. That's why you're here in the first place. What *are* you going to do with this?"

Billy looked at Matt and gave a patented grin, as he ignored the accusation, "Matt, I heard you don't like the media too much, but this is a chance for you to do some good. I'd like to interview you for tonight's news."

Matt thought about Billy's request for a moment and put on a show of looking at his watch. "I'd really like to, Billy, but I don't have the time to make the round trip to Oklahoma City for the interview."

"Matt, how unfortunate. That said, there's a camera truck parked in the back lot with a crew waiting for my signal to come in."

Matt did not find Billy's statement funny at all.

"What do you imagine Bud Tamsen is thinking?" Jeff asked.

"Probably the same thing a lot of others are thinking—that he's sorry he got caught in the web of the Black Widow," Frank said, with his own memories of the creature.

"Oh, wait," Billy expostulated, "I almost forgot to tell you. A grand jury is being assembled to indict the esteemed medical doctor, Charles Campbell." He said this with great emphasis on the word "doctor."

"Don't you need overwhelming evidence against someone to assemble a grand jury?" Jeff asked.

"That's true," admitted Billy. "They're going to indict him on fraud and extortion. The man will likely lose everything. He'll probably serve prison time. Losing his medical license will be the easy part.

"Aaannd," he stretched out the word, "GNN made me an offer I couldn't refuse. I'll still be based in Oklahoma City with occasional travels to, oh, you know, Hong Kong, Paris, that sort of thing."

"We're sorry about the bad luck, Billy," Jeff said straight faced. "But glad I could be part of it."

Frank said to Matt, "Okay, Mr. Collins. I've been

dying to ask: How did you know to pressure Wendy about her purported pregnancy?"

Matt sighed, "Ah, that. As you know, my wife, Linda, is also an attorney and when I get home at night we both love to discuss our cases. Sometimes that's *all* we talk about.

"As the trial continued through the second day, we went out to dinner with a couple we knew, both of whom are medical doctors. The husband, Wade, is Linda's OB/GYN. Like everyone else in town, they were following the case and recognized Wendy's face from the TV. That was when the cameras were rolling while the witnesses and attorneys would enter or leave the courthouse for the day.

"'I saw a picture of Wendy on TV'," said Wade. "'She's quite an attractive young lady. I wonder who the father is'."

"I looked at him like he was crazy. "Her father is Bud Tamsen, Wade. Okay, her stepfather. Come on."

"Wade said, "'No, no. Not that. I mean the father of her baby'."

"Then I got out of him that she came in for a pregnancy test—a test that turned out to be positive. "She was six weeks along'."

"So Linda turned to me and told me, "'No, dear, I know what you're thinking and you can't use that in court. That's confidential doctor-client information'."

"Of course, I told her. I agree. If I state it as a fact, then, no, I can't reveal it. However, if I ask it as a simple question, then, it's a simple 'yes' or 'no'."

The others shrugged. Point taken.

Frank suddenly announced, "By the way, guys, Cheryl and the kids and I are moving to Alaska in a couple of months to start a new life. They need a good environmental attorney in Anchorage and I've accepted the job. While I'm at it, I'm going to catch up on some salmon fishing."

Billy turned philosophical, "Damn, Frank. That's great because what I'm getting out of that news is that you and the fish are one and the same. Neither of you has to swim upstream anymore."

Two weeks later, Matt, Frank, Jeff, and McKinney showed up at the hearing. Mary Sue did not appear, against orders.

Matt requested the hearing judge to issue a contempt of court citation against her. The judge agreed to issue a passive warrant; if she ever got stopped for a traffic ticket, or if the law had any other occasion to run her name in her presence, she would be handcuffed and hauled off to jail. Five thousand dollars would have to be posted for her release.

At that moment, Mary Sue came into the courtroom, somewhat breathless and reported she was meeting with a real estate company for sale of the house.

The men departed and shook hands all around. Frank couldn't resist giving Carmen a big hug, maybe a little longer than necessary.

FIFTY-TWO

Cleveland County District Attorney Darryl King scratched the back of his head with his right hand while holding the newspaper in his left.

Jeff sat casually in an armchair facing the D.A., having been called in to give a report on his own opinions on Hudson's Disease, as the press had dubbed it, because, in one sense, it all began with him.

"FYI, Mr. King, after I hung up the phone from your call, I received another one from Jim Hughes, the principal at Dunham Elementary where Sandra Hudson works," said Jeff.

"What did he want?" asked King.

"Don't know. He said he wanted to do the right thing and to discuss the Hudson case with me if I could keep quiet about some things," answered Jeff.

"Like what?" asked King.

"Don't know. I told him I had an appointment and would get back with him," said Jeff, shrugging.

King pickup up the morning paper. "Sandra L. Hudson, it says here, our first case of hundreds, maybe thousands. Hope neither of us catches what's going around. We don't need any more school problems, doctor."

Jeff leafed through the stack of documents King had given him to peruse. "I wonder what the L. stands for," he queried, offhandedly.

"Lovelace, I think I read somewhere," answered Diane, King's paralegal—a thin well-groomed older woman whose partnership with King went back several years. .

"Lovelace, Lovelace...why does that name ring a bell?" asked the D.A.

Diane replied, "You mean as far as cases are concerned? Well, maybe fifteen years ago we prosecuted a child molestation case with a defendant named Lovelace. The guy got major time."

"Oh, yeah. Abused his daughter from the earliest years right up until the time he got her pregnant at thirteen. She lost the child prior to birth. Whatever happened to her?"

"I don't remember," said Diane. "Let's see if we can find the file." She walked to the next room to search for a file in a row of tall cabinets.

King had followed Jeff's adventures with the players in the toxic mold trial and engaged him for several minutes on the subject, until Diane returned carrying a thick manila folder. "Got it." She placed it on the desk in front of her employer and looked over his shoulder while he leafed through it.

"Here it is," said King. "Ronald Lovelace: sentenced to thirty years for child molestation and having sex with a minor. That minor was his own daughter. He died in prison. Inmates got to him, apparently they treated him like he treated her."

"Breaks my heart," said Diane.

"Apparently, it broke his daughter's heart, too. She was in love with him and went to counseling for some time," said King.

"Does it have the daughter's name there?" asked Jeff.

"Let's see. Yep. The police report says it's Sandra. The authorities never released the name to the press because of her age. The court sent her to a foster home until an aunt and uncle claimed her. Then she dropped out for some time."

King read and spoke at the same time. "The daughter ran away and the wife filed a complaint against the husband. They knew what had happened to her and it gave the husband ideas of his own and he decided to try a go at her, too. She wouldn't have any of it and ran away as soon as she turned eighteen. The complaint didn't hold because the girl disappeared."

"Ouch," said Jeff.

"You almost can't blame her," muttered Diane.

King immersed himself in the report. "Hello. Hudson is the name of the aunt and uncle. The case worker stayed on it and found that she reemerged in a homeless shelter and then went into theater arts. Apparently she did well for herself and got a solid education at Oklahoma State University out in Still-water, then moved here to Norman. It doesn't say where she went from there."

Jeff stared at the King and his paralegal. "Sandra Lovelace Hudson suddenly makes an appearance under a new guise. I think she knew the 'M' word would bring attention to her. Isn't that interesting?"

King dropped his feet from his desktop. "Yes, it is."

"What are you thinking, Darryl?" asked Diane, narrowing her eyes and backing up a step.

"I'm thinking we need to read some of the original reports regarding health complaints at this school. See if there is a history of problems there."

"Do we have time for that? We have a hundred schools in the state closed down, with health officials across the country screaming bloody murder about their own schools and careers, as if the whole thing is our fault. Maybe we should concentrate on the surge in juvenile crime," Diane concluded.

"Oh, that's exactly what I intend to do," said the prosecutor. Get me her medical file, please."

"Okay, I'll nibble. What are you going to get her on? The last time I checked, complaining about a smell isn't against the law," said Jeff.

Once Diane brought in Sandra's medical file, King asked occasional questions of Jeff regarding the many tests he and others had conducted and the possibility that one of them might be wrong.

Six weeks after the first reported incident and

three weeks after completion of the tests, Health Commissioner, Richard Redding, announced at a press conference that all laboratory tests in the Dunham Elementary School cases were negative. In addition, nobody found any contaminating mold or any other findings of interest. He directed the districts to reopen their schools at the beginning of the summer session, which would begin on schedule.

The Norman school district did not look forward to dealing with class action suits brought about by parents on behalf of themselves and their children.

Numerous attorneys had contacted Sandra Hudson regarding suits against the school and the district. Although she never said "yes," she never said "no." "Let's wait and see," she responded. She had gone to see Anthony Kressler to represent her and gave him Frank Bennett's blessing. She also mentioned Jeffrey Shenero's name, whereupon Kressler told her to wait until he contacted her.

"What did you decide, Darryl?" asked his paralegal.

"I had Bob Markus call on her."

"Isn't he a former prosecutor turned defense attorney?" she inquired.

"Correct. I told him our situation and asked him to offer to represent her in any legal trouble, in order to see where she stood."

"And?"

"And, she didn't rule out a lawsuit."

"Markus pointed out to her that the Tamsen trial

went gone nowhere for lack of evidence and asked Sandra if she had concerns about her case evaporating."

"What did she say?" asked Diane.

"He told me that she said something peculiar; that what happened at the Tamsen trial had absolutely no effect on her case, and in her eyes, she'd already won."

"Won what?"

"That remains to be seen," replied King.

"Wait a minute," said Jeff. "Frank Bennett told me that Hudson came to his office wanting to hire him to file suit against the school district and against me not knowing Frank and I are close friends," replied Jeff.

"Looks like her game is evolving," contributed Diane.

"So now what?" Jeff asked.

"I'm going to call her in and have a talk with Miss Lovelace-Hudson. I'll tell her the truth; that we can't pin a thing on her, but if she even thinks about pulling a stunt like that again, I'll make sure the press gets an anonymous copy of her background file—which I wouldn't and couldn't do, of course. But that should put a lid on her.

Diane shook her head slowly. "Nothing is going to fix what happened to our schools, and if it isn't Hudson, it'll be somebody else."

"True," King said. "The little boy cried wolf. I doubt if we'll jump so fast next time.

"Wait a minute," he suddenly said and sat up.

Maybe that's her whole game; shutting down the schools, I mean. Maybe she considers her little venture as a form of therapy; an unusual guise of anger management."

"You got me there," said Diane.

"Hudson is as much a terrorist as any of them, whether she wants to believe it or not. By the time I'm through with her, I'll make her believe it, and if I can find a way to put her in jail, I will. I'm going to make Miss School Teacher a project of mine." King paused in his diatribe for a moment. He stared out the window and a very slow smile crossed his lips.

"You know, Diane, suddenly I have a better idea. The nation is on a terrorist alert as a result of our teacher's prank. By the FBI's definition, it looks like her intent is to intimidate a population. That puts her in the category of a domestic terrorist. The problem is not going to die of its own accord. She needs to confess publicly to her actions and her intent behind those actions. She'll be lucky to get a job as a homeless person after that. Remember the lady who claimed to have found a human finger in a bowl of chili she bought at a fast-food restaurant? Well, if she can do time, so can Hudson."

"Okay, Darryl, but if she confesses, do you think anybody will believe her, or will they think it is another conspiracy, another cover-up thanks to pressure from some government agency. It might make things worse."

"Not if it's accompanied by a well-publicized attempt at prosecution," Jeff added, finding he had free time to assist the D.A. with the Hudson case, until a few days hence when he would take over his teaching duties presently in the hands of his grads. He definitely didn't believe the pair suspected his connection to Billy Kirk.

"A conviction wouldn't hurt, either," murmured King.

"If we can put enough heat on her, we might get her to break. The nation will see how easily it got suckered into her game. Hopefully, things will wind down." King held an index finger into the air. "As a matter of fact, it comes to mind that we have some new conspiracy laws on the books since nine-eleven." King made some entries on his desk computer and checked his watch.

King turned to his paralegal and said, "Diane, call this principal, Hughes, over at Dunham Elementary. Tell him you're from my office and that Jeff—Doctor Shenero is here and we'd like him to help us. Ask him to come in immediately. That should start things rolling. If he wants to know the reason, say you don't know. Don't panic him. If what he tells us can shed light on her behavior, he may not have to become involved at all. With the doctor here in our office he may feel more at ease.

"Then call Hudson. Have her come in, say, a couple of hours. Same thing, but don't mention Jeff's name.

"Finally, to be safe, contact Norman PD and have an unmarked unit watch her leave the school and follow her here. They are to notify us of any deviation from course."

"My sense is that Hughes knows more about her than anyone," Jeff added, thoughtfully.

Then King said, "Jeff, you've worked with both of them, either directly or indirectly. If you can, why don't you stick around for this to ensure nobody makes up any stories?"

EPILOGUE

The well-publicized conclusion of the Tamsen trial brought the Hudson case to the forefront once again. Hughes could not escape the appearance of Mary Sue on television. His conscience replayed the vision of her with his secret sex partner when he met them both at the Sandra's apartment.

With the burden of a troubled conscience, Jim Hughes decided to throw himself to the wolves and put an end to whatever remained of his marriage and perhaps, his career.

He called Jeff and wanted to meet about information he possessed about both women, if, perhaps, his name might be kept out of it.

In King's office, with Jeff present, Hughes related his torrid relationship with Hudson and the infamous meeting with the two women. King gave no promises to Hughes.

After Hughes' departure, events unfolded rapidly. Jeff told of Hudson's visit to Bennett's office seeking a lawyer who would help her file suit against the school district and himself, as well as against unspecified other.

Because numerous out-of-state schools were closed due to Sandra's activities, the case was turned over to a federal prosecutor. The FBI and Homeland Security were summoned because the case smacked of domestic terrorism. The charges against the two women as co-conspirators were deemed to be terrorism-related.

Hudson declared herself to be not guilty on all charges. This set up a jury trial.

King called in Mary Sue, who, when threatened with conspiracy to commit terrorism, confessed completely to her involvement with Hudson. As they wrote her words, she tearfully related the tale of their first meeting after many years and their frequent phone conversations about their mutual interests and Sandra's interest in destroying the nation's educational system.

Darryl King had a case and he summoned a grand jury. They agreed there was enough evidence to arraign both women on a number of charges.

Billy Kirk was anonymously contacted and given background information in an agreement to hold all inside information so that sources would not be suspected.

Hudson was charged with terrorism under the U.S. Code of Federal Regulations which defines the act as "the unlawful use of force and violence against person of property to intimidate or coerce a government, the civilian population, or any segment thereof, in furtherance of political or social objectives."

The public defender pleaded that she needed psychiatric evaluation to be coupled with immediate treatment because of her background, which he detailed. A psychiatric evaluation found her to be sane in that she planned her activities over a period of years. In his evaluation, she intended to make the nation pay for the loss of their children; perhaps not in the way she lost her child, but to make up for it in terms of numbers. A plea bargain was denied in that the psychiatric believed she intended to punish the children.

During her testimony, Sandra expressed concern that Dr. Shenero became involved because of his reputation, but continued forward with her scheme. Her testimony was frequently interrupted by her theatrical tears.

On a reduced sentence based on her cooperation, Mary Sue was sentenced to 12 years for collaboration to commit terrorism. She was sent to Terre Haute, IN, a medium security prison.

Sandra Hudson received a sentence of 30 years for premeditated domestic terrorism and numerous other felonies. She was incarcerate at the maximum security section of the Marion, Ill. penitentiary. Both facilities are part of some 35 federal prisons earmarked for terrorists. Both women faced tens of millions of dollars in lawsuits.

Jeff Shenero returned to his teaching, research,

and consulting business, still eager for adventure, but more cautious than before.

Frank's wife, Cheryl, obtained an administrative job in Anchorage. She and Frank and their children moved to the city. Alaskan Oil hired Frank as their environmental consultant, thanks to strong recommendations by Oklahoma Power and Gas, and especially from Cheryl's father.

Anthony Kressler took on another bogus toxic mold job, virtually identical with the first, but got his law license completely revoked because he co-mingled his client's funds with his own—-an absolute no no in the eyes of the law. Immediately following the revocation of his license to practice, he received another DUI and injured another person during an accident due to his neglect, and spent a fortune on defense attorneys to no avail. He spent six months behind bars and faced several lawsuits.

In an interesting turn of events, with the assistance of McKinney, Kressler and Associates was also ordered to return to All American Insurance the quarter-million dollars he obtained on behalf of the Tamsens, unless he wanted charges of co-conspiracy placed against him.

Jeff closed his eyes in the sanctity of his department office, mentally preparing for an upcoming class lecture. Carmen worked at her desk, giving him some space. After some time, he sat up, then stood, rubbed his face with both hands and declared

"Time to get to work."

Carmen tried to be lighthearted. "Fun is over, boss. At least you got some bad people off the streets."

"That's all we need. More goddamn terrorists," he muttered.

Little did he know the prophesy in those words.

Synopsis of other books by Mark R. Sneller

The Mars Virus
(Sequel *to Dying to Read*)

Cancer researcher Jason Randolph and his geologist friend, Don Jennings, decide to search for life in a meteorite the geologist found in Antarctica years before. What's the worst that can happen? Everybody tried it, from NASA to the Russians, *and nobody found a thing.*

Suddenly, in Lincoln, Nebraska, a nightmarish discovery by the scientists threatens not only mankind and all life on Earth, but the stability of the planet itself, while Randolph and Jennings try to make hay before the sun stops shining.

Dying to Read

A terrible sickness awaits those who read newspapers and magazines. The ink holds aflatoxin, a deadly poison extracted from a mold. Many children and pets of the readers become affected when they get touched by those who handle the print items.

Mold expert and professor, Jeffrey Shenero, get pulled into a diabolical and original plot designed and carried out by terrorists. Countless persons are threatened and many have died.

An epidemic and national panic ensue as Shenero and his mathematician friend, Paul Anderson, stumble onto the truth and the nature of the plot. Attempts are made by members of the U.S. Government who are working in concert with the terrorists, to attempt to persuade Shenero and Anderson to think twice about revealing their findings.

Jeff learns that poisonings by the terrorists are in progress in other aspects of American Life, not only in print, but in the poisoning of everyday household products. Mass murder is on the agenda, even as they come after him.

In a gripping adventure full of eccentric characters, the mold expert gets help from his brilliant students and his alluring secretary, Carmen who must make a hard choice of her own.

The settings are in Norman, Oklahoma, and Tucson, Arizona.

Greener Cleaner Indoor Air 2ⁿᵈ Edition

Re-edited and enlarged, the 2ⁿᵈ Edition boasts over 120 articles written by award-winning scientist Dr. Mark R. Sneller. Greener Cleaner Indoor Air is an invaluable reference guide promoting longer life. Covering virtually every aspect of the range of particles (and toxic gases) we breathe every day, you will learn how to reduce, if not eliminate, them from your home air and save money at the same time.

Considering the book to be of such value, the country of South Korea purchased the rights to download the e-version to its citizens.